£1-99
BRS

Gift Aid
20   70887686   4402

Fi...

and

Fathe

By

Luke McEwen

Published by Unchained Pen Ltd

A CIP catalogue record for this book is available
from the British Library.

ISBN:978-1-910304-02-0

FOR TOBY
MY SON

A Glimpse of the Future

At 12.45 pm, Mr Jeff, headmaster of Chichester Community Primary School, found the first moment in a long morning to retreat to his office. The school was recovering from an outbreak of food poisoning, which had happened the day before. The school's policy of confining children in the sickroom had paid off, for there had only been a few further incidents. He plucked up the courage to look at his in-tray. On top was the expected pile of sick notes. He was glad it would be Mrs Ford, the school secretary, and not him that matched them to the absences, checked and filed them.

He picked up the one on top, Sam Steepleton's, and then the next, Lucy Meddows'. He went through all of them, ten or so, in quick succession. There were a few coincidences... or rather, problems. First of all, the only one that was written, not printed, was on the same pink paper they had in the art cupboard. The date format was strange too. They had written Thursday the 12th, using the same stylistic choice with the definite article. Then there was the issue of spelling of 'diarrhoea'. All of the sick notes had used the American spelling, there was no 'o' in the middle. Finally, Mr Jeff found the most convincing clue. Every third of the way down the paper was a single black dot. It was the kind of the print error you get when the print cartridge on a laser printer is broken. The letters all appeared to be printed with the same malfunctioning printer.

'Mr Jeff, come quick, you've got to see this!' It was Mrs Ford, calling from her office. Mr Jeff was there in seconds, and found Mrs Ford pointing to her monitor. 'Isn't that Steve Bridle? That awful man! You know, Oliver's dad?'

It was the one o'clock news. Mr Bridle, a parent of an excluded pupil, was wearing a Star Trek outfit and shouting at police officers as he chained himself to the cross trees of a lamppost on Westminster Bridge. In the background were the Houses of Parliament.

'I knew he was a bad sort! Thank goodness Oliver left.' The phone rang and Mrs Ford turned away.

Mr Jeff watched as Steve and the police were surrounded by a dozen school kids in pink t-shirts, chanting slogans and causing chaos, and there on a boat were Sam and Lucy too! Mr Jeff froze in a statue of fear. Mrs Ford put the phone down and Mr Jeff tried hard not to show a reaction. His worst fears had been confirmed. He flicked the monitor off. 'Poor guy. Well we knew he had problems.' He turned on his heel, walking back to his office. Should he call the parents? Should he call the police? No! The police were already there.

At 2.30 pm, Mr Jeff made up his mind. He told Mrs Ford he was leaving early for the day but would be back for the Nativity play. But as Mr Jeff left the school, he didn't turn left to walk home, he turned *right and made his way to the train station. As he walked briskly along the busy road, he tried to imagine the circumstances that had led them to demonstrate in London; then his mind wandered to the his own day off from school, many years before.*

His friend, Kirk, was unhappy and wanted to escape to France. They were ten at the time and they'd walked out of school by 8.55am, turning right to the school gate, not left to the assembly hall. No one had seen them go and they'd spent the day walking over the fields, scrumping apples and planning their journey. By four o'clock they'd got really hungry and decided to abandon the plan for another day. His mum had been very upset with him. He'd had to make explanations to a policewoman and the headmaster. But in the end, it was all forgotten. Life had carried on as normal. It turned out Kirk's parents were breaking up and he didn't know how to handle it. So he started to see a lady at the school to talk about 'his issues'. Mr Jeff, Andy as he was known then, had enjoyed his day out, but he'd never done it again. He'd had his day in the sunshine. A day of making escape plans. Life was, in fact, just too good and there was nothing really to escape from.

At the station, Mr Jeff bought a platform ticket. He picked a seat set back from the main thoroughfare but close enough to see everyone going through the exit. At 15.06, he watched the 13.32 from London Victoria arrive and observed the passengers disembark. There they were: his charges. One by one, he marked them off. All accounted for. He stayed in his seat until the

3

platform was clear, his heart lighter now the danger was over. He had no children of his own. His pupils were his children and now they were safe.

'Sam, You Only Need One Good Friend'

Six weeks earlier

Mum was right: year six was working out to be great. I suppose it's because I'd been kicking around the school for quite a few years; I knew what was what. It's like I had the whole place sussed. When you're eleven, life's just so much easier than when you're six and you're the newbie. You know the teachers to avoid, and which ones you can have a laugh with. Even if some of the children aren't your friends, you've found a way to get along. Sometimes that just means keeping your distance, sometimes that means just letting them be in charge. School was starting to be good fun. Mum explained that it's best when most of the kids are younger than you. You get to be who you want to be, without older children giving you a hard time.

And the best bit? I was no longer in the same classroom as my twin sister, Kirsty. We have what my Dad calls a 'love–hate' relationship, although last year when we were both in Miss Benny's class it was pretty much a 'hate–hate' relationship. Kirsty describes herself as the older sister. She will actually tell people that. As if it's a way of explaining why she should come first or why she's taller. The truth is that she is only seventeen minutes older than me! I'm so glad I moved to Mrs Stubbs' class. It's surprising in a school of three hundred children how little I have to see her. Mum insists that we go to and from school together. Apart from that, I had it all working for me in my final year before going to big school.

It started to go wrong when Oliver had a fight at school. Oliver and I never really got into fights. We didn't mix much with the footballers, the techy geeks, the readers, the gamers or the girls. We stuck to ourselves.

Oliver had got to school late that day and Mrs Stubbs told him off when he didn't say sorry. He was a bit quiet when she was questioning him about why he was late. In the end, he said his dad had overslept. Then Mrs Stubbs pointed out that Oliver was looking 'a little grubby' and asked him if the mud-stains on his knees were the same as last week's. Mrs Stubbs is herself always immaculate. She could be in one of those soap adverts with perfect families in perfect clothes, so she was being hard on him. Oliver didn't cheer up all day and then at break, this kid, Mat, bumped into him in the playground and Oliver overreacted and said, 'Oi! Watch it!'

Mat had a go back. 'What's wrong, cry baby? Why don't you go and cry to your mother!'

Mat didn't know that Oliver's mum had died a year ago. Oliver hit Mat on the nose, hard, and Mat fell to his knees. Which was surprising, since Oliver's short and Mat's tall and beefy. By the time the dinner lady came, his white shirt had turned red. Mat's a popular kid and all his friends came running. They surrounded Oliver and made him feel totally rubbish. The dinner lady helped Mat to his feet, and took him inside after she called the other dinner lady to sort Oliver out. The other dinner lady turned out to be Mat's mum, so he got a right telling off. The headmaster sent him home and his dad had to get on the train early to collect him.

I guess it could have been worse. Surprisingly, it was Lucy who calmed things down. Oliver and I had only spoken to her once before, but she came to Oliver's defence. Well kind of – she actually told them both off for fighting. But rather than argue with her, they stopped.

'Fighting won't solve anything, Oliver. You need to control your temper. You're not the Karate Kid! And Mat, you need to take more care about the things you say. The world would be a better place if everyone was a little nicer to each other.'

Lucy's tiny. Small compared to Mat, anyway, so she was brave to get involved. I think Lucy was annoyed at me too. I know I wasn't doing anything, but perhaps I should have tried to stop the fight.

Oliver and I get on really well. He's my best friend and because I didn't have many, Mum was really pleased we'd met up. She told me that in life you only need one good friend. We would only play fight, no proper name calling or anything. I called him 'Lolly Olly' but he thought that was funny. He called me 'SamIam'. He said that would be how Yoda from *Star Wars* would say it. I liked that, I never saw that as someone calling me names. We look quite different: I keep my hair short and my clothes clean, whereas Oliver has lion hair and doesn't bother too much about how he looks.

We first met at school last year. Oliver was the new boy. He comes from Southsea in Portsmouth. He had to take the train there and back each day, and his dad would go with him. No one else at school had to do that. Oliver got excluded from two schools in Southsea, so he had to come here.

We were the same, Oliver and me. He liked cartoons, I had a shelf-load. I liked picture books, he had a collection of Pokémon stories. We both didn't bother with footy or any ball games. We might play tag, but most of our games were LARPing. That's what Mrs Larkhill calls it, anyway. She teaches us drama. It's the same but we call it LARP, live action role play. Oliver and I don't just keep it to playtimes, we could stay in one role the whole day. The teachers know we're doing it. We'll be doing a project together on the life of a tree, say, but to Oliver and me the tree's a hiding place for treasure. The tree doesn't die from old age, but it's been cursed by a witch.

It's got us into a trouble quite a few times. Mrs Stubbs says we aren't concentrating, but she just doesn't realise what we put into our game. Our stories are so complicated, you've got to remember what you were doing in the morning and keep true to that. So say if I was the evil wizard and I had made a magic sleepwalking potion called 'Sleepinzoo', I couldn't change it to 'Walkinjuice' in the afternoon. Sometimes

Oliver will bring in stuff from a game we played from over a week ago.

I get on really well with Oliver's dad, Steve, too. We always talk about *Doctor Who*. He's seen every episode, even the episodes going back to when it started. And if you're lost in the plot, he can tell you what's going on. He'll tie it all in with what happened in the earlier weeks or in the previous regenerations of the Doctor. Steve's really tall, and he usually wears boots too. He often bends down to have a chat with me. He's a bit like Oliver in that he doesn't mind if his hair's a tangle. He's also got this jungle beard, so the complete opposite of my dad, who has hardly any hair.

I often stay at their house for a sleepover. Oliver has a tiny bedroom and it's stacked high with stuff. He has the greatest collection of toys. Not necessarily the new stuff, but great collections of characters from the films. On one of his shelves he'd put together a whole scene from *Lord of the Rings*. His dad helped him. He's into model-making too. They used a load of orcs and trolls from Warhammer and painted them with these special paints. It looks brilliant. We spent a whole afternoon re-enacting the attack on Amon Hen. We painted a load of blood pools in the scene and used his model trebuchet, which he made from a kit, to knock over the figures.

I really enjoyed my sleepovers at Oliver's. We had a kind of routine. Kirsty would tell Aunt Dora I wasn't coming back to hers after school. I'd go back with Oliver and Steve directly from school. It was great fun on the train. I didn't realise how many different schools there were. The carriages were full of colour from all the different uniforms. There was a great atmosphere too, just like being in the playground. Steve would always have a beer from the trolley. I don't know how he managed to finish it so quickly. It was only four stops before we had to get off. He never asked us if we'd like anything. I don't think he has much money, which was fine because my parents wouldn't usually buy anything from the trolley either. My mum is good at taking food and drink with her on our family outings. She says that's the way you make sure you get the right food, but I wonder if she just wants to save money.

Oliver never stops talking to his dad. He'll tell him everything that's happened in school, even the tiniest of things. Steve doesn't seem to be listening but then neither would I. I like Oliver, but he should know that his dad wouldn't be interested in the small detail from his day. Like what Mrs Stubbs was wearing or what everyone was eating for lunch. When we're home, Steve is a lot more fun. He'll get us playing a game on the TV or doing some model-making. It generally starts off that he'll send Oliver to get a beer from the fridge while he and I set up a game. But after a while it'll just be Oliver and me. Then later we'll all walk down to the fish and chip shop. Steve always has a laugh and a chat with the guy who serves. Steve says it's good to have a bit of banter with them and then they might put a few more chips in for us. We tend to stroll there and almost run back. Oliver and Steve don't say much until we've got everything set up and we're in front of the telly. Usually Steve will have something recorded for us to watch. Steve likes his films. He says that you can learn from films, that it's like going to school at the end of the day, but more fun and with no effort.

Steve was a Trekkie when he was young: he used to dress up as Captain Kirk and go to these meetings where they'd play games, talk about the episodes and the films and buy things to add to his collection of Star Trek stuff. It's a big collection, most of it's in the TV room on a shelf next to the sofa. Oliver is only allowed to touch the collection if his dad's in the room. It was Steve and Oliver that first introduced me to cosplay, in the summer. We went to Brighton in fancy dress and did acting. That was the most awesome of days.

As you walk into the lounge there's a picture of Steve standing with Oliver's mum, both dressed up in costume and crouching and sticking their arms out. Their fingers are guns and they're shooting at the cameraman. I always look at that picture when I go in. How strange that Angela, that's Oliver's mum, wasn't there any more. They never really talk about her, but there she is in the picture watching over them. In the picture, Angela is trying to look serious, but you can tell she's also trying not to laugh. She was very pretty. She looked more like Oliver than Steve. They have the same blonde hair, the same face when they smile as if they're smiling on the inside too. That's my mum's expression.

I asked Oliver about his mum. He said she'd got

11

cancer a long time ago when he wasn't even at school. Then she got better, but then it came back and she died shortly after. She was only in hospital for a little while, so he only visited her a couple of times. They'd speak about school and getting a pet dog at Christmas and she'd told him to be extra good for Steve, but he felt like he didn't get to say goodbye.

Oliver didn't want to go to the funeral but his dad said it would be better if he did, and now he could see his dad was right. Oliver met some new family he didn't realise he had. There was also a guy who really wanted to talk to him but he wouldn't say how they were related. The guy was mean-looking, and first off he thought he was one of the men from the funeral directors. Anyway, Steve had been watching and came along and picked Oliver up. He hadn't done that in years. Oliver said it felt right because they'd had a hug.

After our chips, we have to wash our hands. I don't have to do that at home, but then Mum makes us sit at the table and we have to use a knife and fork. Steve always asks if we have any homework and we always say we don't. Although there was this one time when we did and he helped us do it.

Steve once explained the film rating scheme to us. He said it was a number that showed how much you could learn about the real world. If you wanted to learn quickly about life, then you had to understand films inside out, know about the characters and why they did what they did. It worked both ways, so the more you knew about life, the more you'd recognise stuff in the films. Steve says 'it's like being a hunter finding pearls of wisdom. Each film has a gift and as you watch, your job is to find the buried treasure'.

He said that *Blade Runner* was the most amazing film because to most people it looks like a big gun battle between the androids and the special police, but really it was about religion and what it was to be human. Steve explained that they had made the androids so well that they were as good as human! The question the film asked was 'did that mean it was wrong for the police to kill them?'

I asked our vicar about this at church. I think Steve must be right because the vicar got very annoyed. He started to give me an explanation and then when my mother came over he changed the subject and asked to have a private chat with her. My mum asked me later what I'd asked the vicar. When I explained I hadn't actually seen the film, she seemed very relieved and said that was good, as it was a certificate 15. I was immediately interested. 'Great, that will be really educational.'

Then Mum told me her version of the certificate system. About how the number had to fit in with the age you were, otherwise you were too young and it might be inappropriate. I'm not sure if that makes sense. What's age got to do with it? My sister, despite us being the same age, doesn't have a clue what's going on in the films we see. If we are watching *Doctor Who* I have to explain all the way through.

We don't go to church that often. I don't think I'll bother asking the vicar another question. I didn't mean to annoy him. Perhaps his job is just to speak *to* people, not so much *with* them. When my dad got to hear about my question to the vicar, he asked me loads of questions about what I did at Oliver's. He went on and on for ages, he wanted to know all the little details. At one point he even asked me how many drinks of beer Steve had.

I stopped going to Oliver's so much after that. Dad said that it was okay on a Friday or Saturday, but not a school night. The trouble is that most Fridays or Saturdays we do other stuff at home.

Kirsty and I usually go to Aunt Dora's after school. She's not a real aunt, just a friend of the family. She's a lot older than Mum. She likes cooking cakes and biscuits and does that with Kirsty. Mum says that Kirsty has to be careful not to eat too many of the things they make. Aunt Dora's got a big garden, but she likes her flowers to be kept nicely. I'm not allowed to kick a ball around or anything. Dad likes to call her Andorra – that's a place in Spain where people ski.

Steve keeps his films on a laptop, which he calls 'The Fountain of Knowledge'. He told me he had a thousand films on it and he'd got them all for free. Because he was prepared to share his films with other people, they would share their films with him, and now he'd built up a huge collection. Because he was generous, people had been generous back. That, he told me, was a lesson worth knowing and bet me I'd never learn that at school.

Around the beginning of term we got into a new

routine, where just before we set off for our fish and chips, Steve would make a big deal about choosing the film to see. There were rules for the selection. We couldn't see it if he thought it inappropriate and we couldn't see any 18 certificates. Then 15 certificates are a special treat and 12s are all right as long as we ask him anything we don't understand or tell him if we're getting upset. We all choose together, but if we can't decide then we take it in turn. Last time Oliver chose, so it's my turn next time. Steve doesn't need to have a turn because he can watch them during the day. Sometimes he'll get through three between dropping Oliver off at school and collecting him.

The Book of Lives and Living

The last time I went to Oliver's was on a Friday night. It turned out to be the best part of the weekend, because my mum and dad had a rubbish weekend planned. We had to get the spare room ready for Granny Worthing to come over at Christmas.

The spare room needed new wardrobes and so we set off to buy them, in the car, on Saturday morning. Eight hours later we returned from Ikea, squashed in with loads of boxes, fitted in between Kirsty and me and above our heads. Kirsty had complained from the minute we got in the car. 'Can we have Radio One on, not Two? Can we stop off at Costa? Could you drop me off at the front of Ikea and meet me inside?' And so on and so on. Kirsty's friends had been to Ikea before and so although Kirsty had never been herself, she ended up giving us a guided tour of the store. Then she insisted that we had lunch in the café because that was the full Ikea experience, even though Mum had brought a picnic to eat in the car. When we got back, Dad had asked everyone to help because 'many hands make light work'. But Mum had to get her report ready for Monday morning and Kirsty had to call her friends because, well, she had to, and it was a good father–son bonding activity. So it was Dad and I who built the cabinets.

We got into a sequence. Unwrapping. Cardboard in bin. Tools found. Instructions followed. Dad says 'Right tools for the job.'

We took nearly the whole of Sunday to finish and by the end I was really tired – my dad would say 'knackered.' I didn't mind making the cupboards. Dad gave me five pounds for helping and he made it fun. Well, most of the time. He's like me, I guess. He's quite logical and prefers to follow the instructions, although he'll ignore them if it doesn't work out. We got into a system and got faster and faster. And then Dad said that if we ever needed to, we could always make money by building flat-pack furniture for other people.

My mum cooked a Sunday roast and then afterwards we all got around the telly to watch for a bit, so it didn't end too badly. My mum got her report done. She's a local government officer, whatever that means. That's where she met my dad fourteen years ago. He makes the local council's website. They used to meet for lunch every day but now they've relocated Dad, it's a bit too far for them to meet up. Dad always says he married Mum because she looks like the actress Elizabeth Taylor, but I've seen her in *Black Beauty* and I know I may be biased, but I think Mum's a lot more beautiful.

So it was the Friday night that stood out. Where I got to do my own stuff. I'd gone back to Oliver's on the train for a sleepover, as usual. Steve was in a good mood.

'Hey guys, I saw *John Carter* today, you know, the

film? It's awesome.'

'What's it about?' Oliver asked.

'It's about a guy who travels to a different planet and has adventures, why don't you see it tonight?'

'But you've already seen it today!'

'No, I'm okay, I don't mind. I really think you should see it!'

Sometimes Steve would watch a movie ten times or more. If you ask him about *Blade Runner,* for instance, he can tell you scene by scene from beginning to end what was said and done. He could remember names, types of cars, times of day, colours. Then he'd describe the mood: he'd say if it was dark, spooky, or Hollywood, which means not very real. If something was too easy, fun and happy, he'd say it was saccharine, which is a kind of sugar. He'd tell you why people did what they did. He could work it all out.

'It's a one star, just right for this evening. You haven't got homework, have you?' By one star, Steve meant that it had a learning potential grade of one. He works it out as the film's age certificate, which was 12, minus 11 – my age – so that's one.

'I tell you what, let's eat our fish and chips first, before the film, then we can concentrate.'

We sat at the kitchen table to eat. It was funny seeing Oliver eating like that rather than balancing his food on his lap. He looked grown-up. He even took his toys off the table before we ate, although Steve hadn't asked him to.

'So, this film, *John Carter,* is about destiny,' Steve

started. 'How everyone has a life purpose and an opportunity to fulfil theirs. This John Carter guy really goes for it. He's not interested in TV, working or doing what he's told. He knows there's a special life waiting for him and he's not going to sit around waiting for it to find him.'

'What's a destiny?' Oliver asked. I'm glad he did.

'It's like an invisible force making you succeed or fail, controlling what you do,' Steve replied.

'What if you don't want to do it?' I had to know.

'That's the thing! Can you throw off what life has given you and control your own destiny?'

'That sounds good, how do you do that?' Now I *really* wanted to know.

'Well it's what John Carter does. That's why you've got to see it. I think it's my new favourite!'

'Well mine is *Harry Potter and the Deathly Hallows*. And it's got to be part two!' Oliver said.

'But why? Why is it your favourite?' Steve looked serious.

'It's so awesome. That scene of dead goblins scattered around after everything's exploded and caught fire. I wouldn't watch it at night, though!'

'How about you, Sam?'

'*Shrek.* It's been *Shrek* for ages.'

'Good choice. And the why?'

'It's just so funny, non-stop laughing. But I like Shrek because you're not supposed to like an ogre, but you do. And Fiona, you're worried when she is an ogre and when she can't change back. But it's okay, because they're together.'

So we had different films. It was fun finding out why they liked theirs and it wasn't until I explained why I liked mine that I knew why I did.

The film was amazing. Not much of a title; it doesn't give you a clue what it's about. You wouldn't choose the film from the title. It turned out this guy had an incredible life. Conquers another planet, has amazing battles, travels through space in wormholes and marries a princess. He didn't have any fear, and on Earth before he left for his adventure he had no time for ordinary people or doing things just because everyone else did them. He wanted to explore and see everything. There were times when you'd think 'Oh he'll do that', but he does the complete opposite. Just imagine if he was at school and the teacher said your homework is to draw and describe the Houses of Parliament. He'd go up to London to sketch it. He'd meet with the people there and find out what was going on. He wanted more than everyday life and he went looking for it.

He wrote the whole thing in a diary – he called it a journal. Then, right at the end, he gave it to his nephew, who wrote a book about his life from that. But the big thing was the diary became a major tool in his life. He used the diary to get what he wanted. Oliver and I were glued: it was just the most amazing thing – non-stop alien creatures, weird languages, strange plants. Then there were the costumes, the spacecraft, even the buildings. They were just so unearthly. Which made sense, because it was set in Mars. This guy wanted to have a different life from what everyone else does. Not go to school or work, packed lunch, TV, computer games, shopping, takeaway meals and bed at nine. No, he didn't even want a job. If people tried to persuade him he wanted more than he should, he didn't even bother arguing, he did it anyway.

We didn't even get to halfway through the film before Oliver said, 'That journal is cool!'

'Yeah, I wonder if you can buy that?'

'What, John Carter's journal? Yeah, I'd buy it!' Oliver kicked his shoes off to put his feet on the sofa.

'Imagine if it had all the worlds and maps in it.'

'Yeah, that would be awesome.'

And then towards the end. 'We could make our own?' I said.

'What, his diary?'

'No, ours! We could write about our own adventure.'

'Adventures!'

And as the film was ending, Oliver was already on it. 'Dad, that film was brilliant. Sam and I are going to do our own journal!'

'Cool idea, guys, what will you put in it?'

Oliver went all John Carter and waved his hand out in front of him as if he was following our spacecraft across the sky. 'A book to chart our voyage of learning and discovery, what we've learnt from films and life.'

'Yeah we can go on trips, perhaps Brighton or maybe Paris,' I said and then to Oliver, 'We'll have to take our parents in the beginning but after a while we can explore on our own.' In my mind, I saw it. We'd be a team and together we'd find adventure and do more than whatever it was Mum and Dad and the school had planned for us.

'Here you go, guys, here's some paper to get you going.'

'No, we need one of those blank books,' Oliver said. 'Let's call it *The Book of Lives and Living.*'

'Or *The Manual of Purpose and Doing.*'

Oliver made a face. 'Let's have a think on it?'

'Hey, we could paint the name on the book in dark red as though it was blood, and use one of those pens that make it look old.'

'Yeah and we need to draw our own charts, maps and pictures of the things we see and do.'

'Do one now?' Even Steve was getting excited. 'Come on, guys, do a map of the school or something. Perhaps with all its hidden tunnels or something and when you get your blank book we'll stick it in.' Steve passed us coloured pens and a ruler.

As we drew, our plan developed. My mum had ten pounds of my pocket money so I'd ask her if we could buy one of those special books with the leather binding. The diary would be a secret. I didn't want my sister having a read – she'd just laugh –so we'd keep it at Oliver's and he could bring it in each day. I could write entries up at school or just stick them in when we got together.

It was a great plan. But that was back then, and now it's all changed.

The Fountain of Knowledge is Mine

When Oliver came back three days later, after the fight, everything about him was changed. He didn't smile, he didn't say much, he could hardly look at me. I thought he was going to cry and you could see he was concentrating really hard so that he didn't. 'They've had a go at Dad,' he said. 'They're not happy with me. I think I've had it, SamIam.'

'What do you mean, had it?'

'A lady came around to the house and asked me loads of questions, you know, about home. Where I sleep, what I eat, if I'm happy. Then she asked questions about how much beer Dad has. What sort of things he does, and then... well, she asked if Dad had told me to use violence at school.'

'What did you say?'

Oliver looked worried. 'I told her the truth. You know Mum said honesty's the best policy.'

'Oh!'

'Yeah, but Dad's right, you gotta shoot first.'

'What?'

'Yeah, that's the reason some cowboys made it in the Wild West – not because they drew their pistol faster, but that that they decided to shoot first.'

It seemed a reasonable explanation to me. Makes

perfect sense. I've seen lots of fights at school and it's never fair. The person who gets beat up most isn't the one that gets the blame. Oliver had got the blame, and I know it sounds random if you say 'Mathew deserved it'.

At break, he told me more about what the lady said would happen and it was then he slipped me the laptop, The Fountain of Knowledge. I didn't realise he had it in his bag, but out it came.

'Look after it.'

'What! Why are you …?'

'I don't know if they'll take me away, I don't know if I'll be allowed to keep on coming here. But Dad said for me to give it to you. The lady never saw me put it in my bag.'

'Well okay, just till things are sorted. I'll look after it and carry on with our mission until we can do it together. But I can always come around to your house?'

Oliver was pretty upset, so I decided not to ask any more questions. I was too worried I'd say the wrong thing, and I thought I could talk more when he'd calmed down. But I never got the chance. Sure enough, as Oliver had said, he didn't come back the next day. Or the day after that. I kept on asking Mrs Stubbs where he was, but she said there had been an 'intervention'. That sounded bad, so I didn't ask any more. Sooner or later he'd be back.

Our project – *The Journal of Great Wisdom* – never got started. I didn't want to start it without Oliver. I wanted a joint project. If I started it without him, then it would be weird when he came back. I wouldn't want to join in halfway through if he had started one. Besides, I never got the same feeling as when I first watched the film. Nothing was pushing me to get started. The guy in the film had this thing where he really wanted to do something. He knew his destiny. And after the film, Oliver and I had that feeling too. But I'd lost it. I couldn't be bothered to get my mum to buy the empty book.

It was a difficult month waiting for Oliver to return. School just wasn't the same. The worst bit was the boredom at playtimes and lunch. I got to know the library area quite well. Life at home carried on as usual. Mum was working hard getting her reports done. Dad was busy with his websites. Kirsty was busy being herself, and being the centre of universe, not just Chichester.

School was the same, although they started a Nativity play to rehearse. It was a modern thing, although the music was quite old. We were going to do it with guitars and drums. The kings were going to be Bee Gees lookalikes, Mary was a disco queen, Joseph a breakdancer and little baby Jesus was going to sit up in his crib and sing another oldie: 'The Power of Love' by Frankie Goes to Hollywood. My mum told me to go in for one of the wise men which means I'd have to wear Lycra trousers and a big Motown wig, which is a gigantic afro hairstyle.

But the Nativity felt like a distraction, like I was ignoring something big. As if I was walking down the street with my family and there was a big pink whale in the middle of the high street but no one was talking about it. Class was where it became difficult. No one was talking about Oliver. He'd disappeared, and no one knew anything.

Our headmaster Mr Jeff is really nice. He hardly ever wears a tie. Mum says that's a good thing, but Dad disagrees. I saw him in the playground and we had a talk like we usually do. He always gets us talking about the stuff we like and what's going on in our lives. He's a bit of a film fanatic too. At the end of the summer term they had a film night, and he decided to show *My Neighbour Totoro*. He said it was 'a beautiful film. It showed the innocent freedom of a child's imagination'. Steve told me beforehand that 'wonderful cuddly Totoro was in fact the Japanese version of the Grim Reaper'. I asked Dad about that and he said, 'You could enjoy the film at two different levels', and he liked it because although it was a cartoon, it wasn't Disney. I just thought the cat turning into a flying bus was brilliant.

Anyway, Mr Jeff wasn't in the mood for talking about films so when I got to a good moment I asked him, 'What's happened to Oliver?' His face changed straight away, as if I'd asked him for the answers to next week's spelling test.

'We're not too sure if Oliver will be coming back.'

Before I knew it, he'd changed the subject and was asking about the rehearsals for the Nativity. I couldn't work out what the big deal was. People don't vanish. You can't tell me he didn't know what was happening with Oliver.

26

It upset me that no one else in the class cared. It was only me that wanted to know. I went home and I guess I came across as a bit demanding but as I came through the door I said, 'What's happened to Oliver?'

Mum looked surprised. 'We're not... well...'

'We suspect that that little incident with Mat got both Oliver and his dad into a lot of trouble,' Dad said. 'He must have changed schools.'

'Well can you call him to find out?'

Dad looked at me. Lips pressed tight. 'Well yeah, of course, if I had the number.'

That was weird. How was it we didn't know Steve's telephone number? We'd arranged things by our parents talking in the playground. I didn't even have his address. I knew he lived in the Southsea part of Portsmouth, but that was it. How totally wrong it felt. I'd been to his loads of times, but I couldn't even tell you which road he lived in. It came as quite a shock. I felt really stupid. I wanted to hit something.

I felt like there was nothing I could do. I went upstairs and sat on my bed. It was then that I saw the laptop. I hadn't opened it since the day Oliver had given it to me. I'd been waiting for him. Quickly, I opened it up and signed in. As if it were yesterday, I saw the list of films we'd choose from and imagined Steve guiding me what to see. My eye saw *The Last of the Mohicans*. I thought that was a hairstyle. It was a 12 certificate so a learning factor of one. Not a bad place to start.

The film was epic, a great adventure about Indians and the English army from centuries ago. It's funny

27

taking the side of the Indians against the English army. They come across as mean and silly. As though they'd just turn up and not have to fight very hard. The Mohican guy was well sorted: he knew everything about tracking and surviving in the wild. Anyway, the lesson of the film wasn't about survival or fighting, it was about his friendship with a woman. They get on really well and despite the war going on, they decide they want to live together. But then the woman's kidnapped, just when you think they're going to live happily ever after. And he tells her she's not to worry as he'll find her whatever happens. I saw the film before supper. I put my headphones on so no one could hear it and it finished just before they called me down. So it was perfect timing.

My dad asked me what I'd been up to and I just said I'd been on the computer. So really it was only half a lie – a white lie, if you like. But it still felt bad not saying what I'd really been doing. After all, my dad was strict on watching films. I don't think he agreed with Steve's understanding of how the certificate system worked.

*

It had been a busy week and I was beginning to think about Oliver less, but Friday morning I woke up from a really weird dream. I was kidnapped and no one could find me, no one came. I was running through this forest calling out, but although I ran faster and faster, I never seemed to get anywhere. I woke up

28

in a sweat, and in that moment, I got this really strong picture of Oliver. I put two and two together and understood straightaway what my dream meant. I had to find Oliver. I couldn't let him down. It would be difficult, but that was my quest.

And then, as I sat at breakfast scoffing my cereal, I knew what I wanted to do with the journal. *The Book of the Quest.*

'Mum?'

'Please don't talk with your mouth full.'

'Can we go into town after school?' Before she could answer, I said, 'I want to go and get a book.' I stopped myself in time from saying diary. I remembered that keeping a diary should be a secret. If they knew I was writing it, they might try to read it. 'I want to get a blank book.' I looked her hard, one of my 'this-is-really-important-to-me stares'. 'I want one of those leather-bound books I can doodle in'.

My mum looked at me, her eyebrows battling for the centre of her face.

'Leather-bound, hark at you!' Kirsty was in first. 'Why does it have to be leather?'

I ignored her. 'I've still got that ten pounds, haven't I, Mum?'

'Yes you have.' She finished her mouthful. 'Do you know where they sell them?'

'They sell blank paper pads in Tesco's, Mum, for a pound.' Kirsty was having another go.

'I was going to do a bit of a project.'

'That's fine. We'll go shopping tomorrow morning then. I might have to put a couple of quid in. I think

29

they're more than a tenner.'

'Thanks, Mum, you're the best!' I jumped up and put my arms around her. I hadn't been so excited for a long time.

Saturday 9th November

I waited patiently for Mum to wake up and when she saw me, she giggled and said, 'Alright, let me get dressed and have some breakfast!'

When we got back, I raced up to my bedroom, two steps at a time, closed my door and put my treasure on my desk. When I say desk, it's more of a platform. There isn't enough space for a desk. Kirsty's got the big middle bedroom and I have the one at the end, above the bathroom.   Because it's so tiny, Dad converted this old chest of drawers by taking out the drawers so I could sit on my bed and put my legs underneath the top. It sounds funny, but works well. It's also a great place to hide if Kirsty has one of her moods; she still hasn't worked out I can get in that space – probably because she can't.

I sat and slowly took my book out of the bag, feeling the ridge of the spine under the plastic wrapper. It looked lovely. I unwrapped it and turned each page, as though I might find one that wasn't blank. For a full ten minutes I sat with my hands on the book, staring out the window. It felt like the start of something big. I'd got a new pen too. Mum bought that, one of those italic felt pens to write the title on the cover. First I practised writing it on the paper bag. And then, in my best writing, I wrote on the first page: *THE BOOK OF QUESTS AND KNOWLEDGE.* There it was, I'd started. It looked great; there was a small break in the 'd' in 'and', but I underlined it and the gap disappeared.

'Kirsty! Sam! Supper!'

Wow, where had the day gone? I heard Kirsty come out of her room and then put her hand on my door handle. I put my school bag over my desk, just in time.

'Watcha doin?'

'Homework.'

'They were talking about Oliver yesterday.' Kirsty's in Miss Benny's class. 'Rachel said he's been put in prison for hitting Mat.'

'What?'

'Yeah, well he nearly broke his nose, didn't he? The police take that sort of thing seriously. Rachel said they took his dad away too because he hadn't brought his kid up right.' She looked at me for a response, but I wasn't going to give one. I'd learnt about that.

'Oh.'

I walked downstairs. If I'd stayed in the bedroom, Kirsty would have just kept on talking.

Mum was serving up. 'Have you washed your hands, Sam?'

'Mum, you don't go to prison for hitting someone on the nose, do you?'

'Well you could do!'

'But not Oliver, they wouldn't have put him in prison would they?'

'What do you mean?'

'Kirsty said they put Oliver in prison.'

'Kirsty!' Mum gave her a stare as she put the food on the table.

'Well that's what they're saying at school, I'm only repeating what they said. And the police were called to school after the fight!'

'No they weren't!' I know that's not right, because there have been fights before at school and the police aren't called. You get people who talk about stuff and they make it bigger than it is.

Dad was sitting at the table reading the paper. 'Kirsty, they don't put you in prison for that kind of thing.'

Kirsty put her knife and fork down. 'No, but they have a special prison, don't they? Secure children's homes? He'd have gone there!'

Dad put down his paper. 'Kirsty, Oliver did a bad thing, but it doesn't warrant going there.'

'Well he could have broken Mat's nose and damaged him for life. That's not right! They don't let people like that in our school. They have to go somewhere else and be with their own kind.'

'Kirsty, that's enough!' Mum began to serve the food. 'You're talking about Sam's friend.'

I really didn't want to be sitting down at the table right then, I just wanted to get back to my book. I tried to ignore what Kirsty said, but she was winning. 'Mum, can I eat upstairs. Just for today? I want to do my book.'

'No, we always eat together, Sam. That's what families do. You can go after supper.' There was silence as Mum served out the lasagne.

Dad poured the water. 'So, have you bought your book then, Sam?'

'Yeah, Mum and I got it this morning.'

'What do you want to put in there?'

'Oh you know, funny drawings and things, jokes from school and stuff.'

'And how's this Nativity going? Are you having fun with that?'

Kirsty started again. 'I've heard it's going to be really stupid. They've got some really weird ideas. Rachel's mum said that it might even be cancelled as it's making a joke about Christmas.'

'Well don't come then! And tell your stupid friend to keep away. It's going to be a great show!'

'Sam!' Mum stared at me.

Silence followed; I don't think Dad was impressed with my outburst, but she had to be told. Finally, Dad broke the silence. 'I think it's time to move on, Sam. We don't know where Oliver is, but he's got his family. They've got to work through their own problems. It's what happens in life and we shouldn't interfere. Just accept that he's at another school now. One day you might meet him again, but things change. It's how life goes.'

I couldn't answer Dad. As I looked at the food on my plate, I felt a little bit sick. Why don't people understand? There's no way in the world that I can forget about Oliver. No one was saying anything and I only just managed to eat it all.

'Dad, I'm not going to forget Oliver because... because he and I are the same and I don't know

34

anyone else like him. Do you remember our day at cosplay?' Dad didn't reply. 'Well that was the best day, and life hasn't been the same since then.' Dad was still quiet. Not even Kirsty was saying anything. 'Mum, can I go upstairs please?' Mum nodded and I was gone.

*

Dear Reader of the Quest

The idea for this book was supposed to be more of an adventure into discovering the world. But my fellow explorer has disappeared. He may be in captivity. My quest is to find my friend Oliver, and I hereby make a solemn promise to find him, wherever he may be.

Oliver, I WILL find you.

I don't really have any clues. I have asked the people in charge and they either don't care or they won't tell. My plan is to get a plan. This would be easier if I had my friend with me, but then of course if he was here, I wouldn't need a plan.

I looked at my journal. It looked great. I'd been worried about starting, but now I had, I could see how it would take shape. I needed to write about my day out at Brighton with Oliver, when we'd done cosplay at the Film and Cartoon event at Brighton. I needed to record that day and it would help me from missing Oliver – and perhaps it would help me with making a plan to find him.

I heard Kirsty come upstairs, so I put my school bag back on the table. She opened the door. 'You doin' that silly book?'

'Just homework.'

'Can I borrow your ruler?'

I was pleased that was all she wanted. But it got me thinking. I needed two things: a lock on the door and a place to hide the book. My dad putting a lock on the door, I knew, just wasn't going to happen. He might buy the lock but getting around to fitting it would take ages. I'd seen it before, the big discussion about what, when and how and then the shopping and then you'd watch the stuff they'd bought sit around waiting to be done. I needed something now. I looked at the door – what could I do? I examined the door lever like I'd never seen it before. Funny that I'd been using it for my whole lifetime but now I could see there had been a lock there. There was a keyhole, just no key. okay, so I should ask Dad if he had a key.

Now, the diary. My dad always says that if you want to hide or secure something, the first thing you do is think about the places where people will look. Where would people look in my bedroom: under the mattress, behind the picture, at the bottom of a drawer? These were the obvious places, the places Kirsty would look at first. Dad does a lot of security work for his website stuff. He says you've got to stop people from hacking the website, so you hide the good stuff. You don't make a file called 'Important stuff, keep out', you call the file 'XY dead and dull'. No one would look in there. He calls it 'security from obscurity'. Thanks, Dad! There was the answer. Hide it in my bookcase.

I knew what I had to do straight away. I've got a book in my bookcase that I was given as a kid: it's a Rupert Bear annual. My dad read some of it to me when I was a kid, but I never liked it. I carefully detached the cover from the pages and within a few minutes I had my hiding place. It looked great. The book cover wrapped around my diary perfectly. When I wanted to write in my diary, l could just take it out of the bookcase and then put the cover back in the slot.

It was time to fire up The Fountain of Knowledge so I could put another entry in my diary. I guess I needed a place to hide the laptop too, but that would be more difficult. I looked at the long list of films. Steve had highlighted them with a colour. Gold were must-see films, what he called life-changing, stories you can't forget, moments you'd want in your own life or films which would change the way you wanted to live *your* life. Green ones were films you should watch because they were things you should know, like famous battles or people that had done things. He said that it would help with history and geography, and make you a more rounded person. Red were films about love, and he told me I was too young for them. But they were good to understand earlier than later, to prevent making mistakes. Steve said that before I got married there were long lists of films I should see. He said it was less painful to learn from other people's mistakes than it was to learn from your own. But so few people spent the time imagining what had happened to other people and instead spent time repeating the misfortunes that had happened to others.

He got me to imagine what it would have been like to have been a slave in nineteenth-century America. To have been captured in your village in Africa and then be told to live and work in a way that was totally different to what you wanted to do. To have all of your freedom taken away from you, including who you married, where you went, or even what language you spoke. I'd never thought about it before, but then we saw *Roots* and I understood. I had a lot of questions though, like why did the people think it was ever okay for there to be slavery?

Then there were the silver films. These were feel-good films. Steve said I had to be careful of these. They had their place, but if you only saw this kind of film all the time then you would get a distorted view of the world. He said these kinds of films were best if you'd had a bad day. They were excellent for changing your mood back to happy. It was about balance. He explained that it was difficult to choose a colour for this category, but that silver was the closest colour to sugar apart from white, which he said was arguably not a colour. Scientists would say that white was a colour, and black wasn't. And an artist would say black was a colour, and white wasn't. Anyway, the point was that you can't just make yourself happy by watching sweet films in your life. That was no more helpful than putting sugar in your tea. I don't drink tea, but I know Dad says sugar is bad.

The last category was the black films. These, he said, came with a big warning. He would have preferred to have used red, as red is the usual warning sign. But red was definitely about love as it was all about emotion and passion. These black films were films which showed 'in a very raw way' what Steve called 'man's inhumanity to man'. They were dark films. Films which might question whether you're safe or whether the world is a good place. He told us never to watch them unless we felt in a safe place and could discuss them with an adult afterwards. And just as you shouldn't fill your life up with sugar, you shouldn't fill your life up with too much beer either. You needed balance.

So I realised that I needed to choose wisely. I'd last seen *The Last of the Mohicans,* which Steve had coloured gold. I looked at the list – what would be good now? I was happy, so didn't need sugar. I wasn't with anyone else to discuss the film, so shouldn't see black. I didn't need to know about love, so red was out. Green it was then.

I never got the chance to choose. Mum and Dad were arguing downstairs. I know it's rude to listen to other people's conversations, but this sounded important. I opened my door and walked to the top of the stairs.

Mum was talking. 'Why didn't you tell me before? We wouldn't have bought the car.'

'I wasn't given any warning.'

'Yes you were, you've just told me you weren't getting on with your manager.'

'Yes, but I've never got on with him. I didn't know they needed to make redundancies!'

'So what are you going to do now?!'

'Well, I have been looking on the internet. I've signed up with a few agencies.'

'How long have you known?'

Dad paused. 'About six weeks.'

'Six weeks! And you didn't think to tell me?'

'I didn't want to worry you.'

'Well, I am pretty worried now!'

There was a sudden silence as Mum and Dad seemed to reach a point of 'well that's that then'. A silence in which I shifted my weight. The floor creaked.

'Kirsty? Kirsty, have you been listening?'

'It's me, Mum.'

'Sam? Have you been listening all this time?'

'Sorry.'

'I've told you before, it's rude to listen to other people's conversations.'

'Janice?!' Dad said, loudly.

'Well, can't we have a private conversation in our own home?'

Kirsty had appeared by my side. 'It was hardly private! I could hear you in my bedroom.'

'Don't be rude!'

'Well I'm just saying we couldn't help but hear, you two have been shouting at each other!'

'Kirsty, get into your room.'

40

I saw Dad standing at the bottom of the stairs, his head bowed. Mum was glaring at Kirsty and me, but Dad didn't look at us. He shuffled his feet. The silence seemed to suck up the whole house in that one moment. I walked down to Dad and tried to put my arm around him. 'Sorry to hear... to hear your news, Dad.'

'Thanks, son.' Dad gave me a squeeze.

Monday 11th November

I had a really long dream last night. It seemed that I'd been busy for the whole night and felt exhausted when I woke up. I was fighting an army, protecting my family and friends, being chased and our home had been taken. I was trying to be the hero, but I was getting it wrong. At the end there was a big cage and scramble to escape. It got muddled. There was an evil guard and as I awoke, the guard and cage just melted away and the thought of Oliver came to me. The whole dream vanished in an instant. I couldn't remember any of it. All that was left was Oliver, the way he looked when he passed me the laptop. His face so un-Oliver. Like one of those photos taken of prisoners when they're arrested.

I had often thought of writing to him, but I'd need his address. If I could write to him, I'd just send my telephone number and he could call me. Then I had one of those good ideas that are so good, they're obvious. The people that would know his address were at school, they'd know it for sure. See, I told you it was obvious.

I think it was because it was so obvious that I didn't plan my approach. At the first break, I went to the school office. That's where everyone goes if you want anything to do with administration, which is writing letters and things and where you fill out and hand in forms. They also have diaries to make meetings and, of course, record everything they know about the kids there. Like where they live!

I always say hello to Mrs Ford. She always smiles at me. Her first name is Sue, but she wants us to call her Mrs Ford, like the teachers. I checked she wasn't too busy. People that are busy find it easier to say they can't help you. She wasn't on the phone and there wasn't anyone waiting to talk to her. She's a nice lady, you can tell because she always asks how I'm getting on. She knows my sister too and teases us about being twins and not getting on.

'Mrs Ford?'

'Yes, Sam, how are you today?'

'Good thanks,' and then I remembered. 'Are you all right too?'

She smiled. 'I'm very well thank you, is there something you needed?'

'Yes please. I'm trying to get in touch with Oliver. I was going to send him a letter. It's been a while since he was here and I don't think he's going to come back.'

As I spoke, Mrs Ford's eyes seemed to get smaller. 'I'm sorry, Sam. I'm not allowed to give out that information. Have you asked your parents? They must have Mr Bridle's number.'

'I don't think so, Mrs Ford, they would have said so by now.'

Mrs Ford looked at me with a different smile, it wasn't her usual one, it was flatter only the ends

43

turned up and her eyes didn't say 'smile', they were saying 'problem'. That meant 'no address'.

'Okay, thanks anyway.'

'Bye, Sam. Go and have some fun in the playground.'

'Okay, bye, Mrs Ford.'

When I walked away, it felt a little strange, as if I'd only got half the story. Which I suppose makes perfect sense, because I didn't get any part of any story. Oh well, more thinking to do. I did what Mrs Ford suggested and went back to the playground. It was quite different since Oliver had left. I'd tried to join in with a few games, but I didn't really feel like it. If only I liked football then it would be okay, I'd have something to do.

At home I thought I'd check, perhaps Mrs Ford had a point. 'Dad, do you have Oliver's telephone number.' As I asked this I had another one of those feelings like 'well that's obvious'. Of course they had his number that's how they used to call me up when I had a sleepover.

'Why do you ask, Sam?'

'I want to speak to Oliver.'

Dad's face started to look like Mrs Ford's. 'Sam, I think it's best if we just leave that alone now. There's obviously been some kind of problem and we shouldn't get involved. Oliver's probably not coming back to your school and since he lives in another town, let's just move on. It's time for you to make new friends.'

I sat down heavily on the sofa and folded my arms.

This just didn't make sense. We sat there in silence for a minute. My dad just kept on reading the paper. I knew he had nothing more to say. I could keep on asking but just like Mrs Ford, there was some kind of rule and I just had to accept that's the way things are.

Upstairs, my journal was laughing at me. There it was, my quest written out, and I was getting nowhere. Not even the easy bits were easy. I sat on my bed and thought. Nothing came. So I pulled out the journal anyway.

Dear Reader of the Quest

My plan has been blocked. The people in charge are not giving me the information I need to contact Oliver. There must be something they know that I don't, and that is the reason this is becoming so difficult. I don't have Oliver's address or phone number, surely there is another way to reach him. The quest continues, I will find another way.

Since I didn't have anything else to add, I thought a picture would be good. After all I hadn't even filled up a page yet. I got out my italic pen and did a fancy Q to the beginning of quest. I did a picture of a poster on a lamppost of 'Help! Oliver Bridle – Missing' and then a picture of his face. The face was good, but looked nothing at all like Oliver. And then I realised that I couldn't remember his face. That was worrying, was my brain telling me to forget him too?

So then I remembered I needed to tell the diary

about my day out with Oliver and Steve and why Dad asking me to forget Oliver is ridiculous. I put a new heading in the diary.

A Magical Day of Cosplay

Dear Diary

Dad just doesn't understand how important Oliver is to me and perhaps you don't either. I need to tell you about the longest, bestest and most magical day ever and then at least you will understand.

'Sam?!' Mum was calling from downstairs. 'Come on, lights out.'

'Okay, Mum.'

As I lay there in the dark, I thought of what Dad had said, but soon my mind drifted and I was remembering my day. The magical day of cosplay.

The Magical Day of Cosplay

It was the summer holidays and I'd gone for a sleepover at Oliver's. Dad dropped me outside after work. Dad never comes in to meet Steve, he waits in the car until the front door opens. The first time he did come in, but it was awkward. I don't think our dads have much to talk about.

Because there was no school the next day, I was going to stay for two nights. A double sleepover whammy. I thought we'd just be playing at his home, or going to the common to watch the hovercraft come in and play in the park. But once inside, they explained we were going to a cosplay event in the morning, so we were getting ready for it. I just concentrated on the word play. That sounded fun. But then I realised that cosplay was something specific. The word comes from costume play. You have to dress up and pretend to be a particular character, like at Halloween. So it was going to be a fancy dress party, except with hundreds of people you didn't know and it wasn't for an hour or two, but the whole day.

'The event is a Comic Con. Con stands for convention.' Oliver explained. 'Dad's won prizes for his costumes.'

Steve got into character. He was going as Thor. 'Who would like a cup of tea?' he said, big and

47

booming. As if it were a very important decision that could change the course of world history.

We went upstairs to the spare room. As Oliver pushed open the door, stuff fell out into the hallway. The room was bulging, full of clothes and props. Steve grabbed a box and handed it to Oliver so we could get in. He held up a jacket against me, like Mum does when we go clothes shopping. 'No, that's not you.' Then another, this time a full head-to-toe outfit. I put it on – it was Aladdin. Steve looked at Oliver.

'Dad, can Sam use that brilliant one I used last time?'

'You're right! Okay, give me a few minutes, I've got to get to the window.'

Steve explained that tomorrow was about spending time with your tribe and being the person you wanted to be. It was a lot of fun choosing costumes and playing around. Two hours later, we'd finished. I was going as Peter Pan and Oliver was doing Harry Potter, which he said is what he usually does. Steve had me primed up with sentences to say and actions to do. So there we were, with Steve with his massive hammer, me with a silver sword and Oliver with his wand. Oliver had been talking in Harry Potter language the whole evening. By the end, I was turned in to a mouse, cursed, made invisible, turned pink, burst into flames, covered in boils, and levitated to the ceiling. Which I pretended to do by climbing to the top of a pile of boxes.

I practised drawing a lightning scar on Oliver's forehead, which was difficult because he wouldn't sit still. Then someone came to the door. They wanted to talk to Steve about God and his beliefs. Steve stepped back into the hallway so he could raise his hammer. 'Am I not your true and only God? The God of Thunder! Do you question my authority, lowly creature? Get you gone!' With that, he took a step forward and the caller looked as if thought Steve was the real Thor and ran away. Steve stepped out the door shaking his hammer and shouted, 'Do not darken my castle gate again with your vile nonsense.' Oliver and I fell on the floor weeping.

In the morning, we set off without breakfast and walked to the train station dressed in our costumes. Steve had brushed his hair and tidied his beard. Although it was early, there were still quite a few people around, and most of them were staring at us. At the station, Steve asked us in his Thor voice, 'The first task is before you, brave warriors. Which of you will make good the purchase of the tariff to the yonder city of Brighton?'

'Dad wants one of us to buy the tickets,' Oliver explained. 'He likes us do that sort of thing, you know, to build our confidence.'

'I'll do it,' I said. Steve looked at me with a Thor look of indignation. So I tried again. 'Mighty Thor, I will carry out this deed.' Steve winked and gave me the money as we got in the queue. I asked the man for the tickets and he asked me for £33. I was just going to pass over the money when I heard Thor behind me.

'Kindly Earth warrior, can you please clarify if the special proclamation of Asgard, that two shall travel as one, is still law in this kingdom?'

The man looked up at Steve and tapped into his keyboard. '£22... your grace,' he said, without smiling.

Steve bellowed from behind, 'Tis a great service you have bestowed upon us, thank you and may your day be one of glory.' Oliver and I hid our laughter till we were out of the queue.

It was like that the whole way there: Steve refused to talk in any voice that couldn't be heard by the whole of the carriage and that included talking to the ticket collector, the guard, the lady on the snack trolley and then any passenger that sat next to us.

One guy played along with Steve and they kept it up for ages, talking about stuff in the news from an Asgardian's point of view. The other guy was playing Loki, Thor's brother. Then Steve was trying to get Oliver and me to act. Steve asked me if I was missing Neverland. I managed a few sentences, but I hadn't done it before, so I guess I was just shy.

Oliver was getting into his role by waving a paper bag under my nose. 'Rat poison sweet?'

'Oh, yum!' They were actually chocolates.

'Hey, we only really needed two tickets. I could've used my invisibility cloak.'

'It is not befitting of the integrity of a God to avoid buying a ticket!'

'Well, in Neverland no one has the need for tickets. Trains haven't been invented yet,' I said

Steve gave me the thumbs up. 'That's it, Peter! You're getting there.' And then he rose to his feet and his voice was even deeper and louder. 'Sam, I bestow upon thee the power of imagination and supreme confidence so you can be a brave man. So few get to be true men before they die. So few come to realise their destiny or find their true voice. Don't wait for the time when you feel you've found these things. Believe that you have found them and you will be victorious in life, love and death.' And with that, he put his hand down for me to kneel, and then he tapped me on the shoulders and my head with his hammer. 'Rise, warrior Sam, for you are now a great man.'

I don't know what came over me, but I stood on the seat, waved my sword in the air, and announced to the carriage, 'To live will be an awfully big adventure. Second to the right, and straight on till morning. That is the way to the Neverland!' And then I did a big dramatic bow like Steve had shown me, starting above my head and then cupping and rolling my hand to my knees. The lady next to us clapped and that started the whole carriage off, till someone wolf-whistled and cheered. It was excellent!

We had to walk from the station to the Metropole, which was a big hotel on the sea front. The closer we got, the more people we saw in costumes. Then we saw the beach and then the hotel. It was huge. Outside was a sign across the front of the building: *Film & Comic Con Brighton. Costume Role Play at the Hilton Brighton Metropole Hotel.* I could see the i360 Tower and the pier with the rides on the end. We joined the queue. It was going to be at least a twenty-minute wait. Everyone was excited, talking about their costumes, what was on and who was there.

Then people were coming up to Steve and asking him what he was doing that day. I didn't understand what they meant. Was Steve performing? How did they know Steve? I looked at Oliver, puzzled.

'Dad does a stall at these cosplay events.'

'A stall?'

'Yeah, you know, like a table. A table which is a shop. Mum and Dad used to sell clothes. People had their picture taken with them, and they'd put on little mini acts. They've got loads of fans.' Oliver dropped his wand. 'Argh!'

I made a face at him, like *why did you do that?*

'I'm always like this before a show, my hands just shake with excitement! Why aren't you doing a stall today, Dad?' Oliver asked.

'It'll be different without Mum. Let's just take it easy today.'

Then I saw Captain Hook walking past us on the way to the end of the queue. Without thinking, I shouted, 'Oi, Captain Hook! How did you get that hook, then?' What had I said? He was on me in seconds.

'Raise your sword, you blackguard!'

I just got it up in time before he brought his down. I guess he knew mine was plastic because he was gentle. People stood back to give us space.

'I'll kill that Peter Pan who cut off my hand.'

'Tinkerbell and I will get you walking your own plank, Captain Hook.'

After a battle, I danced around the back of him and

tapped him gently on his bum with my sword. I think he was a year younger than me, so I wasn't frightened. It didn't last long, I think he wanted to get in the queue. So we both laughed and bowed to each other. People in the queue were taking photos and were clapping.

Steve patted me on the shoulder. 'Hey, Sam, you're a natural, you've got a chance for a prize today!'

When we got through the door and went to buy our tickets, something really random happened. A man at the door approached Steve and shook his hand. Then he spoke into his walkie-talkie and said, 'The Leather Man's here.' And that was it! He led us through the doors and we didn't have to pay!

We heard the noise of it all before we stepped into the massive hall. There was so much going on, and there were hundreds of people. The first thing we saw was this huge screen with Bumblebee from *Transformers* fighting with a Decepticon in New York. They were chucking each other at buildings and causing mayhem amongst the crowd. Then I saw how it worked. There were two real life people wearing sensors and every time they moved, Bumblebee and the Decepticon moved.

'Dad, can we have a go?' Oliver asked.

'Come on, guys, we can still have plenty of fun without spending £20, and it looks like a forty-minute queue.'

As we walked through to another hall, we caught the end of a parade. The costumes were amazing. Oliver and Steve were pointing out their favourites and Steve was shouting out stuff like 'brilliant costume, Spiderman', 'well done, guys' and 'great effort'. And then right at the end, 'Hey, Legolas, brilliant crown!'

'Cost me five coat hangers, thirty glue sticks and ten hours!'

'No, it's brilliant, absolutely worth it!'

Afterwards, Steve explained about the costumes. 'The guy in red was more OC, original characters, or possibly steam punk fusion. But did you see Batman? I spoke to him and he had his body armour built by a car body shop. They used carbon fibre. It must have cost a fortune!'

Oliver explained, 'Mum and Dad made their own costumes and they used to sell them on the internet. Someone paid Dad £2,000 for his King Arthur outfit. He went up to Dad as he was coming off the stage. He had loads of money in his hand and just said "I gotta have it!".'

Then Steve said, 'Did you see the X-Men one? It's a great costume, but bits of it came from Argos. The roller skates were effective, it looked as if he was floating, and those coloured contact lens were scary, eh? Like snake eyes!'

Oliver continued, 'We used to hire out costumes too. People came around to the house to try them on and they'd end up staying for the evening, just talking and mucking around.'

'Hey, Oliver, do you remember the last time we were here at the Metropole?'

'Yeah, that was the year we saw Gillian Anderson,

from *The X Files*. Dad and I ran from a whole load of stormtroopers, but Luke Skywalker appeared and said "Stand behind me", and he had a real lightsaber. Well, you know, not real, but it looked like the real thing, it couldn't kill anyone.'

'Don't forget that car.'

'Yeah, they had the car from *Back to the Future* and you could sit in it.'

'We got an autograph from Akira Toriyamao, you know, who did Dragon Ball Z.' I guess Steve was talking comics.

'Then I got this amazing magazine that the Disney stand were giving out for free! Oh and a woman went up to Dad and gave him a hug, and said he was awesome. I can still remember Dad's face now like "who are you?". Dad said she was a groupie.'

'Don't forget the food, Ollie.'

'They had a food stall selling Gagh, Klingon food. It was a plate of serpent worms. They were jet black and we had a whole bowlful.'

'What did it taste of?'

'Spaghetti, it was just pasta, but it looked great!'

'Hey, Steve!' There were three people behind us looking excited and wearing outfits from the *Thor* film, which I recognised as Loki, Odin and Sif, and then I saw someone not in costume. Was that Natalie Portman, the one that plays Jane Foster?

Oliver pulled on my sword. 'I think that's Natalie Portman.'

'No, she wouldn't be here.'

'She could be!'

'Hi, Bill, long time no see!' Steve said, shaking his hand. 'You're looking good, who did your make-up?'

Bill put his arm around Natalie. 'Thanks for that! This is Brenda, she's fab at make-up.'

I looked at Oliver, disappointed, but in awe she looked so much like her. She had that mole on her cheek, what Mum calls a beauty spot.

'Come on! Let's get a few pics together,' Bill said.

Steve went into Thor mode. 'Jane Foster Earth lady, willst thou stand by my side? My left is my best, and you will honour it with your beauty.'

'Why thank you, great lord,' she said and did a funny curtsey. 'How masterful!' She winked at Sif.

Then they lined up and everyone around us stopped talking and formed a big circle around them. It was magic! About fifty cameras came out from nowhere and loads of flashes were going off. Then this professional guy crouched down. He had one of those long lenses. And from behind him, a guy with a huge spotlight. 'No. Bring it from the side can you?' the photographer said, directing the lighting guy. Thor, Loki, Sif and Jane went into movie mode and pulled poses in slow motion. Steve did this thing where he raised the hammer over his head with his other arm outstretched. He looked huge, I didn't realise how muscly he was.

Thor barked at the cameraman, 'Take your best shot, Earth being.'

The crowd laughed and I was pushed forward as more people were trying to have a look. Someone shouted, 'Hey, Thor, give Loki a hit. Slow mo!' Steve turned and hammered Loki, who brought his sword to meet it. Sif and Jane held each other, their hands on their hearts. Then I saw a man with a massive video camera on his shoulder and a sound guy with one of those microphones on a long stick.

I heard a person behind me. 'Yeah, that's The Leather Man. I bought a costume from him and his wife.'

'What, the X-Men one?'

'Yeah, he did the leather work... shame about his wife. Did you hear about it?'

'So young, it's just so bonkers. She was thriving one minute and then just taken.'

'So do you think the costume's increased in value?'

Then this guy in a suit and a microphone walked up to the Asgardians and had a chat. They stood up straight and looked at the video camera and the crowd went silent. The suit guy put the microphone to his mouth. 'It is with great pleasure that we welcome Steve Bridle, The Leather Man, to the show, a warm favourite of so many. We've tried to persuade Steve to do a little stage show and a talk on the main stage today. Any change there, Steve?'

Steve smiled, but wagged his finger.

'For those of you that don't know, Steve usually does a light and sound show with his... with other characters and there's lots of fun in the small sketches that they do. Also, I'd like to support Steve's costume-making and...' Suit Man was drowned out by everyone clapping and wolf-whistles. It was funny seeing Steve

57

from the crowd. It was as if he was someone else.

Oliver told a boy next to us, 'That's my Dad!'

Steve hushed everyone and held his hand up for the microphone. 'Thank you so much, everyone. Hopefully we'll get a chance to chat later, but I just wanted to say... well to explain really why I'm not doing a show this year.'

Steve suddenly stopped talking and was searching for our faces and then looked at Oliver. The silence was getting long.

'Angela has passed. I know many of you know that already, but I'm sorry if that is a shock. I came along today to see you all and be with friends, but to be honest it's been hard and I'm just going to chill out for a while.' Steve paused and people were calling out 'We're thinking of you, man', 'Lots of love, Steve', 'She was lovely', 'We miss her'.

Steve went to speak, and it was quiet again. 'I need to say one thing.' He paused. 'Guys, you're here because you love who you are when you love what you do – cosplay. Remember to live! Keep on living your lives completely and in your own lifetime.'

Their clapping was huge, people were calling out, and the crowd were pushing in tighter. I got separated from Oliver.

'Guys, above all I wanted to remind you... love each other. Love each other completely and do it properly, no half measures.' Everyone went berserk and was shouting out more stuff. 'I will be back... fully back, you know like last year, just give me time. I know Angela would have loved to be here with you.'

Steve hesitated again as if lost in a memory.

Suit Man stepped in. 'Thank you so much for those words, Steve. Perhaps we can persuade you to join the Marvel photoshoot a bit later on the cosplay stage, or one of the masquerades?'

Everyone was clapping again and as suddenly as the crowd had formed, it dissolved.

Steve waved to us, shook the Asgardians' hands and came over to us. 'Right, guys, I'll go and get our lunch.'

'Can't we eat here and have that random food?'

'I need to save a few pennies, Ollie, they want one-fifty for a coke here. Besides, that sandwich place around the corner is yum and I can grab a quick beer.'

'Oh yeah, those baguettes!'

'Steve, Mum gave me a fiver for lunch.'

'You put that in your piggy bank, Sam, you never know when you'll need it. A fiver isn't much money, but when you haven't got £5, it's a fortune! You hold the camera.' He placed the strap over Oliver's head. 'Keep it safe. Right, who wants what?'

After Steve walked off, Oliver started to go to the next stall.

'Shouldn't we stay here?' I said.

'It's all right, Dad always finds me. Come on, let's see if we can get an autograph.'

I think Oliver and I were almost the youngest there. It felt exciting being on our own, unreal! The crowd, the buzz of everyone chatting and laughing, it was as if they'd sprayed happy gas on the whole event and people were sucking it up.

'You didn't tell me your dad is a cosplay God.'

'Yeah, well, until you've been to one of these things you just wouldn't get it. Dad used to do Film Studies at university. He met Mum on a cosplay event. She went as Snow White, he was Prince Charming. Mum nearly fell of the stage, but he caught her. The audience shouted "Kiss, kiss, kiss!" and that was it – they were together. Dad says it was as if someone had cast a love spell over them. You know... they were just always laughing together all the time.'

Oliver rubbed something out of his eye. 'People would come to their stand to have their picture with them. Dad used a green screen and when he got home he'd put film sets behind the people. No one knew what the backdrop was until they got the photo in the post. He'd spend ages fixing the images and people still contact him from years before. Dad says it was Mum that was good at the money-making. I don't think Dad's interested in running the website. It's changed now Mum's gone.'

He grabbed my arm. 'LOOK at that!'

'What?'

'The woman in blue.'

'Wow.'

Just ahead, a brightly coloured lady with a blue suit was coming towards us. She seemed to be floating. Her arms stretched out in front of her and she was smiling, her teeth brilliant white against the blue. Everyone around her was just staring, their mouths open. Then I realised why. She wasn't wearing anything. But it wasn't as if she was naked. She'd painted her body in electric blue and then stuck on beads and things to make it look like scales. She looked like a dream.

'Peter?' The lady was right in front of me. 'I can see you're on a journey. A journey of discovery.' She held out her hand and touched me on the shoulder.

'Who are you?' I mumbled.

'Why, I am Mystique. I know Tinkerbell.' She fluttered her eyes, even the lids were blue. And then the eyes gold again. 'Peter, what is your real name?'

'I'm Sam, Miss.'

'Sam, that is a masterful name. It suits you.' And she cupped her hand around the back of my head. She turned her head, and I followed to see what she was looking at. That was when she kissed my cheek. Her eyes were incredible, like the sun – they were so bright. 'You will find what you're looking for, Sir Sam. Your soul is loving and loyal and you are destined for a great adventure. Enjoy that journey and always be true to yourself. Be true to yourself and you will find true happiness.' And then she drifted off, before I could think of saying goodbye.

Oliver was giggling at me. 'You've got glitter on your cheek and blue paint.' I touched my cheek. 'I've got her on camera!'

'Wow! Wasn't she awesome! Her costume was out of this world!'

'Was there a costume?' Oliver grinned. 'You're one lucky guy! Look, she's not stopping for anyone else!'

The First Time I Met Lucy

As we walked around, we saw loads of different characters. Batman and Batwoman, who looked really good, except it would have been better to have seen Batman with Catwoman. Superman and Superwoman were there too, but you never got them in a comic together, that didn't look right. Olaf from *Frozen*. The Green Lantern man. Iron Man. R2-D2 and C-3PO. Morpheus from *The Matrix* in a long leather coat. A guy being an ape from *Planet of the Apes*. Lots of *Harry Potter* characters, mostly Harry, too many really. Oliver's was way the best as his black robe looked as though it was straight out of the film and of course he had the best scar. Oliver said next time he'd come as someone else and we should look for good ideas. There were a few Hermiones, a Malfoy and one of the character who-must-not-be-named. Loads of Japanese anime lookalike girls, with blue or red hair and wearing school uniform. We saw the actual actor who had played Doctor Who, but two generations before. Real actors from *Stargate*, *Star Wars* and *Battlestar Galactica*. I don't know their names. Then I saw Wendy Padbury, Doctor Who's companion, and we could have got her autograph, but the queue was a bit long. She's Kirsty's favourite and she'd have loved to have come and met her. I'm kinda glad she didn't.

She wouldn't of got any of this and wouldn't have dressed up. Only about one person in ten was in a costume; I guess that made Oliver and me pretty special.

There were amazing stalls everywhere. Clothing and magazines, props that you'd see in the films. Like you could buy the ring from the *Lord of the Rings*. They were selling the actual book *The Death Note* from that manga series. There was a place which engraved your name on a bullet. Why would you want that? They had comic stalls, only the actual artist was there, signing them! Books about the films, mugs, posters, everything!

Oliver and I were having our photo taken standing next to a Xenomorph from *Alien*.

'Hi, Sam.' I turned and saw a girl. She was shorter than me and she had blonde hair in bunches. She was from school. I'd seen her many times before but she wasn't in my class and I didn't know her name.

'Hi, Lucy,' Oliver said.

'Hi, your costumes are amazing, I didn't know you were into cosplay. I would have dressed up, but we're just here because of my dad's work. I didn't know what it was about.'

'Yeah it's my first time too. Oliver's the expert. What's your dad's work?'

'He's looking for actors to be in the event he's organising. They need a superhero to present prizes and stuff. Hey, Oliver, we saw your dad on the big screen being interviewed. His costume was amazing. Awesome interview! That must have been excellent for you?'

'Yeah, I guess. I've got used to it.'

'So does your dad let you go around here on your own?'

'He's not far away, where's yours?'

'Just here.'

At that point, Lucy's parents turned around – they were holding hands. 'Hey, you've found a friend.' Lucy's dad said.

'Yeah, this is Sam and Oliver from school. Oliver is Steve's son, that man being interviewed.'

'Oh right, nice to meet you guys. Which one of you is Oliver?'

'Hi.' Oliver waved his hand.

'You've got a famous dad. Is he around?'

'Somewhere.'

' I love your costumes,' Lucy's mum said.

'Thanks, my dad carved the wand.'

'I bet you've been having fun with that.' Lucy's dad said. ' It's a shame you're a bit too young, you could have been just what I was looking for.'

'Can I get a picture of you three together?' Lucy's mum held up a camera.

'Great idea, Mum.'

'Get closer.'

As the flash went off, I struck a pose with my sword and arched my other hand up to balance, and then Oliver got his wand in action and pretended to zap me over Lucy's head. So then Lucy pretended to stop us fighting by putting her hands on our chests. Lucy's parents were laughing as they took more

64

photos.

'I love your scar,' Lucy said to Oliver

'Sam did it!'

'Cool!'

'You could come as Hermione next time,' Oliver said.

'Well, I don't want to be a Weasley!' I said, and they all laughed.

'My dad believes that the person you choose is who you would like to be in real life, and you have to be careful and understand your character. Like if your character has faults you may have those in real life.'

'Good advice!' Lucy's dad said.

'Well then, I'll be Queen Boudica.'

Oliver and I looked at Lucy, confused.

'First English Queen, that took on the Romans. She was brave, in charge and led her people.'

'That's my girl!' Lucy's dad said.

Then from behind us we heard a loud 'Argh'. It was the same guy from the queue that morning, Captain Hook, but now he was with Tinkerbell and a crocodile. He raised his sword and shouted. 'Arrgghhh, clear the decks me hearties, that Peter Pan is mine and I'll have his guts for garters. He'll pay for the pain he's caused me!' Seconds later we were into our sword fight again. Tinkerbell wove in and out of everyone and the crocodile was trying to bite Captain Hook.

'Feed him to the crocodile!' I shouted.

Lucy and her parents were watching from the side, and Oliver got busy zapping the crocodile with his wand. We got a crowd around us, and after a few minutes we'd run out of breath. Captain Hook did a huge dramatic death scene as he grabbed my sword between his arm and his side and took at least twenty seconds to die.

Then a man with a clipboard and camera crew took loads of photos.

'Well, we'd better get off,' Lucy's dad said. 'It's getting late, how are you getting home?'

'By train... with my dad,' Oliver explained. They waved goodbye. It would have been fun to have spoken with them more.

'Bye Sam, bye Oliver,' Lucy called out.

'That was great, guys.' It was the guy with the camera crew. 'Here's a ticket for the Transformers game.'

Amazing! 'Thanks'—I could hear my dad saying 'if you don't ask you won't get'— 'but can I have one for Oliver too so we can do it together?'

'Sure you can, here you go. It's a priority ticket too, so you can just jump the queue.'

Wow! We rushed over to the game – there was still a long queue, but we went straight to the front. Captain Hook and his friends were just behind us and they had tickets too. We both wanted to be Bumblebee, but Oliver said I could, as I got us the tickets. It was brilliant and went on for ages. We really got into it. You could look up above you and see the giant screen. At the end, they give you a video of what you'd done.

When we came out of the game, Oliver was hyper.

'That was abzolutily-confabu-lastically-brillianto! I've never had a friend before that liked cosplay!'

I'd never seen Oliver so happy and I realised I'd never had a friend like Oliver before.

Steve found us, as Oliver said he would, but it was late and we were starving. Oliver was right: the baguettes were yum. When the show finished at six, we went to the roller coaster on the pier. We got loads of looks for being in costume. Steve had to leave his hammer with the ticket collector. We walked back to the train stations, and Steve bought some beer from Marks and Spencer's for his journey home. We jumped on the train minutes before it left the station.

Steve was quiet for a while. Then after he had a drink, he started talking. 'Angela said that people can be victims of society. Filling their lives with unworthy passion, unjust figureheads and unrighteous values.'

Steve waved his can of beer around as he got into it. 'Because it's so mundane, with no war or real problems, you know, they confuse their world of buying things and being entertained as having a proper life. She said the danger was they could live their whole lives without ever living!'

I wasn't sure what Steve meant, but I wondered if Steve met my family, that's what he'd think of them.

'That's why Angela loved cosplay. She said it sets you free from the random circumstances that decide who you know, where you live and what you'll do. Cosplay is your chance to be who you want to be now. To show others who and what you believe in. Character choice is knowing the mind of that person

67

and wanting to share their fears and passions.'

Then Steve went quiet again. I think he was still thinking of Angela. We didn't get back to Southsea till just before ten. Steve printed the photos from the day and he gave a few to me. Oliver and I were so tired, we didn't have the energy to talk in bed.

You Went to Brighton?!

The next day, Dad picked me up from outside. He didn't knock on the door – he tooted his horn and waited in the car. Before I left, Steve told me I'd done really well and he was looking forward to the next one.

Dad was quiet, so I told him about our day.

'Cosplay! What's that?'

So I explained.

'Brighton? You went to Brighton?!'

'Yeah, it was great.'

'You should have told us, Sam!'

'I *am* telling you!'

'Before you go! So, what did you do?'

I thought of things to leave out: standing on the seat in the train and how we treated the man that came to Oliver's door. 'Well, we watched Steve on stage...'

'Steve was on stage! Where were you when he was on stage?'

'In the audience.'

'Well, who was looking after you?'

'Steve, he was right in front of us.'

'Well, anyone could have carried you off.'

'It wasn't like that, Dad!'

'It never is, son! Not till it's too late. So what did you do?'

I had to think hard now, but I told him about getting autographs and looking at the costume stalls, meeting the actors and playing games.

When we got home, Mum gave me my usual hug. 'Did you have fun?'

'Yeah, Mum, it was great!'

'They've been to Brighton!' Dad said, with his hands on his hips.

'What!'

Here we go. 'Sorry, Mum, I'd have said before but I didn't know we were going.'

'They were going around on their own while Steve was on stage.'

'Steve was on stage?' Mum looked interested.

'Yeah, he's famous, Mum.'

'What for?'

'Dressing up and stuff. Oliver's mum used to sell costumes with Steve. It's how they made money.'

'Well, that's very industrious,' Mum said. Dad just grunted. 'But was Steve with you all the time?'

'Well...' I couldn't finish.

'Sam, you're too young to be there on your own,' Mum said, holding my shoulder.

'Oliver was there.'

'Yes, but anything could have happened.' Mum continued.

'What would you have done if a stranger had tried to take you?' Now Dad started.

I thought about telling them I had a sword... no! 'There were lots of other kids there, Mum.'

'Next time we need a call from you, Sam. It doesn't

need to be long, just the basics.'

'Well, if I had a phone, Mum, I'd ...'

'Sam,'—Mum didn't let me finish—' we've talked about that, we'll get you one for Christmas. The thing is, Oliver's father could have called us.'

'Okay, Mum.' I walked upstairs. It would have been better if Dad had gone in when he dropped me off and talked to Steve.

In the evening, it was just me and Mum in the kitchen.

'I'm glad you had so much fun yesterday.' I looked up and she was smiling.

'Mum, it was amazing. There were loads of people enjoying the same thing, dressing up and stuff. I thought it was just me.'

'It's good to find your own thing.'

'Mum... do you think you can change in just a day?'

'Sorry?'

'You know, be a different person?'

'Yes, you can. But I think you've just found out what you enjoy doing, that's all.'

Mum carried on stirring the food and I thought of the weekend. Oliver and Steve had made it so much fun. It was nice to be home, but it felt too normal, something was missing. As if I'd left something behind at the show.

'Hey, Sam!' It was Kirsty, calling out as she came bouncing down the stairs. 'Why didn't you show us your photos?' She was holding them.

'Oi, Kirsty! Don't go in my room!'

71

Kirsty ignored me. 'Look Mum!' And there it was, the picture of the woman.

'Sam! What's this?' Mum held the picture.

'She's Mystique, Raven Darkhölme.' I explained.

'I don't care what she calls herself. Why is that woman... that naked woman, kissing you?'

'She was really nice, Mum!'

'What's up?' Dad came in from the lounge and took the photo. 'Sam, what was this place?'

'What else happened, Sam?' Mum was doing her face.

'Is that glitter in your hair? X-Boy!' Kirsty said.

'Sam?' Mum examined my head.

'She touched my hair, that's all.'

'That's all, what else, Sam?'

'She said stuff and she was gone.'

'What stuff?'

'She asked my name ...'

'Did you tell her?' Mum was staring at me.

'Well, yeah.'

'Sam, what have said about talking to strangers? I'll have that.' Mum took the photo from Dad. 'How many naked women were there?'

'She wasn't really naked.'

'Well, she's not wearing any clothes, Sam! This is the sort of thing we try to protect you from!'

It carried on. I couldn't persuade them I hadn't been in any danger.

The next morning, Mum called me a third time to get up, and I knew that's wasn't good. You could hear it in her voice. I was about to get into trouble, so I dragged myself downstairs with my eyes half shut and with my towel under my arm. Mum was in the kitchen. 'You've lost your place now, Dad's in there.'

'Oh.' So I stood there, leaning against the kitchen worktop, resting my eyes.

'What happened, didn't you sleep?'

'No.'

'What's wrong? Is something on your mind? Are you worried about school next week? Is something…'

'No, everything's fine, Mum. I'm just so excited.'

'Excited?'

'You know? Doing cosplay. So many ideas going on.'

'It was a big day for you, wasn't it?'

I remembered Mystique and what she said. 'Mum what does "be true to yourself" mean?'

'Well, respecting what's important to you. Looking after it and protecting it.'

'What sort of things?'

'It can be anything – your values, your loved ones. Whatever you care about. Don't let anyone or anything distract you from being the person you want to be.'

'Did I tell you I had a pretend fight with Captain Hook? Oliver said it looked really good. I can't stop thinking about it. I got to make stuff up and muck around with different people. Hey! I didn't tell you we saw someone from school there, we had a great laugh with her. Ollie, Lucy and I were mucking around in front of professional video people.'

'She wasn't there on her own was she?'

'No, she was with her parents. I met them too.'

'Have you got a picture of that?'

'No, Lucy's parents have though.'

'Oh... well who's Lucy?'

'I don't really know her, Mum, we just met up and we got on straight away.'

*

So that was my memory of that awesome day. Even talking about it with Mum was special. But now it's as though Mum and Dad have forgotten that. Dad's never understood. Mum does. Was that the day Dad decided Steve wasn't to be trusted? I just thought Dad was jealous because he didn't come.

Tuesday 12th November

The day started with a really tense dream. The school had turned into a jungle and I was searching from room to room, running down the corridors and bursting through classroom doors and frantically looking under tables and inside cupboards. There were teachers and other kids about, but I didn't ask them to help, I didn't even tell them what I was doing. I'd ended up in Mr Jeff's office and was trying to trick him into giving me Oliver's address, but he kept on changing the subject and offering me sweets. I woke up baking hot and I'd been pressing my hand into the mattress, which made it really ache.

I didn't like my dream. Mr Jeff was one of the good guys. He never tries to keep people under control by threatening detentions and suspensions. You'll always get a friendly 'hello' from Mr Jeff, he wouldn't treat you like one of the little people just because he could. When Mr Jeff had caught me running in the corridor, I could have got a detention, but instead Mr Jeff got me to explain why it was a bad thing to do. Whereas when I had dropped a cup of water in the dining hall, Mr Gambit had called me a 'silly boy' in front of everyone.

I decided to go to school a little earlier today. I usually set off with Kirsty, but just lately we've been getting out the front door and walking with our own friends. I'll start talking to Robert and she'll start talking to one of her friends, so there's no real point in walking together. As I walked to school, I passed a whole load of other kids walking in the other direction towards the station – they were secondary school kids going to school out of town. They wore black jackets with red along the seams and blue and gold ties. I was only fifteen minutes earlier, but I guess it changed who I saw. Imagine having to go to school on the train. That seemed scary, going without a parent, I mean. Steve had told Oliver it wouldn't be long before he'd be going on his own.

It was in that moment, when I saw the kids talking politely to each other in their super-smart uniforms, that my idea popped. I'd take the train to Oliver's house! It was *that* simple, and the more I thought of it, the more it made sense.

During the day, my idea became more and more sorted. The idea turned into a plan. I thought about buying the tickets – I'd done that before. How to find his home? I didn't know his address, but I could walk from the station to his, no problem. I could even describe the houses and buildings on the way.

When I came back, I'd need to work out the train times. I could do that. Steve showed me. He got me to work out the timetable when we missed the train once.

'First off, you find the timetable for your journey.' Oliver was looking at me, he'd already been told how. 'Then you find the column that leaves about the time you want to go. Then you make sure that on that column it stops at your destination, Chichester.'

'Wow, that's pretty easy, really!'

'That's the thing, Sam, it's always easy when you know how! Growing up's all about knowing the things you need to know about!'

The more I thought about it the, more I saw how I could do it.

And then, right at last break, I saw Rachel, and remembered all the things she said to Kirsty. And Kirsty saying those lies to Mum and Dad, and trying to wind me up. That was it! I was going. Tomorrow!

*

That night, I was having second thoughts. I imagined the journey on the train. That could be difficult. When I bought the ticket, was it different if you were on your own. Was I allowed to go on my own? Who would I talk to? What if Oliver was in prison? I thought of Dad saying someone could carry me off. Then there was the little problem that my parents wouldn't want me to go. They had his phone number, but they hadn't suggested it. They didn't want me to call him. If I went to Portsmouth on my own, I'd have to do it in secret. Usually Mum leaves work at five and picks us up from Aunt Dora's. Unless either Kirsty or I have gone to a friend's, which we either tell Mum or Aunt Dora about. So what would I say this time?

I looked up and saw the Rupert Bear annual. I got the journal out and thumbed through the entries.

My quest is to find my friend Oliver, and I hereby make a solemn promise to find him, wherever he may be.

There it was in black and white. This was my first test and I couldn't give up now. I'd have to work it out and make my plans in *The Book of Heroic Deeds.*

Dear Diary

Plan for Project 'GO TO SOUTHSEA' Code name: 'Cosplay'
Mission: Locate Oliver
~~Sub mission~~ Second objective: Get Oliver's address

Stuff to arrange:
Tell Kirsty where I'm going (but not really) so she can tell Aunt Dora. This is called a decoy ~~or possibly a lie.~~ or lie.
Take stuff
Be brave. Be John Carter, but no interplanetary travel.

Stuff to Take:

Money – (Piggy bank, £5 from cosplay day.) Keep in pencil case.
~~Apple~~ Packet of crisps
~~Bottle of water~~ Can of Coke
Note pad

Pencil

Penknife – to make traps, pick locks, hunt things etc.

Bobble hat – Army camouflage one, not Granny's

Jumper

Compass – only if I can find one

Whistle to call help? Or just run like mad

Wednesday 13th November

Before I left the school playground, I checked my bag one last time to see if I had everything. As I'd packed that morning, I was thinking of Dad telling me what I should take. He always says when I forget something to remember it next time. When things go wrong, you have to see the gift. The gift is a lesson. It's only by learning lessons we get better. So it's kind of okay to get it wrong!

At lunchtime I told Kirsty I was going home with James and his parents would drop me back home. That way, I could just come through the door about six and if Mum was busy she wouldn't even ask about James. It felt bad, lying. I had tried to think of a white lie to say instead. Like I'm going to see a friend, but that wouldn't have worked – Kirsty would have just asked me where, who, when and how.

It was an exciting feeling walking to the train station, I was nervous too; I didn't know what to expect when I got to Portsmouth. But one way or the other I was going to get to see Oliver.

The station was busy, lots of kids going home. Some were mucking around. I just ignored them and tried to concentrate on buying the ticket, but that was easier than I thought. There was a machine in the station foyer. I'd seen Steve punch in the details so many times and although it was a month ago, it felt like yesterday.

As I stood waiting on the platform, I thought of how many times I'd gone down there to stay over, and how I missed the little routine we'd made. I remember the last time we'd all stood here and Steve had told us what he called his Philosophy of Sad Films. He said that life is full of good and bad and most of the good stuff comes early on. Birth is always celebrated, even the unplanned babies. You start with discovering the wonders of life, taste, smell, touch, sights and sounds. Then you discover joy. You have your first kiss (yuck), you pass some exams (eek), and experience progress. Someone gives you a job. You find a sweetheart. There's a marriage, some children and the years of life continue to pass. You get to watch your children grow. There may be a promotion. But then there is the bad stuff and it isn't always in that order, mostly it gets mixed up.

But as you get older, it seems there are more losses than gains. You lose a job, you lose a girlfriend, you lose a wife. If you're really unlucky there's a war, famine and disease. But if you're lucky enough to live a long time then this is what Steve called a 'mixed blessing'. You'll see many of your friends die, you might even see your children die before you go. But the trick is, he said, how you handle the bad stuff and how you handle the good. In a lifetime there are many moments, and to have a full life you want as many as you can. You also need to have the bad ones so you can appreciate the good. I think Steve told us that so that we wouldn't be so frightened when the bad stuff happened. He said that's why people watch sad films, because it gives them what he called 'perspective in their own lives'.

Getting on the train was the usual panic and chaos. I got a seat by the window. And then a couple of kids I'd seen on the train before recognised me.

'Hello, mate! You're Ollie's friend, aren't you?' He was wearing a cap.

'Yeah that's right!'

'We haven't seen Ollie for ages. Do you know what's up? Has he moved school?'

'Yeah.' I hesitated, not knowing how much to give away. 'I'm going to see him now. I haven't seen him in a while either.'

Then another kid with a crooked tie started, 'Well I heard Ollie moved away, he's gone to another school, near Winchester.'

'Why didn't you tell me?' said the boy with the cap.

'I didn't know you knew Ollie.'

'Yeah, my parents know his dad. Steve isn't it?' he asked.

'Steve, that's right.'

'Well what are you saying then? Is this guy,' he said, looking at me, 'wasting a journey then? What's your name then?'

'Sam.'

'Is Sam wasting his time? My name's Jack, by the way.'

The other kid looked doubtful, and he hesitated. 'Er, well look, I don't want to be the bearer of bad news but Oliver definitely doesn't live in Portsmouth any more. Like I say, he's at some school in

Winchester.'

My face must have said it all. I felt stupid and lost.

'Don't worry, Sam, there will be a reason, there'll be an explanation.' Jack was trying to be nice, but I felt an ache in my stomach. I didn't want to be on the train any more. 'You haven't got his number?'

How crazy did it look? I didn't even have a number, what kind of friend was I? 'Yeah, it's silly, but I never got his number, I know where he lives. Where he lived.'

'Well that's a start then, isn't it?' Jack was being positive, he reminded me of my mum. 'Look, if you go around there you can knock on the neighbour's door, maybe they'll have an address of where they've gone.'

I smiled. 'Yeah, you're right, that might work. Thanks.'

We talked for the next twenty minutes, all the way to Portsmouth. Jack was into Minecraft like me, but he liked football. It was dark when we got off the train and it felt cold. I was hoping Jack would offer to come with me, but I guess he had his own stuff to do. He wished me luck.

So there I was, on my own, in the station. Portsmouth suddenly felt like a big city. When I'd last been there, it had felt like summer but now it definitely felt wintery. The place seemed unfriendly, like there was hidden danger. But I knew Oliver's house was only five minutes' walk, and I remembered what Steve had said on the train, going to cosplay. 'Believe that you have supreme confidence and you

83

will have it'. I imagined Thor's hammer in my hand. I stuck out my chest like Steve, and before I knew it, I was turning into Oliver's street.

There was the street name on the corner: Kings Street, of course! I should have remembered that. The street light made Oliver's house look strange and unwelcoming. It was so different to last time when we were playing in the street. So they'd gone and I hadn't known. It was weird, like I had no right to be there. I decided I'd knock on the door of each side of Oliver's house and, if necessary, across the road. Someone had to know. As I walked to the neighbour, I got a shock: I saw a tiny blade of light coming through Oliver's window. Was this the new people? Would they know where they'd gone?

I was a little nervous about knocking on the door and I thought about Dad saying not to talk to strangers. The night suddenly seemed darker, the autumn air colder. I knocked quietly on the door, no one came. Should I go? I knocked louder on the door and I saw the hall light came on. As I waited, I noted the number on the door, fifty-two.

Without opening the door, a voice called from inside. 'Hello... who is it?' It was a man's voice.

'My name's Sam, I'm looking for the people that used to live here.'

The door burst open. 'SamIam! Wow, hi.' Steve patted me on the back. His face was beaming. Even with the hall light behind him, I could see how pleased he was to see me.

'Hi, Steve, you're here. Brilliant!'

'How lovely to see you, come on in.'

Walking through the door took me back to the happy times I'd had there. 'They said on the train you'd moved away to Winchester.'

Steve said nothing and led me into the lounge. He already had the TV on mute. There was the picture of Angela and Steve in the Star Trek costume. It was as though nothing had changed, but then I saw Steve in the proper light for the first time. His beard had gone all jungle, his hair all haystack. There was something about him that looked as though he spent the whole night in bed with his clothes on, like Mum looks when she goes camping. Then I noticed the plates that hadn't been taken out to the kitchen, and there was a pile of clothes on the floor by the sofa. On the sofa was a heap of unopened letters mixed in with a load of newspapers.

Steve followed my eyes, 'Oh! Yeah! It's not been a great time, SamIam.' He looked down and then with a rapid movement, cleared up the newspapers from the sofa. 'Have a seat. I need to tell you something.'

I sat on the small place not covered by stuff.

'First though, how did you get here? By train? Do your parents know you're here?' Fortunately, he carried on talking before I had a chance to answer. 'Are you thirsty, hungry, can I get you anything?'

'I'm fine, thanks. Are you okay, Steve?'

I almost wished I hadn't asked, Steve looked at the floor again, searching for his words. Slowly, he put his hand down on the sofa and lowered himself. He scratched his beard and finally looked at me. 'I've lost

Oliver.' He crossed one arm across his chest and rested the other against the side of his head. 'It's all changed.' He swallowed. 'First Angela, and now Oliver.'

'Oliver's dead?!' I stood up.

'No! Sorry! No, Oliver's been taken back by his dad.'

'His dad! I thought you were his dad!'

'I am his dad!' Steve raised his voice. 'But not his biological dad.'

'What does that mean?' I couldn't believe what I was hearing – it sounded like he was making out Oliver was some kind of science project.

'Sorry! Listen, it's difficult to explain. I met Angela when she was pregnant.'

'Oh! Yeah... okay... I see what you mean.' I sat down again.

Steve glanced at me from the corner of his eyes. 'Oliver's biological dad, the one Angela was married to,'—his eyes darted again—'when he found out Angela had died, he used the law to get Oliver back.'

Steve bent forward, his arms resting on his legs. 'He'd never met Oliver! Not been interested in eleven years. I've lost them both. It's just me now.' He sighed heavily, like the world was crushing the breath out of him. 'You never realise how good you've got it, until it's gone.' He stood up and walked to the telly.

'So he just took him then... to Winchester?' I couldn't work it out.

'I don't know if I should tell you this, you might not understand. You're the first person I've talked to about this.' Steve stared at me. 'At Angela's funeral, Oliver's real dad'—he made a face—'Mr Chartwell came up to me. I'd only seen him in a photo before. He just came out with it. No "sorry to hear about Angela", or anything. He just said, "How much do you want for the boy? I'll give you £5,000". I was shocked and just tried to walk away, but he said, "I'll give you a few days to think it over, but I promise you now, Oliver's my son and he'll be with me, not you". He said if I gave him any trouble then he'd make sure I lost my house and he'd make sure I ended up penniless trying to get him back.' Steve went quiet again.

'But, you didn't take the money?'

'No! No!' Steve looked at me wildly and walked to the window. 'No, but after the fight… the day after I went to the school, I had a call from Chartwell's solicitor saying I was going to be taken to court. Then a social worker called me and said I'd been leading Oliver astray and then the police called to say they wanted to see me about my threatening behaviour at school. He was just waiting for me to mess up. And as soon as I did, he launched his attack.'

Steve got louder as if it was happening right then. 'He told me he had a thick file on me of the things I'd done wrong and why I was a crap father and that he'd throw everything he got at getting Oliver back. I just panicked, it was awful. I'm such an idiot! And now it's over. I've lost. I know I crumbled. I know I could have stood up for myself. He was just so definite and then he started going on about how I was being selfish and Oliver would be happier with him and he could give him a proper home, education and proper head start in life. He promised me I'd be able to see Oliver… but it was all lies!'

There was a knock at the door. Steve looked at me. 'Did you say you had told your parents?'

'Sorry, Steve!'

Steve went into the hallway to get the door, I stayed on the sofa. I'd been to Oliver's house enough times to know he didn't get many people knocking on the door.

'Oh! Hello… yes… don't worry, he's here.'

Uh-oh, I was in for it now. How did they find me?!

'Sam?' It was my dad calling from the front door. Within seconds, he was in the lounge. 'What on earth do you think you are doing? Do you know how worried we've been?' Dad was inches away from me and had bent over to get his head closer to mine. 'Have you any idea what trouble could have happened to you? What happens to boys who get lost in big cities?'

At that point, Mum walked in – she came over to the sofa and pulled me up for a hug. It was a proper squeeze, I could hardly breathe.

'How did you find me?'

'Because your sister could tell you were lying straight off and you've been banging on about Oliver for weeks.' She let go of me. 'Come on, everyone, let's just go! I just want to get back and sit down.'

'Mum, can you talk with Steve?' I tried but the three of them just looked at each other in silence.

'Where's Oliver?' Mum asked.

'Well, he's not here.'

Mum and Dad just stood there waiting for Steve to say something more, but Steve had gone quiet.

'So it's true then? We heard something at school that Oliver had gone, he's been taken away?'

Steve's face dropped, his frown seemed to want to join up with his bottom lip.

And that was that, we just walked out. Dad stood between me and Steve. Outside, I started to turn to wave, but Dad was short with me. 'Get in the car.' It was a quick journey home: Dad was in a hurry, which was just as well as no one said anything until we pulled up outside.

'Straight to your room!' Dad said.

Dear Reader of the Quest

My mission to Portsmouth has failed. Just as I was finding out essential information from Oliver's father, my hope of getting to the truth of Oliver's disappearance was prevented by my capture by my parents. Something peculiar has happened to Steve, he has gone all tramp-like and his house now resembles something like Kirsty's bedroom. How can someone take someone else's son? Why isn't Steve on his own mission to find Oliver? Why hasn't he called the police?

I began a new section in the back of my journal for addresses and added Oliver's address: 52 Kings Street.

Then I drew a rough map of the walk from the station to his front door. I left a column for telephone numbers. I didn't have it! I realised I should have asked for it. Why did my parents ignore Steve? They were usually so polite and friendly to everyone they met.

Thursday 14th November

At breakfast the next morning, Mum and Dad were quiet with me. They made a point of talking to Kirsty and not me. I guess they were still upset, but it was Kirsty who kicked off.

'So, Sam, where are you going today? London, Brighton? Maybe you should take a packed lunch with you. You know how delayed you can get in that commuter traffic.'

'That's enough, Kirsty!' Mum said, 'Sam, I want you at Aunt Dora's by three-thirty every day. You'll walk to school with Kirsty and come back with her, without fail.'

'Mum! I can't babysit him every day.'

'It's only till your father's job finished next week and then he'll be here.'

Kirsty and I looked at Dad, who was finishing a mouthful of his cereal.

'Sam?'

'Yes, Mum. I will.'

'I'll be back at work soon though.' Dad finished another mouthful. 'I'll be applying for one or two jobs today.'

'What kind of thing, Dad?' It was a chance for me to change the conversation. Dad kept on munching. 'You could do that job idea we talked about the other day.' He looked up but hadn't remembered. 'You know, the idea about putting Ikea cabinets together for other people.'

Mum made a funny noise.

'I could help you.' Dad needed convincing. 'You said we were really good at it, that there was money to be made.'

'I'll keep to my profession for the moment, Sam, but it's a good idea.' He looked up at Mum, who was smiling and staring at the table.

*

At school, quite a few kids knew where I'd been. By the first playtime I had kids coming up and asking about my trip to Portsmouth. They were fascinated and asked loads of details, like how I got the ticket, and how I knew the way. Some just wanted to know what my parents said and what trouble I got into. Lucy, who I hadn't spoken to much, said that I'd been very brave and that it was good that someone was trying to find out where Oliver had gone. She said that it showed great loyalty and that was a great quality. I've always liked Lucy, I've just never found the right way to start a conversation with her. I wanted to tell her all about it, but the bell went and I only had a minute as we walked back. When we got to her classroom door, I realised I'd gone down the wrong corridor. Her teacher Mr Gambit looked up and saw me.

'Bye then, Lucy!' I said calmly, but in my head I was thinking 'Idiot, you'll be late'. The last thing I wanted right now.

Sure enough, I was last in to the classroom. I don't think Mrs Stubbs was very impressed with me generally, though. She didn't say anything, but I could tell as she didn't chat to me during the lesson. We were doing a project on time travel. A local author, H.G. Wells, who wrote the *Time Machine*, had lived at Uppark House, which is only about ten miles from Chichester.

Mrs Stubbs got to the doing part of the lesson. 'Now imagine what you might do with a time machine? Who would you go with? What do you think you'd see? Would you go forward in time or back?'

'We should ask Sam, Miss, he's the expert in travel,' Daniel said. Everyone laughed. It seemed like absolutely everyone had heard about my adventure! I got on all right with Daniel. I thought it was funny too.

'Alright, enough everyone.' Mrs Stubbs didn't smile or look at me. 'Can you write about your time machine, please. Where would you go?'

I loved the idea for the project. 'Miss? In his book, the machine doesn't actually go anywhere.'

'Oh! That sounds interesting, tell us some more, Sam, have you read the book then?'

'No, Miss, I've seen the film, it's really old, from the sixties I think.' I didn't dare mention I'd seen it at Oliver's house and we'd sat up for an hour after the film talking about what we'd do with a time machine. Steve had pointed out the limitations of the machine in the book, so I could explain to the class.

'All it did was take you through time, it didn't fly

and it didn't have any wheels. In fact, in the end the Morlocks drag his machine into their den.' Steve had explained that the film was about how mankind splits into two separate species. One the Morlocks, savages but hard-working, and the other the Eloi, who are so clever and lacking in fear or the need to do anything, that they have become just food to be eaten by the Morlocks.

Mrs Stubbs looked worried. 'Oh I've seen the film too, the original. Didn't you find it scary?'

'The Morlocks were scary, weren't they, Miss? And eating the Eloi, that was random! Imagine finding yourself in the cave when the siren went off and then being clubbed over the head?' Oops, I don't think I was supposed to say that.

Mrs Stubbs was looking at me as though I'd sworn. 'Yes, not really a suitable film, Sam. Okay, well for the non-film aficionados, lets imagine a time machine that can travel about. Let your imaginations have free rein and see where it takes you.'

It was a great project. I wrote loads of stuff, knowing that later I'd write it into *The Book of Quests and Knowledge.*

> *If I had a time machine, I'd use it to locate Oliver. This could be done in a number of different ways. For example, today I could simply go back to the start of term on our first sleepover and ask Oliver for his address and telephone number and then give him mine. He might think it strange. In fact, thinking about*

it, I'd have to go back and locate myself and explain that I needed to get contact information. Actually, that could be a disaster. Firstly, I might suffer from a complete shock from meeting another me. I might think I was mad and have a breakdown, what other time travel films call a psychotic event. Also, there is the danger that I make a small change, accidentally of course, and that changes the whole course of mankind's destiny. Time travellers call this the ripple effect.

Of course, it could be an opportunity to tell Mr Bridle he is in danger of losing Oliver – maybe he'd take action and stop the whole problem. Perhaps I could go back in my machine and stop Angela from dying in the first place, but then Oliver wouldn't have changed schools and I wouldn't have met him. So what am I saying here? That I wouldn't stop Angela from dying because I would lose a friend? That sounds wrong.

First off, I need to know whether I could save Angela. I could go into the future, find the cure and then come back to the past and give it to her, in some secret way of course. So in conclusion: If Angela doesn't die then I don't meet Oliver. That is the ripple effect. Time travel seems a lot more difficult than I'd thought. And it does seem completely wrong to think of me not saving Angela with my time machine. But if I did so now or in the future, I would not be writing this now.

'Okay, well done, everyone. I look forward to reading your work, can you…'

'Miss,' I said, 'we've only just begun, I've got loads of stuff to add.'

'Sam, I'm glad you enjoyed it, but you were writing for half an hour!' She came up behind me and held the back of my chair. 'Okay, can all of you please get ready for P.E.?'

As I looked around, Mrs Stubbs was reading what I had written – she had picked up my book. 'Yes you've written lots, that's great to see, Sam.'

I helped tidy up the desk with James, who I sit next to. As I got ready to leave, Mrs Stubbs passed my book back to me. She didn't really have an expression. I'm not sure if she liked it. Maybe I'd gone too fast and made too many spelling mistakes.

The First Time Mr Jeff Disappointed Me

At lunchtime, I sat with Daniel. I didn't usually, but I was still trying to find some friends to play with instead of Oliver. Daniel was a footballer, even though his clothes and hair were always immaculate. He says a lot of cool stuff in the classroom. We'd known each other since the fifth year. I invited him to my birthday last year and so he invited me when it was his birthday. James was there too – he and I didn't really talk last year, he was in a different class. But now we sit next to each other, and we get on all right.

'So what was it like?' Daniel asked.

'What?'

'Getting on the train on your own, weren't you scared?'

'I met a few people I'd seen before, they were friendly.'

'What school do they go to then?'

'Westbourne House.'

'But weren't you frightened getting off the train in the middle of Portsmouth? Without your mum and dad, or any of your friends?'

'Well yeah, but that's adventure isn't it? It was good fun and...' I noticed that Daniel and James were looking behind me.

'Hi, Mr Jeff,' they both said.

I turned around. 'Hi, Mr Jeff.'

'Hello, boys. Sam, there you are, can we have a talk when you've finished your lunch? Please come along to my room.'

'Yes, Mr Jeff.'

'Daniel, that's a huge baguette, are you really going to get through all of that?' Mr Jeff smiled.

'Yeah, I always have this much. It's peanut butter and jam. Would you like to try some?'

'I'll think I'll pass, but thank you very much for asking. Enjoy your lunch, boys.' Mr Jeff turned and left.

'Oh, God!' Daniel whispered. 'I knew you wouldn't get away with it that easily.'

'Do you think you'll get a detention?' James asked.

'Or maybe a school suspension?'

'Excluded?'

'Thanks, guys.' I flipped my sandwich into my lunchbox. 'Thanks for your support.'

Maybe because Mr Jeff was all right as a headmaster, I wasn't that worried. I'd spoken to him lots of times and he was always friendly. He didn't bark orders or boss people about and you rarely saw him lose his temper. Which is pretty amazing, considering what he has to do! He's really smart and has done some great things. Apparently he has climbed Mount Everest. Before he was a teacher, he was a jet fighter in the RAF. Some parents badmouth him: they say he's too modern, too easy-going. I think other teachers are a bit wary of him. But he is really clever. Like he'll know what you're thinking, and he'll always find the right thing to say.

As I approached his office, my positive thinking faded. Maybe I would get a punishment. I knocked on the door and regretted knocking so loud.

'Come in.'

'Hi, Mr Jeff.'

'Hello, Sam, come and sit down.'

I sat in the chair behind his desk. The chair was bigger than the ones in the classroom.

'So, you had a bit of an adventure last night?'

'It was kind of scary, Mr Jeff.'

'And you know that your parents were scared too?'

I thought of their faces last night. 'They were angry.'

'Well, they had spent a couple of hours not knowing where you were!' Mr Jeff interlocked his fingers on his desk.

'They were angry with Oliver's dad too.' Mr Jeff just looked at me. 'They had nothing to say to him, even though they hadn't talked in a couple of months.'

'They love you, Sam. They'd spent all that time wondering if you were all right. They know the things that can go wrong.'

'They didn't say that. On the way back from the car it was complete silence and then when we got home they sent me to my room. They weren't interested in what Mr Bridle had to say.'

Mr Jeff cleared his throat. 'They were angry that you'd lied to them, and probably shocked to see you there.'

'I asked Dad if he could call Oliver's dad. He

wanted to leave it, but I don't know if Oliver's all right. He might need my help.'

'It's not your job, Sam, you're too young to be involved. Sometimes life can be a messy business, the issues aren't obvious.'

I stared at Mr Jeff, I couldn't see what he was getting at, and he'd missed the point.

'People's lives are very complicated. You meet people at school, but you don't get to know about their home life and how things are for them there.'

'But I do know Oliver's! They've taken Oliver away from his dad. His dad is really unhappy about it. He seems to have given up.' It was difficult to explain what I meant. 'When I went to his house, he was different. It looks as if he can't live without Oliver, like he can't be happy without him.'

'Well … what did he say to you about Oliver?'

'He said that his real dad had taken Oliver away, that he wasn't Oliver's biological father. Which meant that Oliver's other dad could use the law. So he's gone back to his biological father, even though they've never met.' Mr Jeff just looked at me – for the first time I'd ever known, he had nothing to say.

'I'm worried that Oliver may miss Steve, and anyway it doesn't seem right.'

Still Mr Jeff had nothing to say.

'Just imagine if you were at home one day with your family and then some guy picks you up in his car and you've got to pack all your things into suitcases… perhaps he didn't even have time to do that!'

'Sam, can we leave this for now? I can see you're

worried about Oliver, but can we agree to come back to that later?'

I nodded.

'And in the meantime can you give some thought as to how frightened your parents were yesterday, when they didn't know where you were? We've gone through that before, haven't we, about the dangers of going with strangers and how not everyone can be trusted?'

'But Mr Bridle isn't a stranger. I've been around to his house loads of times.'

'Yes, but all the people on the train, Sam, arriving at a railway station? Anything could have happened!'

There was silence.

'Do you think Oliver felt like he'd been kidnapped? It must have been really weird meeting another man who says he's your father. Why do you think the other man didn't want to meet Oliver before?' I looked up, I'd done it again – Mr Jeff had his mouth open and was just staring at me, as though I'd just done a magic trick. 'Have you heard from Oliver, Mr Jeff? I mean, how do we know this other man is real, maybe he was only pretending to be his real dad?'

'Enough! Look, Sam, I'm going to have to ask you to have some confidence in the system! Please accept that grown-ups have very good reasons for doing the things that they do. You may not be party to what their wishes or intentions are. Oliver's family doesn't owe me any more of an explanation than they do to you, and we have to accept that these are their wishes.'

He sighed heavily and stared at me, I think he was

hoping I'd say 'Yes, Mr Jeff'. But I didn't agree with what he was saying. My experience of grown-ups was they often *did* get it wrong. And as for 'good reasons', I doubted that too. Steve said that people only did things from one of three things: love, fear or anger, and it didn't really matter which one of those things they did it from. The point was, they rarely did it for good reasons. I could see that Mr Jeff wasn't listening, which is a shame because that was the first time he'd really disappointed me.

Mr Jeff had finally shut his mouth. 'Well?'

'Yes, Mr Jeff.' It was the best thing to do. If he wasn't going to listen, I may as well make the most of my lunchtime.

'Okay then, Sam. Please do just accept that Oliver is not coming back to our school and move on from trying to find him.'

As I got down from the chair, my head went down as if I were nodding. 'Good afternoon, Mr Jeff.' I managed to leave his office without agreeing to his terms.

After school, I walked back slowly, the long way round. It was sometimes fun to take in the playground around by the old cinema. As I finally made my way through the front door, I heard shouting.

'Well I looked for him and he wasn't where he usually is.'

'Kirsty, I don't know how I could have been more clear.'

'Yes, but Sam never said where he'd be.'

Then they saw me.

'Sorry, Mum, I forgot I had to walk back with Kirsty.'

Mum just looked at me for a second and then came over and gave me a really big hug. 'Sam what are we going to do with you?! We love you, what are you doing?!'

It was funny to hear 'we love you' being shouted out like that. As if she got the words wrong and meant to say, 'Sam, you complete prat!'

'I just forgot, sorry, Mum. I'll remember tomorrow. Kirsty, I'll stand where I usually do.'

Kirsty didn't look at me. She slammed her bag on the table and as she left for the stairs, said 'Idiot!'

Mum squeezed harder. Then she held my face by the palms of her hands. 'What's going on, Sam?'

What did she mean? I could see she was worried. 'Mum, I had to talk to Mr Jeff today. He asked me all about going to Oliver's. I tried to explain to him about Oliver going back to his real dad, but Mr Jeff didn't want to talk about it.'

'His real dad?'

'Yeah, his biological dad.'

'Why didn't you tell me?'

'I thought you knew. You told Steve you'd heard about it at school. So where is Oliver now? Which town, Winchester?'

'Listen Sam, we can't get involved. It sounds awful, but it's not our business. Please just leave it now? We've got our own problems.' Mum let go of me and started to work in the kitchen. I watched her as she pulled out ingredients from the cupboards.

Before supper, I spent the time writing up today's diary note. I'm pretty sure I remembered the time machine work word for word. Then I added something else.

5.45 pm

> *Both Mr Jeff and Mum don't want to discuss what could have happened to Oliver. It's as though the topic is banned. I don't really understand why it is such an issue. No doubt, there is a good film about it on The Fountain of Knowledge. I will have a search after supper.*

I decided to watch *Terminator 2: Judgment Day*, learning factor four. The first film was brilliant. Lolly Olly and I spent loads of time impersonating Arnie, running around the playground taking it in turns to be the mad cyborg or the desperate victim. We didn't really follow the film – it was more fun if the victim died a gruesome death.

I decided to put the film on before supper. I reckoned I could fit in half an hour before we ate. But I had to have the headphones on as Kirsty was playing her music really loudly in her bedroom. She could burst in at any second. I must get a lock on the door.

What a beginning! Non-stop action on-the-edge-of-your-seat stuff, I didn't know if the heroes would actually make it to the middle of the film... but they usually do, of course. I managed to bite all my nails off on my right hand.

Mum called us down for supper. As she served lasagne out, everyone watched intently, as if we were all starving. Dad didn't make his usual lasagne joke: 'Did you hear about the Italian chef that died? He pasta way'.

Kirsty didn't moan about any of her teachers, not even a story about how her friends had let her down.

Finally, I thought of something: I told them about the time travel exercise in class. I thought it best not to mention I'd written about using the machine to find Oliver. I got everyone to say what they'd do with one. Mum said she'd go forward in time, buy a paper and then come back and buy a lottery ticket, with the numbers from the paper. Dad said he'd go back to the sixth form and kiss Susan Hartwright. Mum didn't look very pleased. Kirsty didn't understand what she had to do, but when we explained she said it was a silly idea and it couldn't happen anyway. I got away from the table pretty quick and restarted the film.

This part-two film, a sequel, they call it, was better than the first. And guess what: the hero is ten years old. He saves the planet and teaches the Terminator, who is his protector, how to be a superhero with manners. His mum, on the other hand, loses it big time and can't handle her emotions. John Connor, the young kid, defender of mankind, makes sensible choices and keeps their plan on track. Then there's an evil Terminator that's made of molten metal. He's been programmed with zero morals, so he kills randomly, what Mum calls 'gratuitously'. But creepy, though; he can impersonate anyone he touches. So if your dad acts strangely, you know what's happened.

So why did Steve say this was a learning film? It's coloured green on the list. It was full of action and it wasn't too dark, especially at the end where JC tells the cyborg he's not allowed to kill any humans.

As the credits were rolling, I heard Mum and Dad downstairs. This time I opened my bedroom door.

'We can't afford it! You'll just have to cancel it,' Mum said.

'But it's signed for. Besides, it sets the right impression when I go to interviews.'

'What interview?'

Silence.

'Kevin, this is your last pay packet for goodness knows how long. We've got to make that last and you want to sign us up for £8,000 of credit. Christ, it takes me five months to earn that!'

'It's signed for!'

'Well go and un-sign for it!'

'Janice!'

'Seriously, those credit agreements can always be cancelled within two weeks. Swallow your pride, go back and explain. If you want me to, I'll do it.'

If only I could do what JC did in the film. He went to a cash point machine and used a computer to get a load of money for free. If I could do that then I'd be a hero – of this house anyway. I closed the door and sat on my bed. I hadn't really thought how bad it was Dad losing his job. He sounded desperate. Mum sounded angry or was she frightened?

8.28 pm

I saw Terminator Two tonight and think I understand the lesson Steve had in mind. Just because you're right doesn't mean anyone will necessarily believe you. Just because you're old doesn't mean you've got the answers. The authorities didn't believe the mother, or the boy. The boy saves the planet by destroying the technology that will bring on Judgment Day, the technology that the adults thought right to develop. Mr Jeff and my parents just won't listen, but I must carry on regardless. I have my mission. I mustn't be put off by their doubt. In the film, the boy learns to trust his instincts, a feeling, not the authorities.

Friday 15th November

I was running from an evil Terminator, which looked a lot like Mr Jeff. There was no good Terminator to protect me. We were running down the school corridor and I ran into Mr Jeff's office and put the chair I'd been sitting on yesterday behind the door. By jamming the legs into the carpet, the cyborg couldn't get in. I guess in the film he would have blown a hole in the door, but in my dream, it worked and I woke up. Immediately, I thought about my need for a lock on my bedroom. Could I do something similar? It was something to think about anyway.

On the way to school, Kirsty told me to walk twenty feet in front of her. She said it cramped her style to be seen with her little brother. That was okay with me, as it meant I didn't have to find stuff to talk about with her. As I arrived in the playground, I could see that we were a little early – there were only a handful of people. Over the next half an hour, more and more would arrive, until you could hardly find a place to stand where you wouldn't be in someone's way, or in danger of being hit by a football, frisbee, paper airplane or skipping rope. I made my way over to the classroom door – there was a bench there I usually sat at. But before I got there, something really strange happened: Daniel called.

'Hey, Sam, we need someone in goal. Come on!'

It was as if I didn't have a choice, so I just got in front of the goal and before I knew it I was blocking, kicking and throwing. Daniel didn't give me the time to explain that I don't play football. I saved more than went in, which seemed to be okay. No one said 'You're crap' or anything. So I stayed, and when the bell went I was disappointed.

'You've found a new talent,' Daniel said.

'You weren't bad! I thought you were a library boy!' Mat said. I think he was trying to be nice.

'Thanks!'

'You want to use your hands more,' Mat continued. 'You're allowed to if you're the goalie. See you at lunch.'

Wow! I think that was an invitation.

'You're in, mate.' Daniel nodded. And that confirmed it. I'd been an undiscovered footballer all this time.

Mrs Stubbs was in a good mood today. She smiled at me and then we had a bit of a giggle when I said that I'd used my time machine to go forward and get the right answers for my homework, so I was expecting the top mark. We did maths and then some reading and then went to the hall to practise the Nativity. It was the first time we were going to practise the song we were doing as the wise men. We were going to sing some ancient Boney M song, 'Mary's Boy Child'. It wasn't just us three singing – there was everyone else singing as a choir. But they would be in the audience, hoping that would lead to the whole audience singing too. Miss Benny, the music teacher, wanted this as she believes in audience participation and said our parents needed to reconnect with their youth.

Taylor, Felix and I had to stand in a line and do the identical motions. When we say 'Mary's boy child, Jesus Christ', we have to pretend to rock a baby in our arms. Taylor thought it was funny to rock the baby and then pretend to throw it like a rugby ball. Felix was hopeless! When he was supposed to turn left, he turned right. When he had to raise his right hand, he raised his left. Miss Benny was irritated and put Felix between Taylor and me so he could copy us. But everyone said it looked as if all three of us were getting it wrong. Miss Benny rolled up the sleeves of her jumper, took off her glasses and said we'd have to practise in the lunch break unless we got it right. She actually joined in our line for the whole song. I didn't realise she could dance. It was great seeing her doing that! Eventually, Felix got the hang of it and she gave all three of us a high five.

'Well done, boys, and don't forget to smile, that's why I picked you. You always have those lovely big beamers.'

I think she might have picked us three because were all about the same height.

The dance looked epic. Mr Jeff came in when we did it the last time and started to watch. He cheered and clapped at the end. He told us to give it some. I'm not sure what that means, but he seemed really enthusiastic. We've only got another three weeks for rehearsals, but at least we've got our part right. Next week we've got to do a dress rehearsal and I've got to ask Mum for something that looks seventies, which means colourful shirts, big collars and leather. That doesn't sound like anything I've got in my wardrobe.

As I walked into the playground, I saw Lucy – she was coming from the door on the other side of the playground. I didn't have a plan of what I was going to do. I was waiting to see if Mat or Daniel would turn up. Lucy was crossing the playground and I wondered where she was going. It was a good laugh practising for the Nativity; I might ask Dad tonight if he's got some old clothes I could use. Lucy was heading for the door I'd just come through. That was odd. If Dad didn't have any seventies stuff we could get some at a charity shop.

'Hey, you!'

'Oh, hi, Lucy!'

She stopped and stood next to me. 'I heard you're a bit of a film expert. Gina said you caught Mrs Stubbs out!'

'Oh yeah, what? The time travel thing?'

'Yeah.'

'Yeah, time travel. I love it! It really gets you thinking.' My hands found my pockets.

'My favourite is *Back to the Future*.'

'Really! Yeah, I've seen all of them.' Lucy was smiling. ' All four on one day, at Oliver's!'

'Me too! Not all on the same day though!' She chuckled.

'What was your favourite?' She had to say the first

one!

'Oh definitely the first.'

Awesome!

'It's just great the way he meets his mother and she fancies him,' she continued.

'Yeah, awkward.' We both laughed. Lucy laughed like Mum does, more of a giggle than a bellow like Dad.

'Sam!' It was Mat calling.

'My dad often takes me to the cinema on a Saturday morning,' Lucy added. 'He's into his films too.'

'Oh yeah I used to do that, when Oliver was around.'

'Not any more?'

'Sam, come on!' Mat was calling louder.

'Er no, my dad doesn't really like the Saturday morning films, he likes other stuff, but he says I'm not old enough.'

'Oh well, you could come with us if you like?'

'That'd be great!' I thought of sitting next to Lucy in the cinema and sharing a tub of popcorn with her.

'Sam, you're in goal.'

'We'll do that then. You'd better get in goal.' She smiled. 'Go on, we'll talk another time.' And with that, she turned on her heel and walked away.

I sprinted off to the goal. In that very second, the ball came my way. 'Save!'

'Awesome, Sam!' Daniel shouted. I threw the ball to him.

Dear Reader of the Quest

What an awetastic-fabu-lick-acious day. I have been a hiding a secret talent: I am a natural goalie. Maybe one day I'll play for England. My part as a wise king is brilliant, and it's going to be a great show. Lucy enjoys films, and she's pretty. She has her hair in a braid to the side, like Mum does sometimes. I'm a lot taller her than her, but that's okay. One day we will go to the cinema together.

My quest is no further forward, but somehow I feel like it's going to happen. I'm going to make it happen. Don't know how, but I'll get there. I can't wait for the weekend to be over and be back at school. I don't think I've ever felt like this before.

Monday 18th November

Kirsty met her friend Rachel on the way to school today. She told me to walk behind. I could hear them laughing like a pair of geese. Then, as we approached the school, Daniel ran up behind and told me about his weekend. They'd gone to London on Saturday and saw loads of stuff. Museums, galleries, a boat ride on the Thames and then in the evening they went to see a musical. They didn't get back till midnight. Daniel said they did loads of travel on the tube and also the bus. His dad prefers the bus because that way you get to see everything.

At lunchtime, I sat with James and Daniel. And then as if it were scheduled as part of my school week, Mrs Ford came to our table and said that Sarah was here to see me and could I come with her straight away. James and Daniel just laughed. We all know that social workers are called by their first names.

Miss Ford showed me into the First Aid room, which was strange since I hadn't hurt myself. I waited and looked at all the medicines, bandages, and there was a mobile defibrillator, just like the one they had in *Casino Royale*. Then there was a knock at the door. I sat up straight. A woman about Mum's age walked in. She wore a dark red jacket with black trousers and had her hair pulled straight up and sitting in a bobble on top of her head.

'Hello, my name is Sarah,' she said in a near whisper.

None of the grown-ups at school use their first names. Then it got stranger: she shook my hand, which is what my dad does with his friends. I can't remember shaking anyone's hand before.

'I've come to talk to you.' She looked at me and raised her eyebrows. Was I supposed to say something? 'It's Sam isn't it?'

'Yes, Miss.'

'Don't look so worried,' she said, smiling. 'We're only going to talk.'

I wondered what else we would do in the room, would she have practised first aid or something?

'Take a seat.' She pulled up her chair right in front of me, like the dentist does. I sat right back in mine.

'I'd like to ask you a few questions about Oliver.' She got her clipboard out. 'About your visit to Portsmouth on Wednesday.' I just stared so she added, 'On the train,' as though I might confuse it with another trip. 'Were you asked to go there?'

'No, Miss. By who? Who do you mean?'

'Not by Mr Bridle?'

'No! I don't have Mr Bridle's number. Dad has it I think, but I don't think I'm supposed to know it?'

'Oh! Well why's that?'

I got the feeling that I might have said the wrong thing. 'Well my dad said that I didn't need to know any more.'

'Because?'

Hmm, Sarah *knew* why. 'Because Oliver isn't at school any more.'

She looked at me and then wrote something on her clipboard. 'Are you happy, Sam?'

'Yes, I think so, Miss.' I can't remember being asked that before, not by a stranger.

'Happy at home?'

'Yes, I think so, Miss.'

'And was Oliver happy?'

'Yes, Oliver was happy, Miss, we had lots of fun together.' She wrote something else on her clipboard. 'I miss him, Miss.' That sounded weird. 'Is he coming back?'

'No, Sam. Oliver isn't coming back.' She looked at me again, over the top of her glasses with her pen still on her clipboard. Then she wrote some more. She had really bright red lipstick on, the colour Mum sometimes wears when she goes out. Now I could see her hair more closely, it was all pulled up on the top of her head and then did a sort of circle. I couldn't work out where the circle started, it sort of just came out of the middle like a stuffed doughnut. Was it just stuck on?

'Did Steve tell you where Oliver was?'

'No, well…' I tried to remember. It had been me that had asked if he'd been taken to Winchester, Steve never actually said it. 'Yeah, he didn't say.' I looked at her. She was chewing on her pen. 'But I don't think I asked?' Why didn't I ask Steve? 'Where is he, Miss, has he gone to Winchester?'

She carried on chewing. I don't think I was

116

supposed to ask that.

'And do you like Steve?' She looked up, her mouth squeezed, her eyes got smaller.

'Yeah, Steve's great, he knows a lot about everything.' I smiled.

She bit on the pen and I could hear it crack. I think I got the answer wrong.

'Do you know him then, Miss?'

'No, Sam, I haven't met Mr Bridle. Did he touch you, Sam?' Again, the tight face.

'How do you mean, Miss?'

'Did he touch you anywhere?' She squeezed her mouth again. 'Anywhere inappropriate?'

'No, Miss. He patted me on the back, like he always does, you know like my dad does. Is Oliver all right, Miss?'

'Yes, Sam, he's landed on his feet. He's with a very wealthy family in a large house – they are very comfortable. He will be having foreign holidays every year. You really mustn't worry about him.' She put her clipboard in her suitcase and snapped the lock shut. 'It's probably better for Oliver to make a complete break from his friends, so he can start his new life.'

What did she mean by that? I don't know quite what happened but I found myself standing. 'I think Oliver misses us! For all I know he may need us.' My voice echoed in the room.

'Now, Sam, please!'

'Have you actually met Oliver?' She didn't answer. 'You haven't met Steve either have you? When it comes to forgetting Oliver I'm afraid'—I decided to use *Men in Black 3*— 'let's agree to disagree.' I decided it wasn't worth talking to Sarah. She just wasn't listening, so I used a bit of Mum. 'Isn't it about time we started doing what's right and not what's easy?'

'That's enough. We'll leave it there.' She stood up. 'I will schedule another meeting, if necessary.' She turned and left.

A few minutes later, Miss Ford came in. 'What did you say to Miss Preen?'

I looked at Miss Ford, I don't think it was one of those questions I was supposed to answer.

'She looked quite upset?'

'She told me to forget Oliver. That he's better off not keeping in touch with us… with me! I told her we'd have to agree to disagree.'

Miss Ford's mouth fell open. I seemed to be getting a lot of that recently.

*

At home, Mum was cooking supper, and Dad was at the table reading the newspaper. 'Sam,' Mum started, ' I had a call from Sarah Preen, she told me about your meeting today.'

I looked up, where was this going?

'She wasn't very pleased with your attitude, Sam.' Mum was staring at me. 'She says you'll have to meet again, and she wants to see you've reconsidered.'

'What's this all about?' Dad said, looking up from

118

his paper.

'Sam's told this woman she's wrong,' Mum said, plainly.

'What happened, son?'

'Miss Preen, well Sarah, really …'

'Who's Sarah?'

'She's a social worker. I think. She didn't really say who she was.'

'A what? You saw a social worker today?' Dad put his paper down

'Yeah, we have this joke at school, social workers want you to use their first names.'

'I fail to see the funny side of that!' Mum said.

Uh-oh, Mum was getting cross.

'Sam,' Mum continued, ' what did you say to Miss Preen?'

Here we go again. 'She said that she wants me to forget Oliver. That he would be better off by not keeping in touch with me. I just like… well… told her that we would have to agree to disagree!'

My mum's mouth fell open, this was getting ridiculous.

Dad chuckled. 'Well done, son!'

'Kevin! What on earth do you think you're doing?' Mum had her arms crossed. I don't think it helped that Dad had broken into a laugh.

'Leave the boy alone,' Dad said, smiling. 'I'm proud of him, he stuck up for his friend. Good on you, Sam. They'll probably take you away, mind, but hey, you've had your say.'

'Kevin, this is not a laughing matter.'

'Seriously, Janice, it's right that Sam stuck up for Oliver. I feel sorry for Steve, I never realised the full story. I think Sam's got a point!' Suddenly my dad became a lot more animated. He picked up his paper and then flicked it down on the table. 'Just imagine if you were in Steve's position, you've lost your wife to cancer and then five minutes later someone you've never met takes your son.'

'The point is, Oliver isn't his son!'

'Well, he was for the first ten years of his life!'

'Well, I think we're going to have to agree to disagree.'

Dad and I looked at each other. It was hard but we didn't say anything, not even a chuckle. But Mum realised and threw a tea towel at Dad.

'Oi! What did I do?'

And with that, Dad and I burst out laughing, and after a while Mum did too. I hadn't seen her smile like that in quite a while. It was great.

> *Dear Reader of the Quest*
>
> *There has been a development. The authorities have made it clear that I am not to see Oliver. I have tried to find out why that is, but I'm not getting anywhere. I did learn though that Dad is an ally, he thinks that I'm right. He said the same as Lucy, that all I'm doing is looking out for a friend. Dad seemed to have thought about what it was like for Steve. Maybe he wouldn't be so unfriendly now if they met again.*

Tuesday 19th November

I was sitting with Mat and James in the dinner hall. Mat was discussing football strategies and I was nodding at the right places. We were halfway through our boxes when Taylor came running up with Felix in tow. 'Come on, Sam, The wise men now!'

'What?!'

'Come on, we've been practising. Felix is better than me now!'

'But…'

'On your feet, Sam!' Taylor kept on cupping his hand and waving me to come with his big beaming smile. I didn't have a choice.

They were standing in the line next to our table – my place was at the right. They looked over their shoulder and mouthed 'COME ON' for me to get in line.

Here goes nothing. I joined the line and immediately Daniel called out 'Five, six, seven, eight.'

'Mary's Boy Child Jesus Christ'—this was louder than I felt comfortable with!—'was born on Christmas Day.' At the end of the chorus, we turned stage front. Sure enough, the whole of the lunch hall had stopped eating and were just gawping at us. O.M.G! We pointed to the sky, we kicked the dirt, and we rocked the baby. Fortunately, the next bit, which I don't know very well, was begun by turning stage right. Great, I could follow Felix. Felix was in his element and louder than Taylor and me put together. I think he was doing what Mr Jeff said and 'giving it some'. No one in the hall was talking, I saw one boy with his sandwich in his mouth half eaten. It was as if they'd all just frozen.

Then it happened. One of those times in your life when the fantastic became real. For when it came to the chorus, guess what, everyone and I mean *everyone*, sang. It was epic. Us wise men couldn't hear ourselves sing. I didn't know if I could keep this up but I didn't want it to end. Star jump, arms right, arms left, rock the baby. Star jump, arms like a rainbow. But then uh-oh, the next bit was turn stage left, I'd be leading!

I did it! March for four, step heel toe, rock the baby. Step back, heel turn. I didn't want it to stop. And then I saw Miss Benny come through the door. She had a huge smile and was clapping. Then for the last chorus, Mr Jeff came running into the hall. For a second, I thought he'd start shouting but he was smiling, a big smile with loads of teeth. He did a little dance too!

Final chorus. Everyone in the hall was now trying to copy our moves, and I saw Mr Jeff dancing with Miss Benny. Epic, epic, epic.

At the end, we fell about laughing and Taylor started the high fives. It was the happiest moment of my life and everyone in the hall was just laughing, cheering, clapping and smiling. Epic! And then, just at the end of it all, at the far end of the hallway I saw Lucy. She'd seen the whole thing. From right across the room I smiled at her and she saw me, and she smiled back.

*

When Mum got home, I decided to have a chat with her while she made supper. She's always in her best mood when she gets back. I think she likes chilling out in the kitchen after work. I sometimes help her – well I sort of cook, perhaps she wouldn't see it as helping? But she calls me her trainee chef. I can roll out pizza bases, chop carrots, peel potatoes, that kind of thing.

Today, Mum was telling me about her day. She just talked away while I killed the veg. Apparently, all the men at the office are quite badly behaved and whatever I do I mustn't be like them. They take the best jobs and delegate, or give, all the rubbish to her. Also, when things go wrong, some men don't put up their hand to take responsibility but they like to point the finger in her direction. She's got a new office junior who is almost half her age, but he doesn't like being told what to do. I don't think this talking makes Mum happy as such, but I think she just needs to say it. A bit like when I've had a rubbish day at school: say if Mrs Stubbs didn't explain something properly or I don't get picked for the team. It doesn't change anything but it's nice just to tell Mum.

The phone went.

'Hello, Janice speaking.' Mum looked out of the window. 'Oh, hello! No, Sam didn't tell me he had a new friend.' She stirred something on the stove. 'This

Saturday? Yes that should be fine.' Mum then spent ages lifting different lids, stirring, changing the heat, pouring on more water.

What was happening on Saturday? Who was on the phone?

'What film do they have?' Mum looked out the window again. 'I'm sure he'd love that.' She looked at me. 'Shall we drop him off or do you want to collect him?' Mum smiled at me. 'Well, come a bit earlier if you'd like and have a cup of tea.' Mum winked at me. 'Okay thanks for the call. See you soon.'

Mum put the phone back in its cradle. I couldn't see her face. She began stirring the supper again.

'Well?'

Mum didn't turn around.

'MUM?! Who was that?'

'You have a new friend, you didn't tell me.' She was giggling.

'WHO was it?'

'Lucy's mum.'

I had the most awesome day today. I don't think I've had so much fun all in one day. The whole lunch hall plus Miss Benny and Mr Jeff and Lucy watched us wise men do our thing and sang all the choruses. Oh, and... I am going to the cinema with Lucy! Lucy is very pretty. Lucy is actually quite awesome. She likes films too, and she said I was right about looking for Oliver.

Wednesday 20th November

School was a chore today, Mrs Stubbs worked us hard and for one reason or another, I didn't get to meet Lucy, so I decided that I'd earned a proper treat of seeing a film tonight. It was an amazing zombie film. One bite and that meant you turned into a zombie yourself in less than a minute unless you got eaten first. It was supposed to be about the near destruction of civilisation and the hero had to inject himself with a life-threatening disease in order accomplish his quest. I saw half of it before supper and half after.

My parents didn't notice I was watching a film in my room. They were watching TV as usual. They generally start watching after supper until they go to bed. Last week I woke up and had to go to the loo – I came down just after midnight and they were both there, staring blankly at the TV. They didn't even notice I'd come down. I don't really know why they watch so much. A lot of it is soaps, which Granny watches too. I sometimes hear them talking about it together as though it was something that had actually happened. In fact, when we visited last time, Mum and Granny Worthing were talking about one of the programmes and then when Dad came in ten minutes later, he was concerned because he thought someone had actually died in real life. And when they explained to Dad and said it was the TV, he was still shocked that that had happened. It was weird, as if they might be planning to go to the funeral.

Thursday 21st November

I awoke from a zombie nightmare, although curiously I was calm and not frightened at all. Kirsty had caught the virus and we were keeping her in the cellar. We were worried that if we told the authorities, she'd be taken away from us. But the trouble was she kept on escaping and eating some of the passers-by and one of our neighbours, which was difficult to keep a secret. Also, she ate so much that she'd put on weight and had become difficult to control. She got stronger every day, which is why her chains would break and she'd get out. I was put in charge to maintain her diet, and although the zombie virus had taken away her ability to talk, you could tell she was miffed I was in control. Dad was busy trying to earn money to keep her fed without her eating people and improve the security of the cellar. In the end, it was looking good. I had retrained Kirsty to speak a few polite phrases and to control her zombie temper. She was almost ready to be brought out into public, but then I woke up and didn't find out whether she got caught or not.

Perhaps, though, my parents have caught a mild form of the virus and that's why they can't move away from the TV. I guess if the local council finds out, then they'll be tested and a social worker will be sent to put me in care. Was this why Dad got so angry with Mum last night when she asked him about his job search? He almost spat at her with his words. Fortunately, I was upstairs but when he left the lounge, he slammed the door so loud I could feel the floor shake. I need to research and find what other symptoms this mild form may have.

Friday 22nd November

Today our football routine met with a new and awesome, if not brilliant, change. At lunchtime we'd gathered as usual and were about to start when Lucy came up to us, together with the five other girls, and said that we were 'hereby challenged'. Boys versus girls! Then when we said we were Manchester they said they were Portsmouth. Which was surprising as Portsmouth aren't very high up in the leagues. Lucy said their team choose Portsmouth because they were local. Which seemed logical but not very exciting? Like asking for vanilla ice cream rather than chocolate because it had fewer calories.

It was a really good game, but it started badly because Mat said right at the beginning that the girls could have a two-goal start, because they were girls. Portsmouth didn't argue and just smiled and nodded at each other. Mat insisted on calling all the fouls, which he doesn't usually do. He said we had to play proper rules and spoke about 'the offside rule'. But when no one knew what he was talking about, even after he explained it a couple of times, he gave up and said we were a bunch of amateurs. Melissa was really good, she scored almost all of their goals. She's like Jessica Ennis, really athletic. I did find it difficult tackling her, I was worried that I might kick her. So Mat started shouting at me to 'get stuck in and stop mucking about'!

Right at the end, Mat did an amazing save in our goal but landed on his shoulder and asked for injury time. Lisa shook her head, her thick blonde hair wobbling like a lion's. She said that he didn't need his shoulder to kick a ball. So Mat went into a whole new level and went from one side of the playground to the other, avoiding all the tacklers, and scored. The bell went and the boys were up by one goal. As we walked back, Lucy winked and said she didn't mind. It had been a good way to get to see me at lunchtime.

I spent the rest of the afternoon smiling. Mrs Stubbs kept on asking me what I was grinning about and I just said it was because we'd won the football, but I couldn't stop seeing Lucy's face when she winked at me. When I got home I celebrated by seeing a film. I managed to see the whole thing before supper. It was called *The Boy In The Striped Pyjamas*. I don't think I really understood the film. It was a bit sad. This boy, probably my age, makes a mistake and dies completely unnecessarily. But the thing was, he had a friend who died too. They died together. Saying that, his friend was going to die anyway, so you weren't so upset for him. Woah, that seems like a really weird thing to say. Anyway, it was really just an unhappy film. Why did Steve have that on his list?

Mum made shepherd's pie, my favourite. Dad always reminds us when we have it of the difference between shepherd's pie and cottage pie. One is lamb mince and the other beef mince. He keeps on asking us and we always say we don't know, but we smile because really we do know.

Then Mum told us about one of her soaps from last night. A divorced family was battling over custody for a child, and she was saying how it really should go to the mother because it was the right and proper thing to do. She said, 'Mothers have an innate quality that they bring to a child's development, that the boy or girl would need to feel safe.'

She seemed annoyed about the story and Dad was getting annoyed as well. Dad was saying that the child would need their father too, to have a rounded upbringing. Mum said the programme was creating a drama out of nothing – everyone knew the mum would get custody, it was what always happened.

I didn't say anything, but I thought about Oliver going to his other dad. Mum and Dad never got worked up about that. It was strange for them to not show any kind of feeling. Perhaps it's because they thought Steve would always lose Oliver, so it didn't really matter.

Dear Reader of the Quest

My football talents are progressing. I am learning the essential skills that will help me achieve my mission: fitness, team building and strategy. We have organised a team name, my idea! And officially pledged allegiance to Manchester United, although I don't think any of our dads have ever seen them play or for that matter been to Manchester. Brandon's dad has been to Liverpool but we decided that Manchester was the better bet as they were more likely to win the league.

Saturday 23rd November

I answered the door when Lucy knocked. There was something unreal about seeing her on my doorstep, as if she didn't exist out of school.

'Mum says we're running late, so we're going to have a cup of tea after the film rather than before!'

'Oh, hi, Lucy,' Mum said, from the kitchen door.

'Hi, Mrs Steepleton.' That was weird, hearing Lucy say my surname. I didn't even know she knew my surname.

'Oh, call me Janice, if you'd like? Okay, we'll expect you for a cuppa after the film then. Grab your coat, Sam.'

Lucy and I walked to the car. She didn't say anything and neither did I. She walked in front of me but just before she got in the car, she turned and smiled.

'Hello, Sam, do you remember me from cosplay?'

'Oh yeah, hi. Hello, Lucy's mum.' Lucy, and then I, giggled.

'Our surname is Meddows,' Lucy said. 'But it's spelt with two 'd's and no 'a'. It's Anglo-Saxon, and it was given to the people that lived near the meadows. They didn't call them fields then because they hadn't been invented. They often used to call people after—'

'So, Sam, have you seen the film today?' Lucy's

mum said.

'No.'

'Have you been to Chichester Gate?' Lucy asked.

'Yeah, I usually go there unless we go to Gunwharf Quays. I haven't been for a while, though, Dad's not really into the Saturday morning films.' Chichester Gate always shows up-to-date films for one pound on a Saturday morning. But Dad says that's all they were really worth.

'We go about twice a month,' Lucy continued. 'Mum takes me one time and then next Dad takes me. We've been coming for about three years now. Do you have popcorn?'

'Err, yeah. Yeah I do.'

'We always have popcorn, which is why I don't have breakfast before we go. We don't have the cola because that makes me hyper and we sometimes have ice cream if it's my birthday or it's Christmas.' Lucy seemed chattier this morning.

The film was great fun. But it's one of those films my dad would say was a bit Disney: 'Life displayed through rose-tinted glasses'. They weren't good because it made you think that life was really like that and you'd get disappointed. But I liked today's film all the same. I sat next to Lucy. She kept on talking all the way through. I had to keep on looking at her because she was whispering. Her mum didn't want any popcorn, so we had it between us. When we left the cinema, Felix was leaving too and he said hello. He didn't say anything about me being with Lucy. I thought he would as the boys at school can be like

134

that.

Mum and Mrs Meddows couldn't stop talking. It seemed like a competition as to who could say more. But I could tell Mum liked Mrs Meddows. She'd got out the special cups and she'd made one of her cakes, although really it was lunchtime. It turned out that Mrs Meddows used to work where my mum works, and they compared people's names to see who was still there. Mrs Meddows, whose real name is Tina, now works for the BBC in London. Mum was really impressed. Then Tina said that Mr Meddows, whose real name is Tom, works in event management. Mum just nodded. I don't know what that is either.

It reminded me of one of those sports programmes where you've got two people talking at each other and you've just got to listen, so I showed Lucy my bedroom. Mum had told me to tidy it just in case. Lucy sat on my bed and said that although her room was bigger, she really liked the colour. I looked at the wall – until she'd said it, I'm not sure if I'd have remembered the walls were blue, which is silly I know. She said she liked my film posters. I've got eleven in all. The first one we got from the cinema: it's huge and they were selling it off for charity. Then Dad would get me a new one every so often. He said that it was cheaper than wallpaper and easier to make a change when I got bored. But I never changed them, I just kept on adding to them, and now there are so many I had to put the last couple on the ceiling. Mum kept on calling up for us to come down as they had to go, but I hadn't finished showing Lucy my old Lego constructions. I don't think she was really into that, but they are pretty amazing. She said they looked really cool, but perhaps she was just being nice?

'Come on, Lucy, I'm sure there'll be another time to see the rest of Sam's things.'

'Okay, coming!'

As we came downstairs, we caught the end of their conversation.

'… in Brighton, at the cosplay event?' Mum asked.

'Yes, that was a fun day out. Sam had a brilliant costume, very professional. Oh I've got a picture if you'd like to see it.' Lucy's mum got out her phone and I thought of which moment it might be.

'Oh and one of Oliver too!' Mum said. ' Sam, come and see, there's a picture of Oliver.'

There he was, smiling, with his magic wand pointing at me. Tina let me hold the phone to see it. I went back to Lucy, who was looking at my aquarium. But I had half an ear out and heard, 'We were really impressed with Mr Bridle.'

'Steve?'

'Yes, Steve or as cosplay likes to say "The Leather Man". He was clearly very popular and he spoke really nicely about his wife passing away. It was so moving.' She lowered her voice, so I listened even harder. 'It's such a shame isn't it? About losing Oliver. Did you hear about the incident after the fight?'

'No?'

'Well, when Steve collected Oliver he started having a go at Mr Jeff and at the boy's mother who was hit.'

'Not apologetic then?!' Mum raised her eyebrows.

'No, he was furious that Oliver had been teased and started having a go about all schools being the same and not understanding their situation and being insensitive to Oliver.'

'It must be difficult for him.'

'Well, he threatened to write to the papers about Mr Jeff's cruelty and started banging the table. I don't think it helped having the boy's mother there.'

'Well no, she shouldn't have been there. I think it's because she works there she was able to be around at the right moment... if you know what I mean?'

'Yes, she stirred it up all right!' Lucy's mum, put her cup loudly on the saucer. ' She told him he needed to improve his parenting skills! In the end, the police were called and they asked Steve to leave.'

'Wow, that is shocking!'

And then I realised that Lucy saw I was listening and she put her hand on mine, like Mum does.

'And of course,' Mum continued, ' Mr Jeffrey can be a bit of an ass—'

'Mum!'

'But generally he is a great headmaster.' Mum glanced at me.

'Poor Steve, I think he's one of those people you either love or... worry about.'

I had to say something. 'Mum, Steve's really nice, he wouldn't hurt anyone.'

Mum and Tina turned around as though they hadn't known we were there.

'I know, Sam, it's just people were a bit frightened by the situation.'

After they left I asked Mum what Tom did. 'What is event management?'

'Good question. Sounds interesting though!'

Sunday 24th November

On Sunday, I had The Fountain of Knowledge fired up and was just choosing a film when I heard Kirsty stomping up the stairs.

'Sam, Mum wants you to tidy up the front room.'

I ignored her. Perhaps if I didn't answer, she wouldn't know I was in and I could carry on with my film. The door burst open.

'Alright, I did hear you!'

'Well answer then, Simple Sam.'

What a pain it was having her just burst in on me like that. I pushed the door closed with my foot.

'Mum wants you to do it now.'

'Alright!' I could hear her outside, she hadn't moved away. Then I saw the handle move – she had her hand on it. I grabbed it and forced it up. I could feel her pushing down, so I pulled it up more.

'Don't be a prat. Let me in.'

I didn't say anything and I could imagine her seething, steam coming out of ears, and the pressure on the door got stronger. Finally, as the skin under my fingers had turned white and I was about to give up, I heard Kirsty grunt 'idiot' and walk downstairs.

And that was the seed of the idea for my do-it-yourself lock. All I had to do was get something to go between the floor and the bottom of the handle. Like most ideas, as my dad says, the simpler the better.

I went into the garage and looked for a pole. Perhaps a tent pole or a broom handle?

'What's up, Sam?'

'Oh, hi, Dad!'

'What are you up to?'

'Just looking for some stuff to make'—my mind whirled—'a camp. A long pole would be great!'

'Well you can have anything in that pile there, that's all going to the tip. Failing that, you can borrow the rake as long as it comes back by the end of the day.'

'Thanks, Dad!' And there it was in the pile, sitting on the top: an old curtain pole. 'This'll work, thanks, Dad.' And I carried the pole as if I'd found a priceless national treasure.

I stood the pole on the floor underneath the handle and marked off a point just below the metal. Then, when I heard Dad cleaning his car, I raced down to the garage, got the saw and made the cut. I put the leftover bit in the pile, brushed my foot over the sawdust and raced back up the stairs with my new and improved national treasure.

It was perfect. Once placed under the handle there was no way you could move the handle, not a millimetre. I almost felt like shouting at Kirsty to annoy her and see if she could get in. I could shout 'Oi zombie girl' or 'cuddly Kirsty', but I thought better of it and just placed it by the door. From now on, people would have to knock before they came in.

Monday 25th November

I was getting ready for school and Dad was still at home. He was wearing the same clothes he wore yesterday.

'Aren't you going to work?'

Dad looked at me. 'My contract ended Friday.'

'Oh! So, what will you do now?'

'Apply for jobs. I've got to tidy up my CV.'

'CV?'

'Curriculum vitae, it's a list of your qualifications, skills and experience… a list of the jobs you've had.'

'Are you doing that today?'

'This week sometime. I've got to work out which job I'm going to do first, you write your CV to suit the job you're going for.'

That was confusing. 'But aren't your qualifications and the jobs you've had the same.'

'Ah, well.' Dad smiled. 'It's all about marketing. You have to accentuate the good bits. Most people have so much to say, so it's easy to fill up the paper. But your average employer only skims what you've written, so you need to make the things they want stand out.'

'That sounds difficult.'

'Yes, but it's easier if you've studied at school, so pay attention today. Go on then, son, you best get ready.'

'So what kind of job will you go for?'

Dad looked at the pile of papers and then to his laptop. 'Come on, Sam. We can talk about this later.'

It was strange having Dad at home, but nice knowing he was there. I wondered whether it would take all day to find the job he wanted.

On the way to school, Kirsty did something really peculiar: she rolled up her skirt at the top, where her waist is. So although the skirt should be about knee level, it was now five inches above.

'What did you do that for?'

'Mind your own business, Simple Sam.'

That was severe! I was genuinely interested. But I decided not to push the point. I couldn't put a door between us.

We had a talk today at school. This careers officer was in the main hall telling us about 'The World of Work', and then they introduced a man from Rolls Royce. They have a factory in Goodwood, a village near Chichester. His name was Hans Baddermann. He spoke about 'climbing the right ladder', which confused everyone. But then he explained that he was talking about choosing the right qualifications and career path to follow. 'Make sure you climb the ladder that arrives at the place you want to get to.'

He asked for people to suggest jobs they knew about. Some kids came out with accountant, solicitor and doctor. The room was a bit quiet and so was Mr Baddermann. So then he asked what we would all really like to do. The people came out with things like astronaut, jet fighter pilot tester and Formula One racing driver. He folded his arms and rocked on his feet. We couldn't really see what he was getting at.

'No, tell me what you'd enjoy doing, but would still be possible?'

One kid put their hands up and said they'd liked to work for Her Majesty's Secret Service and have a job like James Bond's. Someone bettered it and said that they wanted to be Matt Damon from the Bourne series.

The speaker was still looking annoyed. 'Something you can do in Chichester, that would be fun and would give you the lifestyle you want.'

We then all looked really confused, so he carried on. 'Would you like three holidays a year, to live in a big house, with a games room, a nice car and a swimming pool?'

'Yes, please!' Someone called out.

He frowned. 'So, can I have some sensible suggestions please?'

There was silence for quite a while. I put my hand up. 'Website designer... Local government officer?'

'Great, well done. Who else would like to be those?'

There was silence.

A hand went up. 'Why can't I be an astronaut?'

When we got back to the classroom, it was all quiet. I think we were still trying to work out what to do with our lives. Mrs Stubbs looked annoyed as if we hadn't been well behaved, but I couldn't see what we'd done wrong. No one was talking when the speaker was talking.

'Right, children, I think we need to do a little more work on careers. Let's discuss what we want out of a career.'

James was quickly in. 'I don't want to work too hard, Miss!'

Then Hannah. 'I'd like a lot of money.'

Sophie added, 'A company car would be cool.'

Then I just came out with it, what we'd all been thinking. 'Miss, I don't really understand why people work. There are plenty of ways of making money without working. You can bet on the horses. Those gamblers in the *Casino Royale* film were betting in the millions.'

Then Ben had a go. 'Look at Usain Bolt, he gets hundreds of thousands in sponsorship and he's only got to run for ten seconds.'

'Less than ten seconds!' James said.

Taylor tried. 'Then you get people who get £26,000 a year, just from government benefits, and they don't actually work!'

Mrs Stubbs was quiet, her lips were tight together and she was frowning. She went to speak but James was in first. He sits next to me.

'You're barking up the wrong tree. Why do any of those things, be a bank robber.'

'*Ocean's Eleven*,' I said, as evidence.

'Or steal high performance cars.'

'*Gone in Sixty Seconds*,' I proved.

Mrs Stubbs closed her laptop loudly, the white screen went black. 'I think we'll move on to some maths now.'

When I got home, Dad was there. Of course he was there, but it was still strange he was there. I decided not to tell him about the careers day or ask him if he'd ever wanted to be an astronaut.

Tuesday 26th November

Mum kissed Dad goodbye at the front door as she was leaving. Usually Dad has gone to work by then. Mum turned around, just as Dad was closing the door.

'Do you want to do a white wash? Oh, and why not do a spaghetti bolognese for tonight?'

I can't remember Dad cooking before.

'Okay, love. Have a nice day at work.' This really did feel strange. 'Can you bring me your school shirts down, Sam, and I'll do them too.'

*

I saw Lucy in school today – she was talking to Peter in assembly. They seemed to have a lot to say to each other. I wanted to be with her but she's in another class and we have to sit where we are told. She did look up at me, though, and when I smiled, she waved.

*

When Mum got back from work, Dad hadn't made supper. He said he'd been 'busy with his job hunt'. Mum said 'Okay', but I saw her raise her eyebrows. I offered to help Mum, and she looked happy again. When we got in the kitchen, Mum opened the washing machine door and pulled out a wet shirt, but then just put it back in.

When I was chopping the onion, I asked Mum, as casually as I could, 'What's a good film to learn about love?'

'That's a bit out of the blue?' She was quiet for a bit. 'You mean boy-meets-girl type love? Oops!' She laughed. 'Do you mean love between people that are going out with each other, boyfriend-girlfriend love? Oops!' She laughed again. 'There are lots of types of love. Like the love I have for you, like the love I have for your father, the love you have for Kirsty.'

'What?!'

Mum was smiling to herself.

I thought about the film list: there's only two films coloured red. *Love Actually* and *The Notebook*. I haven't seen these films but they don't sound very revealing and I wanted to know now. What do girls want?

'Well, give me a for instance then,' Mum continued. 'What is the love you've seen that you want to know about?' She laughed again. 'Sorry, I'm not doing this very well.' She seemed really cheerful tonight.

'Okay then, why does Fiona love Shrek?'

'What?' Mum was thinking as she opened the tomatoes. 'Well, wasn't that all about looks? She was a troll and so was he.'

'No Mum, Shrek was an ogre not a troll.'

'Same difference, isn't it?'

'Mum a troll is ....' Wow, I realised I hadn't

considered the difference.

'Yes?'

This needed thought. 'An ogre eats humans. A troll is more supernatural.' I don't think I gave a very good definition. 'Anyway, the point is they didn't fall in love with each other because of looks, because Fiona was human and then she was a troll. Shrek loved her before and after she changed, so it can't be that. Anyway, if it was about looks why did the dragon fall in love with the donkey?'

'Yes and that was a problem wasn't it?' Mum thought as she emptied the can. 'Love isn't always so straightforward. Donkey didn't love the dragon, which was sad for the dragon. Love made the dragon protective, sad and softer.'

Wow, Mum had a good point. 'So why did they fancy each other if it wasn't looks?'

'Fiona liked Shrek because he rescued her.'

'Yeah, but that was only so he'd get his land back from Lord Farquaad, it wasn't a proper rescue. Shrek didn't want to save Fiona, he wanted something else.'

'Yes, but on the way back he did look after her. Also, although he wasn't rescuing her for her, but for his land, she knew that he was dependable, reliable and could rescue her. He could keep her safe. Just like he looked after the donkey too. Also, I think Fiona may be a romantic, a hopeless romantic. She had an idea of how she should be rescued and that she should fall in love with him, so it was very romantic if they did get together. That's how she was brought up, to believe that she would have a fairytale relationship.

The enchantment could only be broken by "true love's kiss".'

'No, Mum, she just wanted the curse to be gone, the curse of being an ogre. She wanted to be kissed by Shrek because if she was kissed by her true love then she wouldn't be an ogre every night.'

'Sorry, you know the film better than me.'

'Why do you love Dad?'

Mum frowned. 'Often with love you don't know why you love someone, you just know when you are and when you're not... in love.' Mum picked up my chopped onions and scooped them into the frying pan. 'You'll know, Sam, don't worry, one day it will happen.'

I heard the onions sizzle.

'But be careful what you wish for, it doesn't always make you happy.'

'Why?'

Mum was smiling again. 'Because she – the person –may not love you.'

Yes this is what I needed to know, how would they love you, how could you make them love you?

'Or you may realise,' Mum continued, 'that you might have to make some sacrifices for your love. In Romeo and Juliet, they are in love but their families hate each other. If they had got married they would have lost the support of their families.'

'What?'

'In Romeo and Juliet, the families are feuding.'

'Feuding?'

'They're battling... arguing, they've fallen out and

they have proper sword fights against each other.'

I thought that my Mum got on all right with Lucy's mum. That was good.

'With Shrek, wasn't it the fact that they had the same sense of humour. Do you remember they both burped and thought it was funny?'

Lucy and I do laugh at the same stuff... giggle, more.

'Maybe because she turns into a troll...'

'Ogre.'

'...at every sunset, she knew it was just meant to be. As if they were soul mates.' Mum was now stirring the supper; she was concentrating hard. 'Maybe it was really because in the end she realised that with Shrek, she could be her true self, and wouldn't have to pretend to be anyone else.'

'Like who?'

'Like a red-headed human princess.'

'Why would Fiona pretend to be something she's not?'

'Because before, she was never happy being an ogre. When she found someone who would love her for her, for who she is, that was powerful. And so the idea of marriage on the same day they first kissed... all made sense. It was perfect.'

I helped lay the table while Mum finished and then she asked me to call everyone. Kirsty was upstairs. I think she heard me; I got a kind of grunt. Dad was watching TV, he'd turned it on at five o'clock as there'd been a really good programme he needed to watch about buying a second property in Spain. He told me to see if Mum could wait ten minutes, as it would be over then. But I had to go back and say that Mum wanted him to record it. Dad kind of grunted.

Mum and Dad were quiet at supper; no one had any much to say. I thought about asking Dad about his thoughts on love but it didn't seem the right time to bring it up. It had been fun talking about it with Mum.

Holidays! Now that always gets them talking. 'Where are we going on holiday this year, Dad?'

'Not sure yet, Sam, probably wait and see what happens.' He looked up at Mum.

'To see if what happens?'

'Sam, you can be so simple!' Kirsty said.

'Kirsty!' Mum looked up.

'Just waiting to see about my job, Sam.' Dad continued.

'We'll be tightening the belt until your dad has a job, Sam. It may mean we give up a few luxuries until then.'

'What do you mean by luxuries?' I saw Kirsty sneer.

'Holidays, eating out, that kind of—'

'It won't be long.' Dad interrupted. 'Something will come up,'

'Well, it'll take a lot longer if you don't apply for something!'

'There isn't anything.' Dad insisted.

'There must be!'

'Show me where then.'

Mum dropped her knife and fork on the plate. 'I think that working and doing all the housework is enough, actually! I'm feeling quite drained.'

This conversation wasn't working out, I tried something else. 'Dad, what do you think about love?'

'What?!' Dad looked quite confused.

'Oh you know, why do people fall in love?'

He looked as shocked as Mum.

'Mum and I were talking about it earlier.'

'Who'd like more?' Mum offered.

'Well, why did you fall in love with Mum?' Dad looked even more confused. 'Why did you get married?' Dad didn't look at me any more. He didn't look at Mum. I think he was thinking. Maybe it was like the Shrek and Fiona discussion – it wasn't obvious. I decided not to try any more conversations. We sat in silence. I thought about what Mum said about getting drained – I think she meant getting tired and then ill. Mum did look a bit tired, and she had had a cold last week. What would happen if she got ill? That would mean that both Mum and Dad wouldn't have jobs. What would we have to give up then? Perhaps Kirsty and I would have to work. Or, would we be taken into care? I think it may be necessary to learn those essential life skills Steve was talking about as soon as I can. Also, I'd better keep my room a bit tidier, anything to help Mum out.

9pm

Dear Reader of the Quest
I saw this film tonight. It had a very high learning number and Steve has warned me to

not to watch it on my own. But I decided at
supper I need to make my learning go faster,
maybe I'll need the information quite soon.
The film was called The Shining. This man
goes to look after a hotel in the wilderness for
the winter with his wife and son. He slowly
goes mad and tries to kill them. I didn't really
understand why the father went mad, I think it
was because he couldn't do his job. I didn't
really understand why the boy was so spooked
with ghosts, whether that was him or the
haunted hotel. It didn't make much sense to
me. I really needed Steve to tell me why I
should watch it.

I heard a door slam downstairs.

'You just monopolise the remote.' It was Mum.
'You've been in all day watching TV, and now I can't
relax over my programme.'

I didn't hear any more, Dad said nothing back.
What if Dad went mad like the man in *The Shining*?
Should I hide the axe that's in the garage?

Wednesday 27th November

It was 10.30, just before the morning break, when Mrs Ford came into the classroom. 'Can we have Sam for a little while, please?'

'Yes, of course.' Mrs Stubbs was as curious as me.

As we walked along the corridor, Mrs Ford walked ahead of me. 'There's a Mrs Blacknell – Susan – to see you. She's a social worker.'

I was shown into the same room. The lady was already in there. She wore a suit, like my mum does sometimes. She didn't smile. Her hair was cut short and her face reminded me of the wicked witch from *The Wizard of Oz*.

'Please sit.' The woman said putting on some glasses.

'Yes, Miss.'

'You're Sam?'

'Yes, Miss.'

'And you know Oliver?'

'Yes, Miss.'

She looked at me over the top of her glasses, 'Do you know where he is now?'

'Not exactly, Miss.'

'What does that mean?'

I thought of Steve's face talking to me at Southsea. 'I think they've taken him to Winchester, but I don't have his address.'

'And have you been in contact with him?'

'No, Miss. What's all this about?'

'I'll ask the questions, Sam.' There was silence as she tapped her pen on the desk. It was a big wad of paper in a green cover. 'And have you been in contact with Oliver's father?'

'Not since I went down there by train.'

'When was that?'

'About a couple of weeks ago.'

'Ah yes, your little adventure.' She tapped her pen again as she carried on reading. I looked down: she had a big bag full of similar files. The bag was black and much bigger than Dad's briefcase. The two sides of the lid were open, and on each file cover was a person's name handwritten in felt tip.

'Sam, I need to tell you that it's a serious matter if you withhold any information from us that may help us find Oliver!'

It was then I heard the bell go for morning break. 'Why don't you ask Oliver's dad?'

She took off her glasses. 'I will ask the questions.'

'Well I'm trying to help!'

'You're just here to answer questions, we don't need your help!'

'Well maybe Oliver needs my help! You people seem to be getting it pretty wrong. Why are you here, have you lost him?' As I said it, I realised. 'He's run away, hasn't he?' I saw her lips tighten.

'And how did you know that?'

'I don't.' But I did now. What was in that file of

hers? I needed to get it. Just like Sarah, she wasn't going to tell me anything. How could I get that file? I needed to draw on all my resources; this was my opportunity.

I thought of all the films that were relevant. I hadn't seen *My Sister's Keeper*. Steve said the age certificate was all wrong – they said it was a 12 but he thought it was a 15. Anyway, in the story a young girl has to see a solicitor and stand up for her older sister's rights to not have to donate her kidneys to her sister. Her mum is really hard on her, making her feel unloved, but she had to be strong and keep true to her sister's wishes.

This social worker didn't seem to be for Oliver. If he'd run away, he wanted to be back with Steve, but her job was to find him and return him to the other dad.

'I'm wasting my time,' she muttered. She slammed Oliver's green file shut and stood up. 'Let's go. I'll hand you back to Mrs Ford.'

She looked pretty angry and examined me as I stood up. No one said anything as she opened the door and waved her hand for me to leave the room. As we walked along the corridors, I could hear her breathing heavily and tutting. Just before we got to Mrs Ford's office, I realised my opportunity.

'It's okay, Miss, I can find my own way back. It *is* break time.'

'Sam....'

I didn't wait to find out what she was going to say. I raced down the corridor, turned left and along and then I was back in the First Aid room. I found Oliver's green file on the table and closed up Mrs Blacknell's case. I put the file up my jumper and within seconds, I was back out of the room and into the busy playground. It was like escaping. I needed to find somewhere to read it.

'Hey, Sam.'

'Lucy!' Of all the people I'd want to meet, and there she was.

'What's up?'

'Brilliant! I need to show you something.'

'What?'

I thought for a second. 'Can you come with me to the library?'

We crossed the playground to the other building. Each step away from the corridor made me feel safer. It's not a real library, of course, not even a room, just a place between the reception and the main hall with the corridor running through it. But there is a corner I know which has a table and a place to sit for two. I explained everything. Fortunately, some other people were making quite a noise and we could talk easily.

'You'd better give me the file.'

'Why?'

'Because when the wicked witch finds out the file's missing, she'll suspect you've got it.'

'Good point.' I pulled the file out of my jumper.

'Wow.'

'Yeah, it's a chance isn't it... to find him?'

'Yeah, and it's exciting isn't it?' Lucy had already opened the file and was looking at the pages. I saw a picture of Oliver, it seemed strange to see him there looking at us. Then Lucy was turning the pages. We found telephone numbers, a case number, a police report, a picture of Steve and a picture of Mr Chartwell. That must be the new dad? Then there was my name and underneath notes by Sarah Preen.

The bell went. 'Let's hide it,' Lucy said. She turned around and pulled a space between two books, placing the file between them. 'Come on.' I followed Lucy out of the library. 'I'll meet you here at lunch break!'

'Great! Thanks, Lucy.'

She smiled at me. 'We're a team!'

I thought of her at that moment as Fiona and tried to say something cool and funny like Shrek. 'We're good together.' Whoa! Did I say that?

'I love the way you're not going to give up on Oliver and not allow the grown-ups to push you around.'

I loved the way she used the word 'love'.

*

When I arrived at lunchtime, she was already there and she was copying stuff out into a notebook. 'There's loads here,' she said, without looking up. 'I've got Oliver's e-mail address and his new school, and you were right, he's run away.'

'Where to?'

'It doesn't say, just that it was his birthday and no one at the school had remembered. He was gone by lunchtime.'

'Wow, yeah his birthday, I'd forgotten too!'

'It says it was a prep school. I think that means they do their homework in the evenings, like every day, even Fridays!'

'Oliver would hate that! He's probably gone home.'

'What to see his dad? His old dad, his first dad I mean!'

'Yeah, Steve?'

'Would he know how to get there?' Lucy said more to herself. 'Would he find his way home?'

'Well yeah, if I could find the way, I'm sure he could. Okay, so we know where he might be, how are we going to talk to him?'

'E-mail, we've got his e-mail address.'

'That's brilliant, but our school will see what we send, they check stuff.'

'Not if we use a personal account, a personal Hotmail account.'

'You've got one of those?'

'Yeah my dad helped me set it up. Don't you have a PC at home?'

'I've got my laptop.'

'Yeah, great!' Lucy gave me a funny look, like I was talking to her and she was listening. 'I can help you set up a Hotmail account if you want and then we can send each other messages?'

'You know how to do that?'

'My dad does a lot with computers at work.'

'So does mine, or did anyway.' I didn't want to explain.

'So we could try e-mailing Oliver. Hang on, what about Facebook or Instagram?'

'Mum won't let me use those.' Although for some reason Kirsty does. 'Anyway, Oliver never wanted to get into that.'

'Okay, that figures. So I'll bring you a username and password tomorrow.'

I was confused.

'For your Hotmail account!'

'Great! Okay, and then what do I do with them?'

Lucy gave me a smile like Mum does, like 'You should know the answer to that question'.

'Can you show me now on the library computer?'

Lucy showed me how to sign on and send her a message. I also admitted that I didn't know how to sign the laptop on to the broadband at home. She told me to look under the router at home. And showed me how to search for Wi-Fi connections. I had to guess that the one with the strongest strength was our signal. It was all a bit James Bond to me, but I suppose important if we were to find Oliver.

Then Lucy reached for the file again, and she pulled on a blue piece of paper sticking out the side. 'Wow, look at this!'

Lucy was holding a letter. It looked pretty official. 'It's from Bio Dad to Social Services.' Lucy pinched up her lips. 'Listen to this: "Oliver is my boy and belongs with me. Mr Bridle is not responsible or able to look after Oliver. Mr Bridle has agreed that it is more equitable that Oliver be in my care now. He has accepted that his record is not befitting that of a good guardian. We discussed his drink-driving incident, his unemployment, lack of savings, and dependency on anti-depressants. Then there is the issue of Mr Bridle goading Oliver to use physical violence at school to resolve disagreements, together with him threatening his neighbours and the police for not getting involved. My wife, Angela, always said that Steve was no good, that he treated her badly and was mean to Oliver. She told me she felt she couldn't leave them alone together. She also mentioned his deviant behaviour, whatever that meant.   Finally, for your records, although Angela called herself Angela Bridle, her name is Angela Chartwell, she never got married to Steve Bridle. I have therefore, and with great care for Oliver's feelings, brought Oliver home to Winchester and he was very relieved." ' Lucy paused and looked at me. 'It's a brilliant letter.'

'It's full of lies! It's horrible!'

'It may be horrible, but it's brilliant because it sounds true. This Mr Chartwell is good.'

'Good?! He's completely bad.'

'He's bad, all right. A bad boy,' Lucy said, more to herself than me. She looked at the letter. 'But he'll get what he wants, and he doesn't care how he gets it.' Lucy took the letter and held the top edge with both hands. She looked at me.

'Lucy?'

Too late – Lucy tore the letter in half. The sound was unbelievably loud.   Then she put the pieces together and ripped it again. Within seconds, only a pile of confetti remained.

'We've got a proper fight on our hands. Come on! We should get this file back to the First Aid room.'

'Why?'

'Sooner or later they'll see it's gone and you're the first person they'll come to.'

We had five minutes before lunch was over. I hid the file in my jumper and we walked down to the First Aid room. Lucy kept a look out, while I walked in and placed the file on the table. As I came out, the bell went.

'See you tomorrow then.'

Lucy did her funny smile. 'See ya.'

In the afternoon, Mrs Ford came to the classroom. She didn't even bother coming into the room. 'Sam, please?'

This was becoming quite a habit.

'What have you done now?' James said.

'He's in big trouble,' Mat teased.

'Leave him alone,' Charlotte said, pushing Mat's shoulder.

I followed Mrs Ford to Mr Jeff's room. As we opened the door, Mrs Blacknell was standing like an army captain inspecting her soldiers.

Mr Jeff looked at me, and he spoke calmly. 'Sam, Mrs Blacknell informs me you may have her file of Oliver from this morning.'

'No, sir.'

'Well of course he's going to say that!'

'Mrs Blacknell, can I first talk to Sam?'

'And can I remind you, this is a most serious matter!'

'Mrs Blacknell!'

'If you mean the green file, I did see the file in the

First Aid room,' I said. 'Mrs Blacknell had it out on the desk, she was reading it while she was asking me questions.'

'Mrs Blacknell have you looked in the First Aid room?'

'I wouldn't have left it there, I put it in my case.'

'Shall we look? It would be nice to rule that out. Mrs Ford could you do the honours please?'

So the three of us stood in Mr Jeff's room. It felt a bit awkward. Mrs Blacknell was scowling at me. I couldn't look at her. Mr Jeff read something on his desk – I don't think he knew what to say, he was probably wishing the problem would just go away. He was just about to speak when Mrs Ford came in the office.

'Is this the file?' She held up the green file.

Mr Jeff looked at me and winked. Mrs Blacknell grabbed the file and as she marched out and mumbled, 'Thank you'.

Thursday 28th November

As I poured my cereal, Mum was rushing around the kitchen. She seemed to be preparing tonight's supper, making my sandwiches, getting herself a cup of tea, loading the dishwasher, emptying the washing machine and finishing a shopping list – all at the same time. Dad and Mum always teased each other about Mum being able to multitask, but this was exceptional, even for her. As she put away the glasses, I put away the milk and my leg caught up with her leg and the glass smashed on the floor.

'Sam! Can you please not be under my feet?'

'Sorry, Mum.'

She just huffed.

'I'll get the dustpan and brush.' I offered

'No, don't worry, I can do it.' Mum wouldn't look at me. 'Can you take your cereal onto the table please?'

'Yes, Mum, sorry.'

Kirsty and I were about to leave for school. We were putting on our coats when Dad came down the stairs in his bathrobe and slippers. He didn't say 'hello' as such, it was a word that sounded like someone from another country trying to speak English. He didn't go right to the loo, he went left to the lounge. Then I heard the TV going on and Dad flicking through the channels. When we got back from putting our coats on, I could hear Oprah Winfrey on.

'Bye, Dad,' Kirsty called out.

'Bye.'

'Bye, Dad,' I said, but there was no reply.

Kirsty and I walked to school in silence. I had to walk behind her as usual, then she met up with her friend Rachel. As they talked, their voices got louder and louder and they started laughing. Kirsty turned around, she had her hand in front of her mouth. I think she wanted to see if I heard what they'd said, and then Kirsty stuck her tongue out at me.

Mrs Stubbs was in no better a mood. I tried to smile at her a couple of times, but it was as though she was ignoring me, as if I'd done something wrong. Eventually, she let me know what the problem was.

'I spoke to a very upset Mrs Blacknell yesterday.'

Was that a question or a statement? Was it one of those rhetorical questions?

It didn't even go right with Lucy. I couldn't find her until lunchtime and then, when we met, Mat gave me an earful saying I was turning into a girl for not playing football. I didn't say anything and looking at Lucy, I think she wished I had said something back to him. But Lucy *did* pass me a piece of paper saying it had everything I needed for the PC.

Then James was just as bad and said loudly, 'Is that a love letter from your girlfriend?' To which Lucy rolled her eyes. I worried about how Lucy felt. It was difficult to talk in the playground and I think she had something on her mind.

As soon as Kirsty saw me in the playground, I walked in front of her. As we got closer, I got faster, until by the time we were home I was running. I wanted to get on the laptop and get my Hotmail account set up. I put the curtain pole under the door handle and set out the laptop. I unfolded Lucy's letter and typed away.

First, I had to get broadband working. That took ages. I kept on typing the broadband password in all wrong. I'd copied it from the bottom of our router, but it turned out I'd written the admin password not the user password, but an hour had gone by before I'd worked that out. Then the Hotmail account. I don't know what I was doing, but it just didn't work. It was amazing to be on the internet, though. I'd never thought about doing that with the laptop. That could be really useful for my searches. Lucy would be expecting me to message her tonight, and I didn't want to let her down.

There was only one thing for it: a film. Today was a disaster and I felt it was a sign, like you need more information, you need to find a key, it can't be this bad, there must be a reason. So I chose a film with a really high learning rate, *The Deer Hunter*. I was pleased in that I managed to see half of it before supper. But I didn't really understand what was going on. There just seemed to be a lot of people shouting at each other and mucking around. This man dances with this other guy's girlfriend, and does so inappropriately, but rather than having it out with the guy he slaps the girlfriend! Why didn't he shout at the man? Then eventually they went to war and that's when I went to the loo.

As I was going through to the loo, Mum was preparing the supper. I was just looking at the floor and she moved in front of me, so I stepped to the left, and then she moved in front of me. I moved to the right, and she moved in front of me. I looked up and she was smiling at me. We both burst out laughing.

'I'm sorry I was short with you this morning, Sam.' And then she gave me a big hug. The day's rubbishness just melted away in an instant. 'I should have said something straight away, but I was in a grump.' I squeezed her back. 'Do you want to help me with the supper?'

'Okay, Mum.' The film could wait.

Mum's phone rang, 'Oh hello Mr Meddows – Tom, hi Tom. That would be lovely. Yes I think it's a good friendship. Saturday then. Come in for a cuppa. See you then.' Mum put the phone down and carried on chopping.

'Muuuum!'

She grinned at me. 'You're going to the cinema with Lucy.'

The day was getting a whole lot better.

After supper, I went on with the film, but I failed completely to get what was going on. There were all these soldiers trying to get other people to shoot themselves. Then there was this big thing about whether to shoot the deer or not at the end. Wasn't that the whole point? He was a deer hunter, why didn't he shoot it? What was I supposed to get from the film?

That one day I may have to put an empty chamber in the gun to buy enough time to escape? What was Steve thinking? There was no point in putting an entry in *The Book of the Quest*, I had learnt nothing.

Saturday 30th November

As I woke up, I could hear Mum and Dad talking downstairs. Saturday mornings are my favourite. I have a bit of a lie in, do a bit of reading, help Dad in the garage. Lucy! I sprang out of bed – she'd be here in half an hour. I got ready in a bit of panic. I hadn't tidied my room like last time, so clothes and books littered the floor like seaweed on a beach.

A second after I was ready, the doorbell went, which made me jump as I was standing right by it. Then there was a rap-tat-tat on the door: they were in a rush. I opened the door.

'Hello, Sam!'

'Oh, Hi!' I thought it would be Lucy.

'I'm Lucy's dad, do you remember me from Brighton? Hey, this is a nice house you have.' He had a big smile and kind of tapped me on the shoulder. 'Are you all ready to go? It's good to get there on time, don't you think? I'd best say hello to your parents and tell them we're off.'

'Er, yeah. Okay. Mum!'

Mum was coming from the kitchen. 'Hi, I'm Janice.'

'Tom, nice to meet you!'

'Nice to meet you!' He shook her hand too.

'I haven't forgotten about that cuppa, shall we

catch up after the film?'

'Great!'

'Great. Okeydokey, Sam, you got everything? Let's go.'

Lucy was in the car waiting for me. 'Okay, Sam, grab a seat in the back next to Lucy.' He opened my door and then went around to the front.

Lucy was smiling and said, 'Hi'.

'So, Lucy says that you're quite the film enthusiast, did she tell you I love films too?' Lucy's dad started the car.

'No, Mr Meddows.'

'Hey, call me Tom. You'll make me feel old.' He chuckled.

'No, Tom.' I could see Lucy's dad in the mirror.

'Yeah, I've got my favourites.' Lucy's dad was chatty like Lucy. But Lucy was quiet today. ' I haven't seen parts one, two and three of today's film, how about you?'

'Yeah, they were great.'

'Go on then, tell us your favourite film?'

I like this type of question. Lucy knew that and smiled at me. '*Avatar*, I think, either that or *Shrek*.'

'*Avatar*! Great film, Sam, but isn't that a bit old for you, it's a certificate 12, right?'

'Yup, 12. That makes it a learning certificate of one.' I explained.

'A whaty?' I saw Lucy's dad watching me in the mirror.

'A learning certificate of one: the film's official rating less my age is one. That's a medium learning certificate and is acceptable.

'Wow, that's an interesting approach. Is that your own system?'

'No it's Steve's, Oliver's dad.' I watched to see Lucy's dad's response.

'Oh right! Yes, Steve. I enjoyed seeing him at cosplay very much. He seemed very popular and gave such a great speech. So what is an unacceptable learning certificate?'

'Anything that's a four or seven…'

'Age fifteen and eighteen right?' Lucy's dad raised his eyebrows.

'Yeah! Steve said we should be very careful about watching them as they could make us upset. He advised never watching them unless we were with an adult that could explain what was going on.'

'Well that is sensible advice. Good for Steve!'

I decided I liked Lucy's dad.

Lucy's dad continued, 'So, I'm sorry to hear about Oliver leaving the school.'

'Yeah, it's not fair! I'd like to find Oliver. It's weird we didn't even get to say goodbye. I want to speak to him and make sure he's okay.'

'Good for you, Sam! I like that in a person. Loyalty! I can see you've been brought up to have a questioning mind. What do your parents do?'

Lucy smiled at me again. I'd never seen her so quiet.

'My mum works for the local authority and my dad's a website designer!'

'Ah well there you go then, educated and creative,

you'll go far, Sam. Sounds like your parents want you to question and analyse.'

We turned into the car park and after we got out it was though someone had turned Lucy on and she started chatting away.

*

After the film, Tom and Lucy came back home. Mum made Tom a cup of tea, and Lucy and I went to my room.

'Show me your laptop,' Lucy said, as soon as we were through the door.

'It's just here – the broadband is working great, but no luck on the Hotmail account.'

'Perhaps I wrote the password down wrong?'

We waited, watching the black screen fire up, our legs under my makeshift table at the end of my bed.

'Hey, Sam.' Lucy looked across at me. 'You know if we get teased at school about being friends?'

'Yeah.'

'Just ignore them, okay?'

'Yup, I will. You too!'

'Yup.'

We looked at each other and giggled. It was good to have got that out the way.

In a few minutes, Lucy had signed into the Hotmail account and shown me how to use it. The screen was a bit different to the one at school. She'd sent me an e-mail from her account. It said: 'Testing one, two, three – can you read this? Love, Lucy.' Lucy told me to try sending one to her. So I pressed reply and typed: 'Yes I can – did you think I couldn't read?' Lucy giggled. Then I added 'Love, Sam'.

'Go on then, press send.' Then Lucy signed into her Hotmail account and showed me she'd received it.

'Wow, that's epic. Just think, we could have been doing that for years.'

'Yeah, I've just started.'

'Who else do you send e-mails to?'

'My Uncle Bret, Aunt Sue and then just Gina and Peter in my class.'

'Wow, that's really cool.' I thought of all the messages I could send.

'So then?'

'So then what?'

Lucy looked at me again sideways. 'Oliver!'

'Yeah, brilliant.' I twigged. 'Have you got his Hotmail account then?'

'He's on something different, not Hotmail. Open up a new e-mail.' She took hold of the mouse and showed me. 'Now type in: "Oliver b 247 at talktalk.com".'

My hands hovered over the keyboard. 'What are we going to say?' But before she could answer my fingers took over.

Hi Lolly Olly, Watcha doin? I've been trying to get hold of you for ages. I went to see your dad in Southsea. ON MY OWN! That gave your dad a shock, including my parents. I got a bit of a telling off by a couple of social workers, but everyone wants me to accept that

173

you've moved away. I hope you still want to be friends. Please reply as soon as possible. Sam.

'Love, Sam'

'Love, Sam?'

'Yes!'

'What, to a boy?'

'Yeah, it's what people put in letters.'

'Yeah, yeah I knew that,' I said. I was thinking of Lucy signing 'love' in her message. I guess I was a little disappointed. 'Don't they do best wishes or kind regards too?'

'Yes, but Oliver's a big friend of yours. Otherwise you wouldn't have gone to all this trouble.'

'Yeah it's been a bit of struggle. Why has everyone made it so difficult?'

'Well, let's hope it works.'

'Sam! Lucy!' It was Mum calling from downstairs.

I let Lucy pull her legs out from under the desk first, then she put her hand on my shoulder to get out. 'Your bedroom's really tidy!'

'Oh, thanks.'

As we came downstairs, Mum and Tom were talking. They were still in the kitchen next to the kettle, leaning against the work counters holding their mugs. Tom was quite a bit taller than Mum – she was looking up at him.

'It's a real shame, I didn't realise they were such good friends,' Tom said.

'I just feel so sorry for him, for Steve. How life can change so quickly, losing a wife and then right after his son.'

'It doesn't sound right does it?'

'Oh, hi you two. Would you like a drink? Do you drink tea, Lucy?'

'No thank you, Mrs Steepleton, do you have any orange squash?'

'I think so. You too, Sam?'

'Yes please, Mum.'

'So, Sam, tell me more about Steve's movie choices. It sounds like he was quite the enthusiast.'

'Yeah, Steve had a list of films. He has a top one hundred, although there are only seventy-three on there. He's still working on it.'

'He *is* an enthusiast!'

'Yeah, and he puts them into categories too! You know, so you can work out what kind of film would be good to watch, especially when it comes to the learning bit.'

Tom and Mum looked at each other.

'It's an interesting idea of learning through film. With the readership of the Bible waning, what other didactic volume replaces its moral framework in our lives? The vacuum is being filled by competing media sources, be that film, television or the modern novel. Consider—'

'Dad! We're eleven!' Lucy said.

'Yes,' Mum said. 'What did you say?' She giggled, so we all had a laugh.

There was a key in the front door, it opened and Dad stepped in. 'Oh hello!' Dad looked at us each in turn.

Mum and Tom stood up straight. Mum made all the introductions as Dad hadn't met Lucy or Tom. Dad went over to the sofa but then he changed his mind and stood next to me.

'Good film, Sam?'

'Yes thanks, it was the fourth one!'

'Disney thing?'

'Yeah.'

'So you're Lucy, Sam's told me about you.'

I looked at Lucy, I think she was wondering what I'd said.

'Yes, Mr Steepleton.'

'Well I better get ready, nice to have met you.' Dad went upstairs. What was he getting ready for?

Tom and Lucy didn't stay long after that. I was kind of sad that Lucy was going, we were all having fun. Tom gave me a pat on the back but as he said goodbye to Mum, he gave her a kiss on the cheek. I don't think Mum expected that.

When they'd gone, I asked Mum if she found out what Tom's job was? 'What was "event management"?'

Mum sucked in her breath. 'It's the application of project-management techniques to orchestrate a successful event such as a festival, concert, party, convention or political rally.'

'Wow!' That did sound awesome. Lucy's dad seemed pretty cool.

Sunday 1st December

I'd checked my Hotmail account last night, and I checked it this morning. No reply from Oliver. It was raining and everybody else was asleep, so I decided to watch a quick film before everyone woke up. I still wanted to know a whole load of stuff about life, so I decided again to go for a really big learning certificate. I knew the dangers, but it was the morning, I had the rest of the day to sort it out if it went wrong. I chose *The Sixth Sense*, number six on Steve's list. I watched it all the way through without stopping; it was pretty gripping and frightening. I wanted the boy to be safe and it seemed that he couldn't be, because he saw ghosts all the time. What I didn't understand is why the guy took so long to realise he'd died. Why did the mum poison her daughter's food? Why didn't people believe the boy when he told them his problem? So it was scary, but left me with loads of questions. And just left me thinking adults are… well… strange.

Mum made us all a proper breakfast. Bacon, egg and sausages; it was licky-licious.

'What have you got on today then?' Mum asked everyone. No one said anything. It looked like no one had made any plans, which was unusual. Normally Mum and Dad negotiate to see which of their ideas they should do.

'I thought about watching a film,' Dad said.

Mum frowned.

'I'll watch something with you, Dad!' I said.

We set up camp in the lounge. Dad and I still had our sleeping things on. We shut the curtains and turned up the sound. I asked Dad if we could have popcorn, but he pointed out we'd just had breakfast. Fair point.

'Okay, Sam, what do you fancy watching?'

'How about we download something?'

'Yup, call it up then, let's go through the list.' I knew Dad didn't like the Disney stuff, so it was a question of finding something we'd both enjoy. Sometimes it was difficult. The last time I think Dad just gave up and just let me have my choice.

'Dad, there's a boy at school who's seen *The Shining*.'

'Really, that's a bit old for him isn't it?'

'I guess so. He said it didn't really make sense. He said he couldn't see why everyone raved about the film.'

'It's a great film, but a lot of horror, a little gratuitous arguably, but a great story line.'

'Why's it so good then?'

'Well ostensibly ...'

'Ostensibly?'

'Sorry, I mean it comes across as a ghost or possession film. And you can see it like that without going deeper. But for me, it's more to do with how we can be close to someone yet not know what's going on in their heads.'

'What they're thinking?'

'Yeah. The caretaker guy goes a little crazy. So you're supposed to think it's the ancient Indian curse, but actually he was pretty mad before he got there. He'd hurt his son and was a recovering alcoholic. Anyway, the point is that the wife didn't have a clue that he wasn't writing his book, that he was just writing a load of lines. So even though she lived with him so closely, she didn't know he was struggling. You have to ask yourself why didn't she discuss the book with him, or have a little peek. The signs were there long before they got to the hotel. His personal control was breaking down well before he got to there. It could have just have been cabin fever, not ghosts at all.'

'Cabin fever?'

'Being cooped up all together for so long. Humans are social creatures: we need a social life to keep us healthy. So really it's a comment on the diminished personal responsibility that comes from poor mental health.'

I nodded enthusiastically. Dad really seemed to know his stuff, although I didn't really understand what he was saying. Did a head cold count as poor mental health? And just think: I thought the film was about a guy getting possessed by evil spirits.

'Wow, there's a lot to it then. My friend didn't say any of that stuff.'

'Films are very personal, and what you see now isn't what you'll see when you get older. Do you remember when you first watched *Ice Age*? You probably don't, you were three or four. You screamed when the elephant squashed the squirrel. Now you just laugh.'

I carried on flicking through the list. 'How about *Escape to Witch Mountain*?' Dad made a face. 'Well how about *The Deer Hunter*?'

'That's not on there, is it?'

'No I mean, what was all that about?'

Dad looked at me. 'Your friend saw *The Deer Hunter*?'

I nodded.

'Really! Surely that's an 18.'

I didn't say anything: perhaps I shouldn't have mentioned that one.

'I don't think he should have been watching that, it's pretty horrific!'

'Why?'

Dad just frowned at me.

'My friend just said the film was a bit odd. He said he didn't really get what was going on. It just seemed like a lot of people drinking too much, then they go to war, then they come back and do more drinking.'

Dad laughed.

I carried on going through the list. '*The Lady and the Tramp*?'

Dad raised an eyebrow.

'So then, Dad, why bother making a film like that?'

'*The Deer Hunter* is essentially about man's inhumanity to man. The film was controversial because they played Russian roulette and that hadn't been done before on TV, not like that anyway. Do you know what I mean by that?'

I nodded, not sure if I was supposed to know or not.

'They caged these men and forced them to play Russian roulette. It made you question how cruel men can be to one other. It's as though man...'

'Any man?' I asked.

'Man as in mankind can just switch off when they feel they are very different to someone else. When we feel no connection to them culturally or politically, we feel we can treat them like animals, worse than animals. Do you see what I mean?'

I nodded.

'That's the significance,' Dad continued, 'of him letting the deer go at the end of the film.'

I nodded again, but I didn't really get it. But I knew Dad was trying. 'Yeah, he said that was strange.'

Dad hesitated as he stared at me. 'So at the beginning of the film he shot the deer and then when he realised what taking a life meant, he couldn't bring himself to do it at the end of the film. Then there was the whole thing about showing ordinary people. They were a town of steel workers, ordinary folk. How weird it must have been for them to have gone to Vietnam and experienced the people, language and food.'

'Where is Vietnam?'

'Near Thailand... under China?'

'Oh right!'

'When the film came out, it was only three years after the war ended. Should America have sent troops, their own people? Was it their fight? What were they doing there? Not only were they asked to fight so barbarically, but to fight against a country they knew nothing about. They had no beef—'

'Beef?'

'No argument with the Vietnamese. They were made to fight someone else's battle.'

Wow, Dad was an expert on this one. It was like hearing Steve speak. I never knew Dad thought like that. I was pretty gobsmacked.

'Thanks, Dad. I'll let him know tomorrow.' I carried on going down the list. 'How did you learn all that stuff?'

'Old age, son.' Dad was smiling to himself. 'You'll get there. Do me a favour though, son?'

'What's that?'

'Don't rush to get there, enjoy it! Enjoy the simple stuff.'

'Dad? He said that it was funny when they got back to their home town from the war, they didn't want to see anyone?' I knew I was really stretching this one, would Dad guess?

'People can't face their former lives after they have experienced so much pain, seen so much destruction, experienced death so savagely, as you do in a war. When soldiers return home they can't reconcile one part of their lives with the other and it's easier to not go back and make that reconciliation.'

I nodded, but this time Dad really did lose me.

'Stop, there you go!' Dad said. '*The Daleks*, 1964, it's got William Hartnell in it, the best of the doctors.' Dad reached for the remote.

'Okay, Dad.' It looked pretty ancient, but I'd seen old stuff before and some of it was pretty good – rubbish effects, but good entertainment. The film was quite exciting even though you could see it was shot in a film studio. The Daleks weren't like the new ones. Halfway through the film, Mum came in with a cup of tea and I had squash.

'I heard you talking about films earlier on. Did you understand what Dad was saying?'

'Yeah, Mum, I didn't realise Dad knew all this useful stuff.'

Mum coughed. Dad slapped her on the bottom and she smiled.

We saw the film all the way through in one sitting. It had a great ending. I kind of forgot it was so old by the end of the film.

'Did you enjoy that?' Dad asked, as he opened the curtains.

'Yeah, it was all right!' The sun stung my eyes. 'Dad, my friend saw *The Sixth Sense*! He said that was a weird film too.'

'Weird or he didn't understand it?'

'Yeah, I guess that.'

Dad looked at me. His lips were vertical on one side and horizontal on the other. 'Hmm, looks like your friend's interest in films is somewhat fanatical. Where does he get all the time?'

'Well he's not into computer games, he doesn't watch football.' I answered.

'So what is it he doesn't understand?' Dad said, turning down the volume on the TV.

'Well, is there a hidden message? Like you were saying with the other two, is it just a ghost film?'

'Yeah well, like most films you can see it like that, you can take it at its raw, simple story level.'

'Like he doesn't realise he's died?' I asked.

'Yeah! You could simple enjoy the film at that level.'

'But there's more isn't there, Dad?'

Dad looked at me and drew in his breath, and then made a clicking sound with his lips. As though the cogs in his brain where whirring and calculating. 'You're very young for this stuff, Sam.'

'Go on Dad, he was completely lost, it would be great if I could tell him.'

'Well, you have to ask yourself what a ghost is.'

'Creepy, scary things?'

'What, white and floating?' Dad laughed. 'The film makes the point that ghosts are people with unfinished business. Things have happened in their lives they can't move on from until they make amends. Or, sometimes all they need is to understand what happened to them. When they find out, they can let go. Let go of their pain, their suffering and that's when they can move on.'

'To heaven?'

'Well, wherever they're going.' Dad laughed again.

'Okay, but why doesn't the doctor realise that he's dead?'

'Because he's in denial.'

'Denial?'

'Yeah, it's a difficult concept, but really it's saying

he doesn't want to see what's there. It's too painful, or it's not what he wants, so he sees something different. He's focused on a different truth so he can't see reality.'

'What?'

Dad laughed again. 'I'm sorry but I did tell you it was too old for you!'

Mum had come to the door with another drink for us. 'For example, if someone that had lost their job and signed up to buy a new car, they could be said to be in denial.'

'Yes, thank you!' Dad said, in a singing way.

'Have you finished now? We should be thinking about lunch.'

'Yes, we're just film analysing, won't be long.'

Yes we were film analysing, I loved it! I just didn't know Dad did that. 'So, Dad, what was the thing where the mother poisons the daughter, what was all that about? She looked like a pretty normal woman. Not evil or anything.'

'Yes, Kevin, what is all that about?' Mum frowned.

'It's the Munchausen's syndrome. Some people get a weird pleasure—'

Kevin! I don't think I want Sam to know about the Munchausen's syndrome!'

Dad went quiet. 'Okay, Sam, let's crack on with the day, come on, it's twelve-fifteen and we're still not dressed!'

'Thanks for this morning, Dad. That was brilliant! The film wasn't too bad either.'

'Yeah well, there are some better films. I can't wait

to watch them with you when you're old enough. But you know you should tell your friend he shouldn't be watching these grown-up films. There is plenty of time to grow up. A lot of what I told you, you only needed to know because you've… your friend has seen something they needed an explanation for. He doesn't need to find out all this stuff now. He should wait till he's older. There's enough stuff to watch that's still entertaining and interesting and isn't frightening. I know I joke about seeing Disney films, but actually it's not bad stuff. Try to get a balance too. Some people all they want to do is watch zombie films!'

'Okay, Dad.'

As we were leaving the room, Dad put his hand out for me to go first.

'Dad?'

'Yes, son?'

'Can we do that again? I really enjoyed watching the film with you, talking as well.'

'Yes, that would be nice, let's aim for next weekend shall we?'

Who'd have thought it? Dad was like Steve. They both knew their stuff when it came to films. Films and fathers!

Monday 2nd December

As we arrived at school, Lucy did too.

'Hey Kirsty, this is Lucy!'

But Kirsty didn't stop. 'Hi Lucy, I hope my little brother isn't boring you.'

Lucy didn't get a chance to say anything to Kirsty.

'She's seventeen minutes older than me!' I told Lucy.

'You don't get on with your sister then?'

'We have a love–hate relationship. I'm still waiting for the love bit.' I shrugged my shoulders.

'Well, what does she like?'

'What do you mean?' Where was Lucy going with this.

'What sort of things make her happy?'

I thought… 'Chocolate! Shopping! Short skirts, ice cream, make-up, talking on the phone, texting…'

'Your sister's got a phone?'

'Yeah, she got it for her birthday, my dad's old one. Mum says I can have hers for Christmas.'

'Cool! I'm getting one next week.'

'What would I do with a phone?'

'Call me!' Lucy said, her hands on her hips.

'Oh yeah!' We giggled.

'Why don't you buy her some chocolate?'

'Why?' That seemed a bit random.

'You know, offer the olive branch. Hey, that reminds me. Have you heard from Oliver yet?'

'There was nothing this morning.'

'Perhaps the address is wrong?'

*

As soon as I got home, I rushed upstairs to see if Oliver had replied. The laptop fired up, the screen came to life, but no, nothing new.

Tuesday 3rd December

At first break today, I found Lucy reading her book on the bench outside her classroom and sat down. She told me all about a dream she'd had last night. We were walking along a river – the one we saw in that film on Saturday.

'You said you'd save me if the bear came along. We made a raft and went way down river. We found a cabin on an island and couldn't get back until the next day.'

'What did our parents say?'

Lucy looked at me. 'It's a dream.'

'Oh yeah!'

'Well what did we eat?'

'Nothing, Sam, stuff isn't real in dreams.' She raised her eyebrows at me.

We both laughed together, but I wanted to know all about the detail. I couldn't help feeling I'd missed out on a really great day.

Mrs Stubbs started a new project – we had to draw out our family tree. If we didn't know all the details, we had to make them up. We learnt lots of useful facts like what were second cousins, and uncles twice removed. Also the difference between step-brothers and half-brothers. Then some weird facts like you can have an aunt that is younger than you are. People used

189

to do family trees in the front of Bibles but now we do them on spreadsheets.

James drew out his family tree, and we worked out that his grandfather was only thirty-four years older than he was. Mrs Stubbs asked if he'd got his dates right, and Daniel said he was pretty sure because his granddad had his forty-third birthday last year. Then Daniel said his dad had had so many brothers he didn't know all his uncles' names, and because they'd moved away ten years ago, they only saw one of them.

Charlotte asked if godparents counted, as she was closer to them than her aunts and uncles. Mrs Stubbs explained that she wasn't necessarily related to her godparents, although she could be, for example, if her uncle had been her godparent. I don't think Charlotte really understood. After all, why were they called parents?

Sophie said she was half Italian because her mum was born in Italy and her father's father was born in Rome. Mrs Stubbs explained that she was three-quarters Italian, which got Sophie really excited. So Mrs Stubbs did these additions of fractions on the board and proved it. It was interesting to know that maths could be useful. Sophie said she had always felt more Italian than just a half, which was probably why she liked pasta so much.

Mrs Stubbs told us about her father, who had traced her family back to Charles the Second, and Charlotte asked if that meant we should call her Princess Stubbs. And from there we got on to the fact that all the royal family were foreign, and in a different world we might have all been speaking German now.

We had to draw out the family tree of someone we knew and I drew out Oliver's. But I got stuck because I couldn't work out how to connect Oliver to Steve. It turned out that quite a few people were struggling too, as about five of us had half-brothers and didn't know how to draw that. It turned out you had to add an extra tree. Some people's pages started to look more like orchards.

Charlotte asked Mrs Stubbs to go through the difference between a half-brother and a step-brother again. Mrs Stubbs tried, but after a few minutes said that she'd show it on a tree later.

Mrs Stubbs told me I didn't know enough about Oliver's family and asked me to start again with my own. I realised that I didn't know my dad's birthday, but I knew my mum's. Then when I put down Kirsty's details, I had to ask if there was a special symbol for twins. There was, and there's even a different one for identical rather than non-identical twins. I asked if Aunt Dora should go on, as she wasn't related, but was called Aunt. Mrs Stubbs just looked at me and made her eyes go big. Daniel worked out that his sister's birthday was next week and he'd forgotten.

Mrs Stubbs said it was good to have an appreciation of family trees since that would help us learn about the kings and queens of history. Daniel said that he didn't need to know because he was an anti-royalist, and would be voting as a republican to get rid of the royal family. Mrs Stubbs looked at him, crossed her arms, and recommended that he suspend his interest in getting rid of the royal family and focus on antidisestablishmentarianism, as it would help with his studies. Also, she said it was handy to know, as it was one of the longest words in our language.

Then Mrs Stubbs explained all about the succession rules and how the next king, the heir to the throne had always been the oldest son, even if there was an older daughter, but it's changed and now it's just who is born first.

She told us about Henry the Eighth who had had six wives, and how three of his kids became rulers. There was Edward and Mary who each ruled for about five years. But it was Elizabeth the First who was really awesome as she had power for nearly half a century, but she never married or had kids. She was too worried about getting married as she'd probably have had to give up her rule to her husband. Henry the Eighth also had all these other kids with his wives but they all died when they were young, like they didn't even make it to their first birthday. Then he also had all these other kids with other ladies who he didn't marry. So in all he had about fifteen kids. Mrs Stubbs said he was a very bad boy.

Taylor said he had an uncle like that but he didn't have any palaces, just a council house, but the best thing was he had a loads of cousins and so Christmas was always great fun.

I wonder if Oliver's biological dad wanted an heir, and that's why he really wanted him back?

Wednesday 4th December

We got to school early and I was talking to Mat when Lucy came up to us with her team behind her. The girls had their hands on their hips and were kind of posing. 'We'd like a rematch at lunchtime. And this time we are Arsenal.' They turned on their heel and walked off.

Mat looked at me. 'This is serious. We need a team talk.'

When Lucy's team turned up, it was more serious than I thought. They had a uniform! They all had pink t-shirts. Then when they started, they were marking out our strikers and when we defended, they were passing at least three times before they went for the goal. When they scored, they high-fived and then, when it got to 2–0, they chanted:

> *Arsenal till I die,*
> *I'm Arsenal till I die*
> *I know I am,*
> *I'm sure I am,*
> *I'm Arsenal till I die...*

They were organised, they had a chant and they had a strategy. They weren't playing for fun, but they were having a lot more fun than we were. We were all getting annoyed, because we weren't able to play the game how we wanted to.

Mat stopped and called a team meeting. 'Okay, don't get angry, get good. Sam, I need you in goal, I need you to pass to the middle not the sides. I'll mark Melissa. Tim, you can take Lily, keep on her left. Taylor on Lucy. Brandon, take Lisa, and Sophie too if she comes out of goal. Daniel, you're going to have to be quick around Adele. Remember to break when we take possession. Pressure on, play for position not the goal.'

Brandon had a tough job since they'd put Sophie in goal. She was the tallest in the class, almost a full ruler bigger than me.

We scored in the very next minute. 'Mat,' I shouted. 'What's our chant?'

> *Jingle Bells,*
> *Jingle Bells,*
> *Jingle all the way,*
> *Oh what fun it is to see,*
> *United win away...*

But seconds after, they'd scored, so that made it 3–1. Melissa did a victory run by putting her pink t-shirt over her head and running around. It was her second goal. I was going off Melissa.

Mat was losing it. 'Tim, come off Lily and mark Melissa with me.'

This worked well: we kept Melissa in check and we kept the game on their end. I had less to worry about in my goal. When the bell went, we'd lost by a goal. Mat was cool, I thought he'd be moody. But he went up to Melissa when Arsenal had finished their high fives and chanting and said, 'Well done, mate, much respect!' Melissa just said thanks and we all walked in.

Then Lucy came up to me as we were walking in. 'Anything from Oliver? An e-mail?'

'No, we'll have to think of something else.'

'Thinking caps on then.'

And as we went through the door, I pretended to put a cap on. Lucy smiled.

When we got home, Kirsty said something peculiar. 'We made biscuits at school. Would you like one?'

I guess my reaction wasn't very polite. I took one from the box as if she was passing me an unexploded bomb. But as she walked away, I remembered. 'Thanks, Kirsty, they look scrummy.'

'You're welcome,' she said.

'You're welcome?' Yeah, she said that. I quickly walked away. I wanted nothing to spoil the exchange we'd had.

Thursday 5th December

When we walked to school, I had an idea. It was a long stretch but it was worth a go. I suggested to Kirsty that we could go back home via the centre of town. She said she'd think about it.

At lunch, Lucy came running up. 'I had an amazing lesson, we covered the suffragettes. It was all about how the women got the vote like a hundred years ago. They did hunger strikes and they were put in prison for demonstrating. They went on marches, had banners and generally made a real nuisance of themselves.'

'Right, that sounds interesting!' I tried my hardest.

'Well, we could do that.' She looked at me. 'For Oliver?'

'Oh right. What, get arrested? What for?'

'Well, hopefully not get arrested, but protest. We could do a petition! Go around the whole of Chichester and get people to sign?'

'Yeah, but they don't know Oliver!'

We spent the break discussing it all. Lucy called it a campaign and said that we needed a name for it. She said that 'we needed definite objectives and an easily communicative message'. I know what she meant but I can't actually say communicative without tripping up. We decided that that it was easy deciding what the message should be. It was Oliver's right to choose which dad he should stay with. There wasn't much more to say. So we knew what to say, but how were we going to say it?

We thought about writing to the prime minister, but Lucy said that was boring. The suffragettes were loud – you couldn't ignore what they had to say. Perhaps we could call the news and say there had been a breach of the Geneva Convention for human rights? But Lucy and I weren't sure if that was the kind of thing the convention was for. As the bell went, I suggested Operation Oliver as a campaign name. Lucy had been thinking 'Finding Oliver', as in the film *Finding Nemo*. That wasn't bad either. Then we both thought that it wasn't much of a secret if it had 'Oliver' in the name.

After school, Kirsty met me as usual and we walked into town. I went into Smiths and bought Kirsty a Bounty bar – they're her favourite. When I got outside, I gave it to her. She asked me why I gave it to her. I'm not sure Lucy's plan worked. She seemed confused and almost unhappy, but she did say thank you. On the way back, I saw this busker. He had a saxophone, and was sitting on a speaker. He was really good. Kirsty wanted to watch him too, so we stayed for a few songs. Kirsty opened her Bounty bar and gave me one of the halves, and we munched as we watched. He had a load of coins in his case. Lots of people were watching. I wonder if Lucy would walk into town after school with me?

*

When we got home, I raced upstairs and looked for the umpteenth time to see whether Oliver had e-mailed me. Nothing from him but there was one from Lucy.

Steve's number: 02392 818 256
Worth a try?
Love, Lucy

When Dad went out for milk, I quietly went downstairs to the phone. It was time to reach out and join forces. I heard the ringing tone and my stomach tightened.

'Hi, Mr Bridle?'

'Yes?'

'It's Sam.' I waited.

'SamIam, how are you?'

'I'm good.'

'It's been such a long time since I saw you.' He paused. 'I miss our film nights!'

'So do I! I really miss not knowing what the films are all about.' Oops that sounded wrong. 'And spending time with you and Oliver.'

'Have you heard from Oliver?' he asked.

'No. Have you?'

'Well.....' There was a silence and then Steve continued. 'Did you know that Oliver ran away from school? Perhaps you don't know, but they sent him to a boarding school. He only sees his... Mr Chartwell about every other weekend. And sometimes he isn't there when he goes home! I can't see why he's been

198

taken away, if he didn't want to be with him. He hasn't made many friends there, at the school. It's all too academic for him, and he loved Chichester. Keep this under your hat Sam, but when he ran away he stayed with me for a couple of days. We went down to the caravan, as Portsmouth was sure to be the first place they'd search. I put him back on the train when I was sure he was a little happier.'

'So Oliver, he's all right is he?'

'Er not quite, he could be a lot happier. I know it's selfish, but part of me is glad he's not happy there. That sounds daft. I mean, I just want him back.' Then there was another silence.

'Steve, we're going to get him back. Sorry, I mean we're going to protest. Lucy and I were going to do a proper protest. We haven't got any exact plans yet, but we think it's wrong and we're going to do something about putting it right!'

'Well.' He paused. 'Please take care SamIam, I don't want you getting into trouble on my behalf. It's funny, though, a coincidence I mean. I've my own plans for a protest. You've heard of fathers dressing up as Batman and climbing public buildings?'

'Er, no!'

'It's a Fathers for Justice movement… campaign if you like. It's about a lot of different issues and it doesn't quite fit Oliver and my circumstances. But it's a good cause and I'm going to do my bit a week tomorrow. Thursday the twelfth. I'm going down to Westminster Bridge about midday when it's at its busiest. I thought I'd do something different to

Batman. Something for Angela. I'm going to wear my old Star Trek costume.' His voice trailed off. 'The twelfth is the anniversary of Angela passing.'

'And are you all right, Steve?' Perhaps I shouldn't have asked. 'It's so unfair. You should be with Oliver.'

'Thank you, Sam. That's lovely to hear someone say that. That means a lot to me.' It went quiet. 'What's the point, Sam?' He went quiet again.

'We're not going to give up, Steve. Just like that film, you know, *The Last of the Mohicans*. We'll keep on going, no matter what.'

'No matter what. Thank you, Sam. Bless you.'

I'd never heard him say that before. I gave Steve my e-mail address just before I heard the key in the front door. 'Bye, Steve, gotta go, my dad's home.'

*

I e-mailed Lucy:

Brilliant! I had a long conversation with Steve. He knows we're going to help him protest. I said that we didn't have plans, but we were thinking. He's protesting on the 12th December in London! And he's going to dress up and everything. I'll tell you about it tomorrow.

Love, Sam

I checked my inbox after supper and Lucy had

replied.

> *Cool! It must have been nice for you to catch up with Steve.*
> *Love, Lucy*

Friday 6th December

I heard Mum tell Kirsty that she was putting on too much weight. I wasn't supposed to hear the conversation. I felt guilty that I'd helped cause that with the Bounty bar, but I know she likes chocolate. She has to go on a diet. I thought about my dream and her being my big fat zombie.

*

Lucy came up to me at lunchtime, almost running. '*Ferris Bueller*! It's a film.'

'Oh, yeah. I think I've seen it on Steve's list.'

'My dad was talking to his friend on the phone and he was going on and on about how excellent it is. Apparently it's about some school kids.'

'Okay, why don't you come around and see it tomorrow.' I'd just asked Lucy out, that was pretty cool, not waiting for my mum to ask her mum.

'Yeah, brilliant! What, rather than Saturday cinema? I guess there won't be time for both?'

'Okay,' I smiled. 'So is my mum calling your mum, or is it the other way around?'

Lucy giggled.

'It's my mum's turn to call.' I continued. ' Hey, perhaps I should ask her to pick you up. That's only fair.'

'Why don't you come to mine?' Lucy said.

'Yeah, that would be cool, is there a place we can see the film then? I could just bring my laptop around. Oh and by the way, what about "Films and Fathers"?'

'Is that a film?'

'No, you know, for the campaign name?' I explained.

'For Oliver? Cool! Like it! Hey, I didn't tell you. My dad did some protesting like the suffragettes!'

'What, ran out in front of racehorses?'

'No, it was like half a century ago but they went to London to protest against some tax on poles.'

I nodded. 'My dad doesn't like taxes either.'

'He was at university at the time and apparently all the universities and colleges sent bus-loads of kids down to London to protest.'

'Did he get arrested?' I pictured her dad with hand cuffs, being led away.

'No, but other people did. And they won! The government changed their minds, they did what Dad said was a "U-turn". Which is bad! Bad for the government because it means they were wrong!'

Saturday 7th December

Mum had dropped me off at Lucy's and stayed for a cup of tea with Tina. We stood in the kitchen while they talked about the good old days again at the council. Tina asked if she knew about the Dr Flagstaff episode and they both got really excited and laughed. Then Mum asked Tina why she left and Tina went quiet but said it was because she lost a baby. Mum apologised for asking and they had another cup of tea. Tina said she was really happy in her new job and told Mum she worked in the newsroom and reeled off a long list of news presenters and people they'd interviewed. She was a junior broadcast journalist-come-planner. I didn't get where the 'come-planner' fitted in, so I asked and Tina said it was 'where they research and investigate in advance the topical news stories they want to cover'. It sounded awesome.

Lucy's house wasn't bigger than mine, but it was in the countryside. We drove into her driveway, which had gravel and a place for at least three cars to park. The garden was smart, like Aunt Dora's. It was quiet – there was hardly any traffic. And at the door we were met by their dog, Magic, who kept on licking my hand.

When Mum left, we'd decided to watch our film. We sat in Lucy's bedroom on her bed with the laptop on her desk. Her room was all pink. There were soft toys all around and dolls, and then there was a huge pink elephant that had a human mouth that seemed to grin at me. I think that Lucy always keeps her room tidy.

'So, do you like my room?'

'Yeah, I do.'

'Dad said he'd redecorate it for me. Make it more modern… grown-up.' She looked worried.

'No, I do like it!' I said, but she didn't look convinced. 'It's just a bit pink for me, but I can see how it works for you.'

She still looked a little worried. 'Okay, let's watch the film then. Apparently we've got to stop the film at twenty-eight minutes and restart at thirty-two minutes.'

'Right, why's that then?' That did seem random.

Lucy raised her eyebrows, 'Well that's the bit that makes it a 12.'

'There's a bit we're not supposed to see. Cool!'

It was a really fun film until suddenly the boyfriend and girlfriend start kissing, but it wasn't like any kissing I'd seen before. They were completely joined at the mouth, like a bird feeding her chicks in the nest. It made my stomach turn, and then I realised that Lucy was looking at it too, and then she was looking at me to see if I was watching. How embarrassing to watch that together!

'Yeuch, that's gross,' I said without thinking.

Lucy didn't say anything.

'That's disgusting!' I continued, trying to get a

reaction from Lucy. ' Why do they want to do that?'

Lucy just looked at me and gave me a funny smile. I'm sure she looked at my lips.

'This must be the bit we're not meant to see.' I turned it off.

'I've got a video of my mum kissing Dad like that from Christmas last year,' Lucy said.

'Really! I've never seen Dad kiss Mum, only like a peck on the cheek!'

'What, never?' Lucy frowned. 'I only took the video as a laugh. They didn't know I could see them. They don't make a habit of snogging in front of me!'

'Snogging?'

'Yeah, you know like the kissing in the film.' I wanted to change the subject now, but Lucy continued. 'Yeah, but they hug and stuff don't they?' I was quiet. 'They cuddle up on the sofa, yeah?'

I thought about it, no they didn't. 'So shall we leave the film then?'

'Don't worry, it's just that bit we're not supposed to see.'

And then, just when I thought we could change the subject, Lucy went on. 'You were shocked when my dad kissed your mum.'

I giggled. 'You noticed that!'

'Yeah, you were staring.'

Wow, she'd noticed that. 'Well, I guess it is kinda funny.'

'Yeah,' Lucy said. 'Dad kisses loads of women hello and goodbye, and Mum does too. When we go to France all the guys kiss each other on the cheek. It's just a friendly hello, it's not like the film.'

The film was really funny. Ferris and his sister together reminded me of Kirsty and me. Which I guess is because in the film they're twins too. Ferris and his friends get away with loads of stuff, driving cars into swimming pools, getting free meals. There was lots of what Steve would call 'knowledge' in the film. Messages about respecting yourself, and getting what you need and to always have fun.

As the credits rolled Lucy stood up. 'So shall we watch the funny outtakes, or shall I show you my favourite walk?'

'What you and me, on our own?'

'Yeah! My mum lets me go on my own. She likes me to take Magic too.'

'Yeah okay, that sounds cool.'

It seemed funny that Lucy should want to go for a walk, let alone have a favourite walk. She lived in Lavant, about three miles north of Chichester, which is at the bottom of the South Downs. After she had told her mother we were going off, we only had to walk out of her back door, open the back gate and we were walking along a bridle path. Imagine living in a house like that! The path was heading towards the top of the Trundle, which is a Roman fort. It sounds brilliant, and it *is* good, but the fort is only a big circular ditch that runs around the top of the hill. If I go for a walk, we'll mostly go there. Kirsty and I have a competition: who can get round the circle first. But just lately, we play a strategic game and only run the last bit. Kirsty pretends to be walking fast and tries to get a head start before the end. But today Lucy turned left off the path to the fort, and we followed the river.

Magic was running around us like crazy. He was a Lassie dog, a collie.

'He likes you,' Lucy said. 'I know because he licked your hand, he doesn't like just anybody. He's only a year old, he's still scared... And I know my mum likes your mum.'

'How do you know that?'

'Because she told your mum about losing the baby.'

I wanted to ask Lucy about the baby but it seemed a bit personal. When she said, 'losing', I guess she meant the baby died. That seemed really awful. 'So tell me more about your dad protesting. How does he do that?'

'Well, nowadays it's more my mum. She's against fracking.'

'Fracking? What's that?'

'You know, where they get gas from the ground by pumping water into the ground and causing the rock to split and give up shale gas.'

'That's good,' I said positively, ' so they get free energy?'

'No, it's not good.'

'Oh?' This seemed like a difficult subject.

'Yeah, there's a problem with water contamination and earth tremors. The issue is that they're not sure what the consequences are of doing it, but they go ahead anyway.'

'So what does your mum do on these fracking

demos?'

'Well, she's only done one so far. She went down to where they were about to start fracking and kind of got in the way.'

'Didn't they tell her to go?'

'Well, no, there were like hundreds of people demonstrating. They walked in the road so that the machinery couldn't get past. Then, they climbed on top and when they eventually got the machinery to where it should be, it was too dangerous to use with all the people around.'

'Why didn't they arrest them?' Lucy's mum seemed so nice, I couldn't imagine her being difficult with the police.

'Well, there are too many and the police don't want to make things worse, so as long as the demonstrations are peaceful they're allowed to do it.'

'Don't the fracking people complain?'

'Yeah, well, they're worried about making things worse, they know that eventually everyone's got to go home and then they can start up again. When she was young she used to go to marching in London to ban fox hunting,'

'Do they hunt foxes?' Wow, Lucy's world seemed so different to mine.

'They used to! And she sat outside some factory that was doing animal testing. She won't buy her make-up from the big stores, she'll make sure she knows how it's made and tested. Then she tells all her friends – well, asks them – to buy from the right shops too.'

'Wow, she believes in stuff.'

'Yeah, she says it's our choice, I mean we should choose… not just follow. Follow what everyone else is doing, because chances are they haven't chosen either, they're just following.'

'Like sheep?'

'Yeah.' Lucy grinned. 'Like sheep.'

'So does she still go on these demos now?'

'Dad asked her to do less. She fell off this big tanker thing and he had to pick her up from a police station. She was covered in bruises and mud, and her arm was in a sling. They treated them both like criminals.'

When we walked along the river, Lucy was telling me about the time she'd had made a raft with her dad and a load of friends and how they'd all ended up getting soaked. She said it was too cold now but in the spring, we could go paddling. When she sneezed, it was just like Mum does: a small one first and then a massive one.

Lucy took me to this place where the river runs through a wooded area. She sat down on the tree trunk and I sat next to her. It was her favourite spot. She said it's where she goes to dream. It was great being on our own and in the countryside. I guess Lucy does that all the time. There was something really free about it, not having our parents there. It was so peaceful hearing the river gurgle past us and watching the sunlight glitter on its surface. There was even a Mr and Mrs Mallard that tried their luck by coming up to us. But we had no bread for them.

I asked Lucy what she thought of the Ferris Bueller film. She said it was clever. The boy doesn't get caught because he's very confident. He does stuff that other people wouldn't try. He looks like someone that should be doing what they're doing. Not someone who shouldn't be doing what they're doing. So he doesn't look guilty or frightened so people don't challenge him and he gets away with it. Her dad told her that's how con artists work. Con artists are a kind of criminal. They work by conning you. They do confidence tricks, which they do by being confident. Lucy explained that the best ones were so good, the people they'd tricked never found out, or not till it was too late for them to do something about it, anyway.

When we got back, I packed up the laptop and Lucy saw the journal in my bag. She asked me about it and I explained all about the quest, what it had been and what it was now. She was impressed.

'Why is it so important to you?' Lucy asked.

'To be honest, it wasn't in the beginning. I thought one day he'd be back. But as time went on and I couldn't get to speak with him, it felt more and more strange. Oliver's there one day, gone the next. My dad said something about it the other day – he was talking about ghosts and how they can't move on until they understand. That's me. I need to know. I can't have that happening, where will it end? I want to live in a world where you know the people around you can't disappear!'

'Yeah I get that. That's the world I want to live in too.'

As we walked down to the car, Lucy stopped at the gate. 'That was a lovely day. Did you like my walk?'

'Yeah, I can see why it's your favourite. It was fun. I guess it's time to say goodbye.' So then I kissed her on the cheek.

She looked at me, puzzled, but then she smiled. 'That was nice, but if you do that at school I'll kill you.'

I looked at her and was about to apologise but she kissed me back on the cheek and giggled. So I laughed and then she laughed and then she kind of bumped into me with her shoulder as we walked to her door.

Contact

When I got home. I put a drawing in the *The Book of the Quest*: a diagram of the raft I would build with Lucy and Oliver in the summer. Then I got out The Fountain of Knowledge and looked up images of fracking demonstrations. They looked scary. Then my inbox pinged, it was an e-mail from Lucy.

> *I've had an awesome idea! You're going to like this, I'll tell you all about it on Monday. Sleep tight. L.*

I wanted to call her straight away. But then, as I was watching the screen another e-mail came in. It was from Oliver.

> *Sam, I got your e-mail, thank you. I'm sorry I didn't get in contact before. I'm at another school now and it's working out well. I think it's easier if I we don't keep in contact and I concentrate on my new life. I hope you are well and wish you all the best for your life. Goodbye. Oliver.*

Oliver didn't care about me. I sat there, devastated. I'd spent all this time worrying about him and he couldn't be bothered to keep in touch. I felt pretty stupid and something else – I felt lonely. I couldn't stop thinking about the times at his house where we'd had so much fun. They were never going to happen again.

I watched it get dark. I could hardly move. It was such an awful feeling and I couldn't see him to ask why he didn't want to keep in contact. I wanted to know what he'd been doing all this time. Mum would call me down for supper soon and I knew I should get ready. I couldn't move away from the window, watching the light fade, seeing less and less, the birdsong growing quieter.

Before supper, I sent the e-mail from Oliver to Lucy. She should know as soon as possible not to put any more effort into finding Oliver. I felt bad for wasting her time. Also, it was one less thing that Lucy and I had together. If Oliver didn't want to get in contact, then that was that. It really hurt, but if Oliver didn't want to be friends and could walk away so easily then it was for the best. That's what Dad would say anyway. Yeah right! Who was I kidding? As I sat there, I started to cry. I tried to stop, but it kept on coming.

Supper was difficult. I didn't want to talk about anything and Mum noticed and was trying to get me to chat. She kept on asking me questions and Kirsty kept on answering them for me, which was making Mum cross. I couldn't get back to my room fast enough. It was hard being around everyone when I wanted to be by myself.

When I got upstairs, I found an e-mail from Lucy. I was a bit worried about opening it. It would be talking about going backwards, ending our little adventure. I didn't feel like doing that. But eventually, after looking through the window some more, I closed the curtains and faced her message.

Sam. How do you know it's from Oliver?

I replied straight away.

It's from his e-mail address.

As I waited for her response, I understood what she meant. Wow, I hadn't thought about it like that. It was clever of Lucy. Was it Oliver's other dad that had replied? There was still hope.

Her reply appeared.

Yes, but we don't know if Oliver's using that e-mail address. Ask him something only he would know.

It was a good idea. What could I ask? What film did we watch together at your house the first time I came around? What's the picture on your wall in the TV room with your mum in it? The trouble is, if it was Oliver's other dad, wouldn't he wonder why I was asking those questions?

Another e-mail from Lucy.

Try this. 'Hi Oliver, I'm really sorry you don't want to keep in contact. Do you want your purple shoes back?'

What?! Where was Lucy going with this? Oliver never lent me any purple shoes. I don't think he ever had any purple shoes. It seemed like a crazy question.

My inbox pinged again, another from Lucy.

If he says 'no', or even if it's 'yes,' then you know it isn't him.

Wow, Lucy was smart!

I sent the e-mail to Oliver, but I changed it.

Hi Oliver, I'm really sorry you don't want to keep in contact. Do you want your Justin Bieber t-shirt back?

Oliver thinks Justin Bieber is lame. If he ever had a t-shirt with him on, he would have told me to burn it. I pressed 'send' and sat staring at the screen. My head was spinning, thinking of all the things that a reply would mean. I didn't have to wait long. 'Ping!' The reply was there.

'You keep it, mate, think of it as a goodbye gift.'

I stood up and nearly knocked the laptop over.

'YES, YES, YES! Lucy, you are amazing!' I got on the bed and jumped. I hadn't done that in a while. It makes a pretty good trampoline.

'Sam, are you all right, what's going on?' Mum was calling from downstairs.

'Sorry, Mum, yes everything's fine. Everything's perfect.'

I wanted Lucy to know straight away. I wanted to know our adventure was back on. My fingers could hardly do what they were supposed to I was so excited. I sent the e-mail to her and put:

You were right! It was from Bio Dad!

'What's perfect?' It was Mum again.

'You're perfect, Mum!'

'Sam?'

'Sorry I was a bit quiet at supper, I was worried about homework, but I've got it sussed now.'

'That's good, you should have said, I would have helped.'

'Thanks, Mum.'

Lucy's e-mail came back.

Cool! Bio Dad's a naughty boy playing games. Game on!

*

As I got into bed, I thought the day would end well, but then I heard Dad and Mum talking downstairs. It sounded serious, so I moved to the top of the stairs.

Dad was talking, 'Well it's only for one night before I sign up with the agencies. I can meet up with Richard from school too, he might have a few contacts with a job.'

'I don't think so!'

'Why not?'

'We can't afford it!'

'It's cheaper than coming home.'

'Not after you hit the town!'

They got louder and louder, and then suddenly there was a big silence. Then it went bad. Mum was screaming, but it was so loud I couldn't make out the words. It was a total freakout, and I took a few steps down the stairs – perhaps I could stop it. But then I heard something crash. I don't remember the rest. There was a threat and then she was talking under her breath but it sounded like a different person. Dad wasn't saying anything. Or at least I couldn't hear him anyway. Mum was really angry.

I crept back into my room and closed the door. What could I do? It wasn't Dad's fault he'd lost his job. But perhaps he could do more around the house and to find a job. Still, if he was prepared to go to London then that was pretty good. Perhaps Mum had been possessed like that film. I haven't seen it but I've heard about it. Where the devil takes control over the little girl and her head twists round and then looks like an evil witch. Mum certainly sounded like that. Poor Dad. It wasn't like him not to say anything.

Sunday 8th December

Mum and I were sitting having our toast, Dad and Kirsty were in bed. The phone rang and Mum picked up.

'Oh hi, Tina. Sam said he had a lovely day yesterday. Yes, Sam said they'd had a long walk. It's great they can just go out on their own in the countryside. Chichester's okay, Priory Park is safe.' Mum was trying to catch my eye – she wiggled her fingers at me. 'For about an hour? Yes I'm sure he'd love that.' I put my thumb up. 'Okay, then. No, I can drop him off. Yes, let's aim for ten. Bye.'

'Thanks, Mum!' I hadn't seen that coming.

*

Lucy came running up to me in the park.. 'Hi, Mr Bueller Or should I call you Ferris?' I tried to remember the girl's name from the film. 'We'll have our own day off... for Oliver.'

'How do you mean?'

'We'll take the day off from school and go to London and make a protest.'

'Great idea!' Was she joking?

'I knew you'd like it. We'll be doing something. You'll be doing your bit and who knows, perhaps it

219

might lead to something.'

'A visit from a social worker?'

'Or the police, I don't know, but it might lead to some good.' Lucy fixed on my eyes waiting for me to respond.

This seemed like quite a big deal. 'Alright, count me in! When were you thinking?'

'The twelfth. You know, Steve's date? It gives us some time to plan. Time to get some money together for getting there.'

'And getting back! Do you know how then, using the train and stuff?'

'We'll work something out, how difficult can it be?!'

*

We worked out a great plan. Lucy said that a good demonstration looked like a party, with balloons, fireworks and banners. We started with the banner. My job was to get something to write on. The difficulty was, I didn't know what I could use. I told Mum I needed an old sheet to make a camp with, and could I draw on it for camouflaging. First off she said, 'What, this time of year!', but in the end, I think she was glad I would be doing something outside, so she said 'Okay'.

All we needed now was money. I didn't really know how much, but when mum and dad do anything like that they get through a load. Their wallets come out all day long. In my piggy bank, which is actually shaped like a Doctor Who TARDIS, I had £4.75. Mum doesn't owe me £10 any more. I know Cameron would buy my Minecraft figures for about £15.

I e-mailed Lucy.

> *I think I can get about £19.75. We'll need a lot more. Any ideas? S.*

Just before I went to bed I checked my Hotmail. Lucy had answered.

> *No, sorry. We need some kind of fundraising event! L.*

My head was on the pillow but I couldn't sleep. Was Lucy serious? It seemed quite a mission! Okay, we wouldn't be saving the country like James Bond, but then James Bond had a whole organisation. They had government money, a structure. They had a whole team of people with specialist skills. There was the gadget man, 'Q'. The cunning boss, 'M'. They had 'intel', which is short for intelligence. That didn't mean they were intelligent, it meant they had databases and knew loads of facts. Theirs was a united team, guys with bravery who'd sacrifice their lives, who had meticulous plans and who would do crazy unexpected stuff. They even had a licence to kill. I knew we didn't need that. No, it was all about the team. That's what we needed. We needed to join our separate skills and knowledge into a supreme, organised campaigning machine.

Monday 9th December

I woke up tired today. I had been so busy in my dreams, I found it difficult to finish them. Mum kept on calling me to get up. I was playing the saxophone in the street and people were putting money in my pockets. I'd go up to someone and stand in front of them and play loudly. Some of them would run away, some would stand there in confusion, but mostly they'd smile and then give me money. Some put it on the hat I was wearing, which was bizarre. Some put it down my saxophone, more bizarre. I wanted lots of money and kept on going up to everyone. It was an exhausting dream.

At first break, I found Lucy in the playground. 'Any ideas?'

'No, you?'

'No, and I can't see myself getting any today, I didn't sleep. I had this mad dream where I was busking in North Street and frantically playing to get money.'

'Wait!'

'What?'

'That's a great idea!'

'What is?'

'Busking!'

'No, I can't play the saxophone, Lucy, it was just a

dream!'

'No, but you can sing.'

'I don't really fancy singing in public. I can't see people paying for that.'

'Sam, the three wise men, what you did in the lunch hall, you can do that!'

In a few minutes, we ironed out the plan. We just needed a little help from our friends. Lucy said she'd ask Arsenal, and I said I'd ask Liverpool and together we'd ask Felix, who was the only wise man that didn't play football. We'd be upfront and say we were raising money to stage a protest to find Oliver and fight for the cause.

By lunchtime, we had everyone together in the playground and Lucy looked at me to start.

'We've asked you to come here so we can talk about raising money to look for Oliver, and help protest to get him back with his dad.'

'Sam!' Brandon said, sneering. 'Not that old thing. Isn't about time you dropped that?'

'You've got us now,' Tim said. 'You don't need Oliver.'

'No! It's all changed. I know what's happened to Oliver now. He's been taken away by his real dad, his biological dad.'

'I thought that Steve guy was his dad, the guy that picked him up after school,' Adele said.

'No, Steve got together with Oliver's mum just after he was born. His real dad, Bio Dad, won't let Steve see Oliver, he got the authorities involved. Even I'm not even allowed to e-mail Oliver. I think he's really rich and it's as if he's legally kidnapped Oliver. He's never been part of Oliver's life before.'

'But why are we getting involved, isn't that what the authorities are for?' Adele said, flicking her long hair back.

'The thing is, haven't they decided that Oliver shouldn't be with Steve?' Melissa added. 'That's that, isn't it? It's not as though they're trying to hurt Oliver. They know what's best for him.'

'From what I heard, Oliver's dad is a bit of weirdo. He didn't have a job and he used to drink too much,' said Tim, opening his hands out for agreement.

'Right, so, what are you saying? We take all kids away from their dads if the dad loses their job and drinks beer?' I said.

'No, the thing is, Steve's not the dad, is he?' Sophie was emphatic. 'He just got married to someone who had a son. Oliver's got nothing to do with him. Oliver's dad should have his son back, it's like his son! You can't go around taking someone else's son because you'll miss him and you feel it's not fair. The real dad's got the rights!' She swept her hair back behind her shoulders.

'Yeah, but so has the stepdad, he was the one that brought Oliver up. Just because his wife dies doesn't mean he should lose his son too,' Mat said.

'Stepson,' Sophie corrected.

'Yeah, all right, stepson, but still someone he's loved and had family moments with... like Christmases, birthdays. He's made a family.' Mat was raising his voice.

'Well, I don't get on with my stepdad. But then I don't know if my real dad would have me back, he's got a whole new family now,' Adele confided.

'That must hurt?' Melissa said.

'It's okay, I go around and we'll all play together, you know with my half-brothers and sisters. I guess it doesn't happen that often. He's gone to Bristol now but he'll only come down a few times a year. Last summer I went there for quite a while.'

'Isn't the point that the kid should choose?' They looked at each other. 'Whatever makes them happy?' For a moment, there was silence.

'My mum would call that idealistic,' Tim said. 'You know, it's a great idea and everything but real life isn't fair. People go around taking what they want. The stronger you are, the more you get.'

'The richer you are the more you get,' Mat added. 'Yeah, I bet Bio Dad's got a pot of cash, those solicitors cost a load!'

Lisa said, 'Yeah, but what's it got to do with us? He's not in our school any more.'

'Wasn't his dad a drunk? Wasn't that why they took Oliver away?' Daniel said.

'Yeah, and we're just kids, what can we do?' Lisa said.

'Oliver's my friend, I know he wasn't yours, but what's happened to him isn't right! He's not with his real dad, the dad that loves him.'

'The dad that drinks!' Daniel poked.

'Well a lot of people do! He lost his wife, they were really in love, he still isn't over losing her and now he's lost his son.' I could see it so clearly, why weren't they listening? I began to feel like I did on Saturday night when I was sitting looking out at the dark garden.

'Yeah, but Sam, it's not his son!' Lily piped up. 'That's the important fact.' She pulled on her red hair.

That hurt, I don't why it did, I guess I thought they'd understand. It seemed that I'd been fighting this battle right from the start, right from when no one was even interested where Oliver had gone. I turned round ready to walk.

Lucy grabbed my arm. 'Sam! Don't! Tell them!'

I looked at their faces. Somehow the football team spirit seemed to have dissolved. I'd lost them. I gave it one more try. 'I don't think Oliver's okay, I don't know if he's safe and …' I paused looking at their faces. They weren't getting it. 'I guess you've never understood, but I can't let this drop, not till I know he's all right. People can't just disappear out of your life, it's not right.' Still all I got was blank faces. 'Don't worry, I can do this on my own.'

'Look, Sam,' Sophie said, 'What do you want us to do? Drive to his school and bring him back here? What difference can we make? We're kids.'

'Does it matter?' Lucy said. 'The point is, we can try. If everyone gave up because it was too difficult, what kind of world would we live in? This is it—'

'But—' Sophie tried to interrupt.

'This is our chance to make a difference. When will we be old enough to stand up for what's right? When will you be old enough to stand up for what you believe in? Oliver wasn't my friend, but he was a part of this school and he's just like you and me.' Lucy pointed her finger. 'That's the point, he's just like us. What would it be like if one of us disappeared? We'd want answers, wouldn't we? We can't live in a world where our friends are taken away from their parents. Where the teachers don't seem that bothered. Where we weren't even told! Where Sam was made to feel like a criminal, interrogated by some social services lady! Where you've got some rich guy who turns up and takes a kid away from his dad, just because he's changed his mind after eleven years and decides he does want to be part of Oliver's life. Without even asking Oliver what he thinks about it!'

Wow! Lucy was good. She looked angry, but she managed to say stuff I couldn't. There was a silence.

'Lucy and Sam are right,' Mat said. 'This is our fight, we can't ignore it.' No one spoke. 'Sophie, you're right too, we probably can't do much, but we should try. Just because Brighton knows Manchester will win, doesn't mean they give up.'

There were murmurs of agreement, people could see that. I wished I'd said that.

'Okay everyone, I'm in. So you want us to raise some money to get you to London?'

After that, it was easy. By the end of break, we had eleven yeses and with Lucy and I, surely that would be enough? Before the bell went, I had a few minutes with Lucy on our own.

'I'm really going to do it, Lucy. I'm going to London and I'm going to make a protest like your suffragette people. I know I can't make plans like you can, but if I can get to Portsmouth on my own, then this is possible too. I'm not going to fail Oliver. I'm going to get this thing done.'

Lucy was staring at me. 'Sam, you're not going on your own.'

'Yeah, don't worry. He's my friend, it's my problem.'

'No way, we are in this together!'

'But I don't want you getting into trouble.'

'Well, I don't want you getting into trouble!'

'But it's silly that we both have to.'

'We are more likely to succeed as a team. Anyway, I'm looking forward to our day out.' Lucy grinned. I guess I was looking forward to that too.

'Okay, then! Let's do it.'

It seemed like a high-five moment, but Lucy put her hand on my arm by the elbow and we walked back to the lunch hall.

'Lucy, you really think we can do this? It seems like a pretty big thing!'

'Mum and Dad say it's always difficult to make changes. There's always fear, that's why people let things stay the same. History is made by a few people, it's always been that way.'

'History?'

'Yeah, change. We need to be the history-makers. We're not scoring this goal by ourselves, we can use everyone. You know the team. We'll all do our little bit and it adds up to a big deal. It's what Dad says: "little acts together make big changes".'

'What am I going to do about Kirsty?' I thought out loud.

'Kirsty?'

'Yeah, I've got to walk with Kirsty to and back from school. It's because of my Southsea thing... trip.'

'Well you can't, you'll be walking to the train station.' We'd got to her classroom. 'Have a think.'

She pretended to put on the thinking cap and we both smiled at each other.

*

As I lay in bed that night, I remembered what Mat had said in the playground. People listen to him. He gets people to play a game, he takes charge. It could have gone either way today. If he'd disagreed then I think mine and Lucy's plan would have been over. It was pretty big of Mat to support us, especially since he was the one Oliver had punched that day and given a bloody nose. I don't know if Mat had forgotten that or it didn't matter to him any more. Perhaps when he found out why Oliver was so sore, when he heard Oliver's mum had died, that was all he needed to know. Whatever the reason, I'm glad Mat's on our side and he's our friend.

Tuesday 10th December

At first break, Mat found me as usual in the playground. He would usually be shouting and organising us into a game but he was quiet. He stood next to me for a moment with his hands in his pockets.

'Sam. I gave a lot of thought about what you were saying yesterday. I've talked it through with the Liverpool lot and we've all decided... we're coming with you. I know it's your gig and everything, so I'll let you do your thing, but we can chip in with all the help you need.' With that, he patted me on the back. 'Right you lot, let's get this game going. Sam, you're in goal.'

It was everything I wanted to hear.

*

I remember once that Mum and Dad discussed the number of people that pass by the Cross in Chichester on a Saturday. The Cross is a building made to help merchants shelter from the rain, about five hundred years ago. The thing is, it's pretty much the centre of town. It had what Dad would call 'footfall'. Every Saturday, something like thirty-five thousand people pass the Cross. None of us wanted to wait till Saturday. As soon as everyone had agreed to support

Oliver and busk, they wanted to do it straight away. But that's where we'd busk – there would be lots of people. More people, more money. Lucy said we'd need costumes and that a bit of organisation would be the difference between £2 or £20. Also, we needed parents to know that we'd be a little late home so they didn't panic, and we didn't get people asking questions. The plan was to tell them we were all practising for the Nativity, which was good because it was true, after all – one of those white lies.

In the end we lost a few people. Adele had a flute lesson she had to get home for. Melissa and Brandon take the bus home every day which if they missed, would mean they'd be two hours later getting back. I suggested to Kirsty that we go into town after school in the morning and she was up for another detour. She wanted to look at clothes with Rachel.

From the start, Lucy took the lead and stood in front of us doing a fairly good impression of Mrs Larkhill. Also she put down a big jam jar by her feet and a card next to it which said 'Collection for Oliver'.

It was a weird feeling to see everyone who you knew at school turn up in the city centre. We said to meet at the Assembly Rooms and even though I knew they were coming, it was still a surprise to see them there. It was a lot more exciting than in the classroom. I guess we all wanted to be there, and we had a purpose. Felix, Taylor and I wore our wigs. Massive afros that quivered like jelly when we turned our heads. We had our seventies shirts on too: mine was bright pink, Felix's was gold and Taylor had an enormous flower pattern that looked like he was wearing wallpaper. Behind us, the rival football teams had united in a multi-coloured festival that looked like they'd had some big accident at a paint factory.

Lucy counted us in and waving a coiled bit of paper as her conducting wand. It wasn't too bad. Felix was in his element – he was in the middle and kept Taylor and me together, and when the football lot came in we made a pretty big sound. By midway through there were at least thirty people in front of us. They were all smiling and a lot of them had their kids there too. A lot had our uniform on. Before the end, a man went up to speak to Lucy and then pointed down at her glass jar. Then in a few minutes he came back with a saxophone. He was the busker. We'd taken his spot. But he wasn't miffed, he was smiling.

At the end of the song, Lucy shouted, 'One more time, now give it some!' She'd make a good teacher. Then, something brilliant happened: the sax man played along. He was giving it some, copying our moves and playing the saxophone at the same time. I found it difficult to concentrate, I wanted to look at him. He'd joined our little line standing next to me. Then, when I faced away from the line towards him, he'd no one to copy but it didn't matter, he stood there, waved to the crowd and was holding something up high. It was a coin. He took the coin and made a big thing about putting it in the jar. He bent down to put it in, but before letting go he stood up again and waved the coin about and then put it in. Within a few seconds, a lady came up I'd never met and put money in our jar. It started loads of people off and people kept on coming up after that.

The sax man joined the line again and was playing a different tune, but it sounded good, like it should have been that way. I don't know how he did it. I'd never heard the song being played like that before and we didn't give him any music and he'd no time to practise. As we were nearing the end, he bent down to Lucy again and said something else. We came to the end, but he kept on playing and Lucy shouted. 'One last time! Liverpool, follow Mat on the conga.' Then she passed Mat the jar of coins. 'Arsenal, let's see your arms wave.' She showed them how, her arms going side to side.

It was epic. Within a minute, the crowd had grown to about five classrooms of people. Mat was weaving in amongst them collecting money and Lucy had put down her school bag next to the card and people put money on top of that too. The sax man smiled at me and shouted, 'You're a natural.'

At the end of the song, Lucy called out, 'Thank you everyone. It's all for Oliver.' People nodded, although they didn't know who he was.

At the end we all did high fives and enjoyed our moment of success. But in a few minutes we'd all gone our separate ways. Lucy waved at me and left, she had a huge smile. The sax man played the same music he did last week, and I watched him on my own.

'Alright, Sam?' Kirsty had appeared.

'Yeah, you? Did you get your shopping done?' She can't have seen anything.

'Yes thanks.' And most bizarrely, she showed me what she'd bought. She'd never done that before. Kirsty missed our finest hour, which was as it should be.

Later that night, Lucy e-mailed me. We'd collected £188.25. Wow! What a way to make money, and I wouldn't have to sell my Warhammer.

*

When I got home, I went on to the railway website. It was £32.60 for one ticket! How were we going to get all thirteen of us to London? I e-mailed Lucy.

> *I've looked online, it's £32 for just one of us. That will only get about six of us there! S.*

Her response was swift.

> *We need to talk to Daniel, he is the expert for this problem. L.*

She was right. We had to use the team. We'd use his knowledge of London transport.

Wednesday 11th December

As soon as I got to school, I saw Daniel and quizzed him.

'You need to get a Super Off-Peak Day Group Travel Saver. An adult ticket can take six children, so you need to do that twice to make it work.' That was the two six-a-side football teams, plus Felix. 'You should get the price reduced to about £80 for each block of adult and child tickets. You'll need to catch a train after 9.10 and leave London before 4.15 to make it work. That's the off-peak bit. You'll need to take the train that leaves on twenty past the hour not twenty-eight, otherwise you'll have to change at Clapham.

'The ticket can only be purchased on the day of travel and there are some special discounts thrown in right now for tourist attractions. You can book the tickets on southernrailway.co.uk and collect them from the ticket machines. That price doesn't include underground. You'll either have to pay by card at the machine or get an adult to buy the tickets.'

I looked at him. 'Who are you, and what have you done with Daniel?'

He giggled. 'My dad's a bit of train boffin, I guess it rubbed off.'

'That's brilliant! You've made our money go as far as we need it to and now there's money for food!' But, what about the problem they would only sell to an adult, how would we fix that?

At first break, Lucy and I had gathered the team together in the library. Lucy laid out the campaign of 'Films and Fathers'. Everyone loved having a campaign name. We were going tomorrow. It would be a tough mission and the first assignment had to be done before the end of lunch break. The plan was to orchestrate a mass food poisoning in the afternoon. Not around the whole school, just a couple of football teams. And we weren't going to use any poison, just a bit of imagination and drama. This would put us in the position of being known as sick and not expected at school the next day.

If we left it to about 2.15 to be ill, then the school wouldn't bother sending us home or calling our parents, they'd just tell us to put our head between our legs and drink water. It was always the same. Tomorrow morning one of us would deliver all our handcrafted sick notes to the school, in time for registration being taken.

So by 12.30, nine of us were in the library as the 'Sick Note Generator Team'. It was a creative hour. We used different fonts, paper, some with envelopes, some without, some just post cards. We started by all getting around the table to get ideas. People with the best ideas got a high five, those with 'not so good' ideas got a polite smile. Miss Gibb, who looked after the library area, was chuffed that it was so full and the facilities were being used. We got some paper from the art cupboard to mix it up a bit, not just white printer paper. Then Adele was voted to do a handwritten letter since she has proper grown-up writing. The signatures were fun. They're supposed to be unreadable and something that can't be copied, so we did wild ones. Lisa said that one was too unreadable, so we had to rip it up and re-print.

The next part of the plan was to be sick, which was where Lucy took over. She'd given it loads of thought. She only wanted eight of us to be sick and there must be at least someone from each class because that's how these things spread. She gave us individual sick plans and explained why each point was important. She asked if anyone had any carrots in their lunch boxes because apparently there are always carrots in sick.

In our class, it was Taylor who started it off. He had saved some of his sandwich from lunch and a few minutes before being sick had mashed it all up. But he did this thing that dogs do where they like nod their head, then he did all the noises and made sure that Mrs Stubbs was watching. He caught it all in his hand and before she had time to come over he ran to the toilet as though he would be sick again. A few minutes later, he came back in and looked awful. He had his shirt all untucked, his face was all red and sweaty and his shirt was all wet as though he'd tried to wash it.

'Oh Miss,' he said, 'I feel really awful.' Even I felt sorry for him.

'Do you want me to call your mum?'

'I think I'll be okay in a minute Miss, I just need to sit down.'

'Okay, darling,'—we all laughed at that—'take a seat by the window.'

Then, straight after that Melissa put her hand up. 'I need to... urch.' She put her hand to her mouth. 'Can I go to the... urgghh.'

I found it difficult not to laugh, she was brilliant.

Daniel and then I followed a bit later. I have to say I chickened out and just said I didn't feel too good. Mrs Stubbs looked worried and sent us all off to the sick room. When we got there, Lucy, Mat and Brandon were standing about and then ten minutes later, Adele turned up. Mat whispered he'd managed to do a smelly fart right by Mr Gambit and he didn't tell him off but kind of looked all sympathetic. Adele actually physically threw up for real. It took her a long time to do, but she said that she'd done it before and if other people throw up, even if they pretend, she finds it easier. We didn't get any medicine or anything. Mrs Ford was really worried when Mat started overdoing it. But Lucy gave him a stare. Mrs Ford wasn't allowed to give us any medicine, but she wanted to give us water and then she started to get bowls and dustbins.

So part one of the plan had been a success. They sent us home at normal time without parents being called. We were on a roll! It was up to us now to make 'Films and Fathers' happen.

Thursday 12th December

Slowly, I came around from my dream. Lucy and I were adventuring up the Amazon in a canoe. We'd got separated from the other canoes and we needed to find a place to camp as it was getting dark, but it was just endless jungle. Suddenly the reality of the day kicked in. This was it, this was our day. I sprang out of bed.

At eight, Mum was getting ready to leave, but she and Dad were arguing. It was something to do with money, but it might have been housework too.

At eight-twenty, just before we were due to leave, I launched my plan.

'Mum, I'm not feeling well.'

'What is it, Sam?'

'It's a stomach bug, it was going around the school yesterday.'

'Oh, did you want me to stay off from work with you?'

I hadn't seen that coming.

'I can look after him,' Dad said.

'Well, let's see how ill Sam is, shall we?'

'I think I can look after Sam, Janice!'

As they argued, I thought of Tim who was at this minute dropping a load of sick letters through the letterbox of the school. I needed to make this work.

'Can you take my temperature, Mum?'

'Mum!' Kirsty said. 'I gotta get going!'

'Alright, Kirsty, you get off then, give me a kiss.' She turned back to me. 'Right, so when did this start?'

'Well it all broke out at school yesterday after lunch. A load of people went down with it and there was like a queue out the sick room door!'

'These things come on so quick if it's food poisoning or bug thing.' She looked at me for a moment and frowned. 'So, do you have diarrhoea?'

I frowned. 'No, not really.'

'Sam, you can't miss a day off school because your dad's at home. It doesn't work like that.'

'Well if he's ill, then he's ill.' Dad said. 'He should be at home and I am around so that works out well.'

'No, it's just that I had a twinge, but perhaps you're right, Mum. Perhaps I was just worried it might be coming on. I'll try and get to school, I can always come home if I'm sick. I can tell them you're at home, Dad.'

'Very sensible, Sam. Okay then, right I'm late, I've got to rush.' Mum went to kiss me and then said, 'Air kiss, just in case.' She was out the door.

'Okay, Dad, I'm going to do my teeth and I'm off too.' I thought about asking him what he was doing today, but no, I had to be at the station in fifteen minutes!

*

As I got to the station I saw Melissa, Lily and Lisa talking with Brandon and Taylor. Mat was in the queue for the tickets. And then I remembered I hadn't told Lucy about the fact that only an adult could buy the tickets. Mat was next to be served.

'Hi, sorry I'm late, I only just got my excuses sorted. Lucy, I forgot to say, Daniel said that it had to be an adult who bought the tickets.'

We all looked at Mat, he was almost there. Lucy and Adele walked towards him, I was right behind. As we got there we heard the ticket man talking to Mat.

'Okay, so I guess you'll want the Off-Peak Group Saver?'

Mat nodded.

The man tapped on his keyboard. 'That'll be £158.60 please, but I'll need your parent or teacher here to get the group price.'

'Umm, well.'

Adele took over. 'Mr Sanderson told us to get the tickets, he's gone through onto the platform, Brandon had an accident and had to go to the loo.'

'Well I can't sell you these tickets.'

'But the train is nearly here.' Adele's voice was quivering.

I had a go. 'Mr Sanderson can't come because Brandon's wet himself and he's trying to get him dry before getting on the train.'

The ticket man looked doubtful.

Adele put her hand on the counter. 'Please, sir, we've got to get this train or we'll miss our slot on the London Eye.'

The ticket man pursed his lips. 'Okay, guys, just this once.' He winked. Without another word, he printed the tickets, took our money and gave us our change.

As we walked to the barrier, Mat asked, 'Who is Mr Sanderson and what is this slot we'll miss?' We all sniggered. I couldn't help thinking that Adele's long blonde hair and cheeky smile saved us.

Just then, we saw Felix, Tim and Daniel all talking outside. They hadn't realised we were inside. 'I'll get them,' Mat said.

When he brought them back, all the guys did high fives.

'Okay then,' Mat said. 'Are we all here?'

'We're just waiting for Sophie!' Lily confirmed.

At that moment, Sophie walked up. 'Here I am! Sorry I'm a little late.'

We hadn't noticed Sophie because she was in disguise. She wasn't wearing school uniform: she wore a smart dress, black tights, smart shoes, and she had one of those proper raincoats. Her hair was all on top of her head, like Mum does, and she had earrings and a necklace too. And she didn't have her school bag, she had an old lady's handbag. We all looked at her, half of us speechless.

'Sorry, you didn't say about coming in school uniform.'

'You look incredible!' Mat said.

'Thanks.'

'You could be… like my mother.'

'Ah, now you've spoilt it.' She giggled.

'That's amazing.' Felix was equally in awe.

'It's only make-up.'

'No, it's like you've morphed into some teacher,' Lucy said. 'Which is perfect, it could be very handy!'

'Hey, guys, let's get on the platform, we've only got five minutes,' Mat said.

As we walked through the turnstile, Lucy asked Sophie what her mum had said. Sophie had told her it was a Dress Down Friday. Which, to be fair, we had done last term as part of a charity thing. We'd all given, or our parents had, a pound for us to go to school in casual stuff.

Once on the train, everyone was a little quiet; it wasn't like when I travelled home with Oliver on the train. I think we were all thinking where we should be. Right now, I thought, Mrs Stubbs will be taking the register and working out we aren't there. What would they make of our sick notes? 'Hey, Tim, did you deliver the notes?'

Tim looked up at me, the movement flicking his wiry mop out of his eyes. He looked as though he'd been caught picking his nose. Then slowly we saw the faint look of his grin.

'Tim!' Adele hit him on the arm.

We saw the ticket collector come through the carriage door. Mat brought his hands together, like he does with football. We gathered round. 'Leave this one to me, guys. Who's got the tickets?'

Lucy passed the tickets carefully into his hand. 'Remember, with confidence.' Lucy winked and as Mat turned to look for the ticket collector he was there.

'Tickets, please?'

'Yes, sir.' Mat offered the tickets as he disguised a big yawn behind the back of his hand.

The collector took the tickets. 'And your teacher, where is he... her?'

'Mr Sanderson's going to the loo.' Mat gestured to the corridor from where the collector had come from. That was clever.

'Oh! Okay.' The collector carried on. I saw Lucy's shoulders lower; she filled her cheeks with air and let them slowly deflate.

Tim burst out, 'Bloody hell, that was intense.'

'Tim, that's inappropriate language. That simply isn't acceptable,' Lucy said. At first, Tim looked shocked and guilty, but then Lucy smiled and we all rolled about laughing.

We all began to relax after that. We had an hour and a half before we had to face London. Felix had brought a magazine with him about gadgets and some of the guys were reading it with him. Melissa, Lisa and Lily had the same thing going on with something called *Hello*, which was full of pictures of people. Brandon got out a packet of custard creams and was handing them around. I was sitting next to Lucy, Mat, Daniel and Adele and quietly we went over our plan as the Sussex countryside rolled by.

'Wow, what's that?' Brandon said, pointing out the window.

'That's Amberley Castle,' Daniel answered. 'It's a hotel now but once it was a place where the Bishop of Chichester would go.'

'What you can actually stay there?'

'Yeah, but the rooms are like loads of money. My mum and dad went on their anniversary. I got to join them for breakfast. They've got this amazing tree house which you can eat and sleep in. It's even got a thatched roof! I snuck in when they were cleaning.'

'So did it have like battles and stuff?'

'Yeah! It began as a manor house, but later they fortified the walls and put in a portcullis. But then Cromwell ordered the walls to be knocked down so it couldn't be used against him. They rebuilt it all soon after the war.'

'Cool, that is awesome!'

'You can just drive in there under the portcullis and then drive out, you don't need to actually stay.'

After a few stops, the tannoy said that we would shortly be arriving at Gatwick Airport.

'I wonder what they called Gatwick before the airport?' Lisa asked.

Daniel answered, 'It was called Gatwick Racecourse. There's always been a station here, well since the 1890s anyway.'

'What, motor cars?'

'No, horse racing.'

'Are we nearly there?' Tim asked.

Everyone laughed but Daniel answered anyway, 'It's about another forty minutes.'

'What about that? Look there's a Gatwick Express, we should have got that?'

'No, it's only about ten minutes quicker and you'd have to buy a completely different ticket!'

After a few more stops, there was a sudden lull in

the conversation and then I noticed we were all looking at this huge building. It looked like a giant hospital or cathedral but with four massive spires rather than one. It was all red brick and the spires were white. Looking more closely, it was derelict – the windows were smashed and one side was all covered in scaffolding.

'What's that?' Lily asked.

Everyone looked at Daniel. 'It's Battersea Power Station.'

'What, in the middle of London?'

'It hasn't been used since the eighties. Apparently, they keep on coming up with ideas for what to do with it. You know, like a concert hall, sports centre, hotel, shopping centre, oh and theme park. That was Alton Towers' idea. But nothing's happened.'

'Why don't they pull it down?' Lisa asked.

'No! It's awesome,' Lily said.

'Yeah, you wouldn't think it was an industrial building,' Daniel continued. 'It's like some kind of palace. Anyway, they're going to turn the whole building into flats. And they'll have to build a whole new tube station for all the people that live there.'

'Cor, imagine living there, you'd be ten minutes from the centre of London,' Mat said.

'More like three!' Daniel said.

'So we're nearly there?' Lily said

'Yup.'

Everyone suddenly became quiet. We all looked around at each other. This was real – it was going to happen. We all concentrated to make sure we had everything and were ready to get off. I broke the silence. 'Right, guys, Daniel's going to get us to Westminster Bridge. It's follow the leader. Daniel has a blue and white rucksack, it's a good target for everyone to aim for in a crowd.'

Lucy asked Brandon to tuck his shirt in, to which he automatically said, 'Yes, Miss.' We all laughed at him, and he laughed too.

At the station, we all gathered in the middle of the platform.

'Hey, guys.' We all looked to Daniel. 'These kids' tickets don't always go through the barrier, so we'll go to the side where the ticket collector is.'

Then it was Lucy's turn. 'It can't look like we're on our own. Daniel, if you can try walking behind an adult, as though they were our teacher, that would work. In fact, we should walk two by two so it looks like we are in a well organised school trip.'

'We are on a school trip!' Sophie said. We all laughed.

'Right then,' Daniel said. 'Follow me.'

'Do you think we'll be spotted?' Lucy asked.

'Hardly, there are eighty-four million passengers travelling each year through this station... but we have to be careful coming back. Victoria is really two stations knocked into one. If you're not careful, you'll end up in Dover!'

'This place is huge, how do you know your way out of here?' Mat asked.

'Well it's simple really, but if you get lost you can just follow this blue line here.' Daniel pointed to three lines painted on the floor. 'It takes you right through the station. Okay, everyone, we have choices. We have about an hour to kill before the meet-up with Oliver's dad on Westminster Bridge. We could go past Buckingham Palace, it's only five minutes from here. We might see the changing of the guard, and then go down through St James's Park. There's a lake and everything!'

'Can we stick to the plan, please?' I asked.

'Yeah, but I do know what I'm doing. And it would be fun.'

'I know, I guess I'd rather not take too many risks. It's a longer way, someone might see us and if we've got to get back in a hurry, we should practise the fastest route back.'

Daniel looked disappointed. 'I guess you're right, it's a shame though.'

'We need somewhere we can go and be out of sight while we wait.' Lucy said. I'm glad she backed me up.

'Well how about Westminster Cathedral? We're going along Victoria Street anyway and it's just off that!'

'Well, have we got time?' I didn't want to sound like too much of a baby.

'Yeah we do, and if we went straight there we'll be too early. It's only twenty minutes' walk to the bridge. We said twelve, didn't we? Also, it's free to go in.'

'Okay, guys, let's do that.' Mat said.

Westminster Cathedral

We walked in our pairs, closely behind anybody
looking like a teacher. Sophie walked right at the back,
holding Felix's hand, who was the smallest, looking
like a teacher's assistant. As we came out of the
station, we were met by huge glass and concrete
buildings. The road was really busy: loads of cars,
taxis, buses and cyclists too. There must have been ten
times more traffic than at home. Perhaps all the traffic
of Chichester could fit into this one road here. The
buses were space-age, not like our boxy ones at home.
These had curved everything, like something out of
Tron.

'Hey, look, there's *Wicked*.' Brandon was pointing
to a huge billboard with a green witch. 'My mum and
dad took me there. I remember now we came right out
of the show and we were on the train in under ten
minutes. Great show!'

'Yeah, clever to fit in with the film,' I said. I knew
as I'd been to the show too.

'What do you mean?' Lisa asked.

'It's like the story before and after Dorothy landing
in Oz, you know, as in *The Wizard of Oz*.'

'So that's at the Apollo Theatre?' Taylor read it on
the side of the building.

'Well actually it's the Apollo Victoria. The Apollo

is on Shaftesbury Avenue,' Daniel said. We all stared at him. 'Sorry, was that too much detail?'

We walked into the cathedral on the way and Daniel gave us a guided tour. Well he started to, but after a while it was only Sophie, Lucy and I left. It was funny listening to Daniel. He'd never spoken much before about his adventures in London with his parents. He was in his element. He knew who made stuff, when they built it and then there were the funny stories about the place, like the fact that it was built on the grounds of an old prison.

The cathedral had a calm atmosphere. Most of the ceiling was quite dark, as though it was covered in soot, yet the walls were all gold and marble with amazing mosaics. In the centre was this massive cross hanging in mid-air with Jesus on it. There were quite few people there, praying, lighting candles, kneeling in front of the altar – it all seemed very peaceful. Just what we needed, I guess? Daniel talking quietly to his little tour group seemed to fit in quite well.

At eleven-thirty, Lucy walked over to Mat. 'It's time, let's do it.'

Mat called everyone together and we grouped outside. 'Team talk, everyone.' We all stepped in closer. 'Right, remember, stay in your pairs, if in doubt run, keep your ticket safe, and if it all goes wrong...'

'We need a safe place to regroup,' Brandon said, 'to meet up if we get separated.'

'Yeah, good point. So look... we'll meet here... on the inside?'

'By the pulpit?' Adele suggested.

'Sounds good, and remember we're here for Oliver, so don't do anything that makes us look just like a pack of kids.'

'But we are a pack of kids!' Felix said.

'Yeah, but we need to behave like we're here to make a statement, not to just have a day off school.'

'Films and Fathers, fighting for a cause,' Lucy said.

'That's right. Activists not delinquents,' Mat said. 'Lucy, Sam, now we've got Sophie looking like a student teacher, she could go with you on the boat.'

'Yup, let's do that,' I said.

'Right,' Mat started, 'remember team, all for one.'

'AND ONE FOR ALL.'

After only a hundred metres, Lisa stopped dead. 'Hey look!' She was pointing at a House of Fraser department store. 'Have we got time to do some shopping?'

'Argh! Or we could go back to school?' Tim said.

'Or just stand still for half an hour. That might be more interesting!' Brandon said.

'Well, we don't get to go to these big shops often,' Melissa added.

'Yeah, like Chichester doesn't have any shops,' Taylor said.

'Okay, enough, kids!' Lucy said. And we all laughed.

After about ten minutes of walking, Daniel continued his guided tour: 'Down there are the Churchill War Rooms. It's where Winston Churchill ran the Second World War…you know, like told the generals what to do. There's this massive table and they have little models of tanks, solders and fortifications all laid out so they could plan what was going on. It must have been like playing a massive game of battleships. It's all like ancient as well, old radios, massive maps on the wall covered in little dots, where they'd stuck loads of drawing pins in.'

We all looked down the road, there was just so much to take in.

'And down there is Westminster Abbey.'

'We're not going in there as well are we?!' Melissa said.

'No, it's like £9 each.'

'Why do they have a cathedral and an abbey?' Tim asked.

'This is for the Protestants,' Sophie said. 'The cathedral's for the other lot, you know, with the Pope. This place is where they put all the crowns on the kings' heads.'

'The coronation,' Daniel said. 'Yeah, and it's where Kate and William got married.'

This guided tour was good: it was taking everyone's mind off what we were doing. No one seemed scared.

After a minute, Daniel waited for us to gather around. 'Right then, almost the end of the tour. This is Parliament Square.'

'Wow, Big Ben!'

'Err, no. You can't see Big Ben. Big Ben is the name of the bell. You're actually looking at the clock tower of the Houses of Parliament,' Daniel said.

'Cool, where all those angry people are,' Mat said.

'Is it free to go in?' Melissa asked.

'What!' Brandon looked excited. ' You're allowed to go in?'

'Yeah, but you've got to arrange it before with your MP. You can go in and see them shout at each other,' Daniel confirmed.

'Right, everyone,' Lucy said, looking for Daniel to stop.

'Yup all over, end of tour, thank you for going with Daniel Travel Tours.'

Lucy smiled at me. 'Sam, shall we rehearse the plan?'

'Okay, so Lucy and I are going to see Oliver's dad, he should be on the bridge. Then when you see us come back, you come on and do your bit. We are going to do our bit from the boat. Remember, if you go to the other side of the bridge you'll see the London Aquarium, it's just this side of the London Eye.'

'Don't take any chances,' Lucy added. 'Watch out for the traffic, keep safe and look after each other. Remember, none of this is worth it if any of us get hurt.'

'Or arrested,' I added.

Just getting across Parliament Square took ages. There were hundreds of tourists at every junction. As we walked along the bridge, I looked around for Steve. Lucy and I were trying to spot him in the crowd. We'd got to the middle.

'Where is he?' Lucy said

'Look!'

253

On the other side of the road, we saw Steve. He was in his Star Trek outfit and was climbing up a lamppost. It wasn't that high – five metres max – and there was a kind of crossbar he pulled himself up onto. It did look pretty dangerous, though. Just imagine if he fell into the river.

'Come on, let's cross.'

It was a wide road but there wasn't too much traffic. As we got closer, we watched as Steve sat on the crossbar, holding on to a big lantern. He wrapped a chain around himself and then attached it to the lamppost with a padlock. Then a few seconds later he unfurled a banner: 'STEPFATHERS FOR JUSTICE'.

'Steve!'

'Sam!'

Now we were up close, I could see Steve wasn't looking his best. The outfit was cool – a prize-winner– but under it he looked thin and his hair was a mess.

'I didn't think you'd really come... thanks!' He fiddled with his banner, getting it to show straight. 'SamIam, don't get in trouble for me,' he shouted down. 'I've lost. It's over. But don't you give up, Oliver needs a friend. He's not happy. Sam, please don't let them break you as well.'

'Don't worry, I won't. That's why we're here. We think you're right.'

'I got in trouble with the police for seeing Oliver, and I might have to go to jail. I might have to go for three months, but it'll stop me getting a job when I get out. I won't be able to see Oliver again.'

I didn't know what to say. 'It'll be all right. I mean,

we'll do what we can.'

'No, it's not your problem, Sam.' And then he turned his banner to show the other side: 'Fatherhood is more than conception'.

'If I don't get the chance, I need you to tell Oliver something.'

I nodded.

'I realise I wasn't a good father, but I couldn't handle losing Angela. Tell him, I know I could have done better. No wait just keep it simple. Tell him "Forget biology, I'm his father, and I love him". Yeah, tell him I love him. I'll always love him.'

Steve broke off as he looked along the bridge. 'Alright, SamIam, it's time to go, the police are coming.'

Lucy pulled my arm, but I didn't want to leave him like this. Lucy pulled again. 'Good luck, Steve,' I called over my shoulder.

We raced away as I heard him shouting, 'Family isn't always blood. It's the people in your life who want you in theirs. The ones who do anything to see you smile and who love you no matter what…'

Just before we got to the end of the bridge, we saw the others coming. Daniel waved to us and immediately pointed to the steps down to the river bus. And as Sophie joined us, we both shouted out 'Good Luck' and then went down to get our tickets.

Once on the boat, I worked out how we would put our plan into action, where we would put our banner and what we could fix the ties to. The boat was a lot bigger than I expected, which was better as it meant that our activity was more likely to go unnoticed. A man made an announcement over the tannoy telling us where the life jackets were. Then it asked for children to be supervised at all times. At which point, Sophie strutted and lifted her head. Lucy and I sat down while she stood next to us with her arms folded. She did look perfect with her adult costume on.

'We're only going to have just enough time!' Lucy frowned. 'We've got to get to the next stop, change and then come back all before 12.15!'

'Well, he'll be up there for a while. It'll be fine.'

'He could be up there for hours,' Sophie added.

I went over to the rails to plan the banner position again. When I got back, Lucy had moved. She'd gone to the other side and was looking over. I went to collect her – we should all stick together. Then I saw her. She was holding a mobile.

'You should have the picture now. The protest is on Westminster Bridge. Can you get a film crew here?'

'Lucy?!' She turned and looked at me, squashing her top lip against her teeth. 'Who's that?'

Lucy stared at me. 'The BBC.'

'What!'

'Yup, well there's no point in doing any of this unless everyone knows about it.'

'You've told the BBC to film our demo?'

She stared at me again. 'You don't want to know,' she said.

'Why don't I want to?'

'Because you need "plausible deniability".'

'Eh?'

'I can't tell you any more. You will be the one they grill when we get back.'

'What's plausible whaty?'

'It's what the people in charge need when they try to get away with doing something they shouldn't have done.'

Wow, this was getting big, but there was no time to think – the boat was docking and we had to get off and get the boat going back towards the Houses of Parliament.

We managed a quick turnaround, getting off the ferry and going straight to the queue of the returning ferry. We were only off the boat for a few minutes. It wasn't long before we heard the man making the same tannoy announcement. But rather than sit down, we got busy. First off, I remembered we had to be on the left of the boat, so that the banner would be seen from the bridge.

I took out the sheet from my rucksack and passed Lucy the other end. We walked to the rail. Lucy stood next to me, hiding what I was doing. I tied one end on. I'd been practising the knot, and it was done in seconds. I let out the sheet as we walked down the railing and tied the other end. Our banner said, 'KIDS' RIGHTS – WHO'S THE DADDY?' Lucy and I walked slowly back to Sophie.

'Look!' Sophie just stifled her excitement. As we approached Westminster Bridge, we saw Steve standing on the top of a lamppost in his costume. There were lots of policemen standing around underneath him. Then we saw Steve get out another banner: it was red on white, just like ours. 'IT'S THE CHILD'S CHOICE'. He had rigged up a pole so that the banner was horizontal with the crossbar.

Then some fireworks went off just beside the London Eye. Wow, well they'd done their bit all right! Suddenly, I felt relieved. Everything we'd hoped for was working out.

Lucy pulled my elbow and pointed. There was a camera on the bridge aimed right at us. 'Sit down!' I shouted. Sophie and Lucy put a hand up to their faces as though they were sneezing. Good idea, I thought, and copied them. We looked back up the bridge and saw the balloons, loads of them. Ten bunches in all, held by ten kids in pink t-shirts. They started next to the London Eye and then we saw them being dragged across the bridge. They were running. The moving bunches looked brilliant, drawing everyone's attention to Steve. When they got to Steve, the balloons were let go, one bunch at a time. Steve waved and cheered at our lot and then as our boat got closer, he saw our banner. He was waving and cheering at us too. Then we saw the police start to run around. Just before the last two bunches got to Steve, they turned back.

'What's going on?' Lucy stood up. 'They're turning back!'

'The police must be chasing them,' I said. Our boat was approaching the boat station, we'd be there in a couple of minutes. Then we caught glimpses of the pink t-shirts running back and forth darting across the bridge.

'Trouble!' Sophie said. She was looking at the boat

258

station. On the floating platform were two policemen. Lucy put her hand into mine. I thought about saying 'Don't worry, it'll be all right', but as we got nearer I realised it might not be. The policemen looked serious and were looking intently over the boat, their hands by their sides. Then they were talking to each other, but I couldn't hear what they were saying. One of them looked right at me. He stared for about five seconds, looked at Lucy and Sophie and then looked away again. Then he seemed to fix on something else and spoke again to the other one. I followed his eyes: it was a tall man with a tracksuit and a hoody jacket.

'They're not looking for us!' I said. 'They're after that guy at the back of the boat.' The boat came nearer. One of the policemen was pointing now at the man. The man on the boat just stood still. I couldn't see his face. The boat was alongside the quay and the policemen made to come aboard, and then suddenly it all happened. The guy at the back of the boat climbed over the side and jumped over the railings onto the pontoon. He landed with a big bang and then he leapt over the fence away from the boat.

'Oi! You! Stop!' the policeman shouted. But the man kept on running and within seconds, he'd disappeared into a queue. Then we saw him going up the gantry. The policemen set off after him, shouting.

'We were lucky there, guys,' Sophie said.

She was right. The man in the hoody had looked like the most likely candidate for banner raiser. I don't know why he started running; he must have thought the police were coming for him. Slowly, we got off the boat, following the gantry up to the quayside. We saw Taylor, Lily, Melissa and Tim about a hundred metres down the road, and then we saw a policeman, out of breath, come right up next to us. All three of us turned to look over the wall into the river.

We heard him behind us. 'PC Five, two, two, six in pursuit. The perpetrators are running west along north side of Parliament Square.' The policeman started a slow jog over the road.

'We should take off our jumpers,' Lucy said. 'They'll take off their pink t-shirts in a minute and if they see them, they'll see they're the same colour as ours.'

Lucy was right. She and I took off our jumpers and just had our white tops. We stuffed them into my school bag. There was loads of room after I had taken the banner out. 'Let's get back to the cathedral, we can't get mixed up with the others. They need to outrun the police.'

Lucy and Sophie agreed and as we crossed the road, we saw Steve surrounded by policemen who had a ladder. I guess he didn't have long. I looked up and saw the balloons way up high. They'd drifted down the river and were as high as the London Eye.

Taking refuge

We tried not to run as it would look suspicious, but within fifteen minutes we were at the cathedral. When we walked in, it seemed much darker in there than before, and my eyes needed to adjust. We walked quietly up to the pulpit and waited. Lucy kept on looking at the door. Then she took a few steps towards it before turning around and coming back to the pulpit. Sophie sat down on a pew and started to brush her hair and get smart again. Lucy's steps got smaller. I tried to catch her eye, but they were either fixed on the floor or on the door.

'How long should we give it before we have to go?' Sophie asked.

'That's not an option!' Lucy said.

'Yeah, I know we should wait, but what about the train?'

'We'll wait all day if we have to, we can't…'

'Hey, guys!' From nowhere, Taylor, Lily, Melissa and Tim appeared.

'You took your time getting here!' I said.

Taylor said, 'We took the back streets, we let you draw off the heat.'

That sounded cool!

Lucy stepped up to Lily. 'So where is everyone else?'

'We saw Mat, Felix and Brandon run to the other side of the bridge.' Lily looked worried. 'They were going north, past the London Eye! The others went the opposite way.'

Again, I wanted to tell Lucy it would all work out all right. I could see her getting worked up.

'We weren't supposed to split up!' Lucy's mouth was tight. 'It was bad enough we went off. So what happened? Why did they get separated?'

Lily answered, 'Well, Steve was on the lamppost, looking worried, I don't think he likes heights.'

Tim took over. 'He was shouting at the police to leave him alone as they were scaring him. Then he told them that if they didn't stand well back, he'd throw the key, you know, to his padlock, into the river. They kept on trying to climb the lamppost, so he got out the key, held it up and then flung it over his shoulder; like into the Thames! Every so often he'd shout out at the passers-by: "It's the kid's right to choose". After we signalled to Steve, we walked to the far end of the bridge, put our t-shirts on and then filled our balloons from the canisters.'

'It was amazing,' Lily continued. 'They were all up in minutes!'

'The t-shirts were brilliant!' Melissa went on. 'Everyone was looking at us.'

'Yeah, we saw,' I said. 'It was awesome, especially the balloons. After we let off the fireworks we split into groups at the beginning of the bridge and just ran as fast as we could on each side of the road—'

Tim interrupted. 'As soon as we began our chant,

this policeman shouted at us. When he could see we were going to carry on, he started to chase Melissa, but she outran him so he turned on Felix. He was only a foot away from grabbing the back of his rucksack, but Mat and Brandon ran between the policeman and Felix with a bunch of balloons. The policeman got caught up in the strings, then they did a circle around him and he had to stop. Then they made off but they couldn't come to the Big Ben side because another policeman was coming towards them.'

'Guys? There's a policeman at the door!' Melissa whispered. We all turned and froze as we saw the man in uniform walk briskly into the first chapel.

'Oh God!' Lily said.

And then Sophie did something brilliant. 'Everyone sit down,' she said. She walked up to this sculpture and turned to face us, but kept on looking towards the door. 'Could you take your seats please, children?' We all sat on the pew in front of her. Sophie put her hair behind her shoulders and straightened her dress. 'The cathedral is full of Byzantine influences, yet it wasn't built until 1903. There are also a number of influences from the Arts and Crafts movement too, notably the fourteen stations of the cross designed by Eric Gill.'

I tried to look behind me at the door but Lucy stopped me.

'Gill was to return twenty-two years later to finish the altar piece for St George's chapel. Very soon after that he died.' Sophie was pointing to the chapel and was doing a very good impression of Mrs Stubbs

263

looking serious. 'It was quite unusual for him to be chosen to complete these sculptures as he was hardly known at the time.'

The policeman was coming closer.

'He had only been a sculptor for three years before receiving the request to make the stations of the cross.' Sophie hesitated, I could hear the policeman's footsteps. 'Now, children, you will notice this piece behind me is much more graceful than the last. Gill did that one first, even before he had the job arranged. The scene depicts Christ with Simon, it is the fifth station.'

The policeman had stopped to listen. I'd forgotten half the stuff from the earlier but Sophie had soaked it all up.

'The artist had only become a Catholic six months before showing his designs. What a lot of people don't know is that he actually used himself as a model for many of the figures.' Sophie hesitated again. Was she was running out of things to say?

'And what is it made of, Miss?' I asked.

'That's a good question, Jack. It's a very good white limestone, not a marble as you might think.'

The policeman moved on.

'Can you get your sketch books out, please, and try to make a copy of this.' We watched Sophie's eyes as she followed the policeman along the far wall – he was behind us. 'Please remember to use light and shade, and to use your hard and soft pencils. Try to use the rubber as little as possible.'

She paused. 'He's gone!' she whispered. She came

back to our pew. 'Thank God for that, I realised as I said it we don't have drawing things!'

'Well done, Sophie, you were brilliant!' Taylor said. And everyone joined in. Sophie had saved us.

'Hi, guys!' It was Lisa, Adele and Daniel – we hadn't seen them come through the door. Lisa was looking really white.

'Shush, there may be a policeman about. He was just here a minute a go. You didn't get chased then?' Lucy asked.

'No, we were on the other side.' Lisa said. 'When we let our balloons go, we legged it. We changed out of the t-shirts in a back street and walked back.'

'And we bought an ice cream on the way,' Adele said.

Wow, that sounded good.

'I know this other way back across Lambeth Bridge,' Daniel explained.

'Did you see Mat, Felix and Brandon?' Lucy asked.

Lisa was in first. 'Not after they ran off the bridge and went up the South Bank towards Waterloo!'

'We need to go, we'll miss our train,' Tim said. 'I reckon we've only got fifteen minutes to get there. We need to catch the 13.32 to be back in time. My mum gets home by three.'

'Well you could go ahead? We could wait here for the others and catch the next train,' I said.

'No!' Lucy said. 'We've got to stick to together. We've got to wait for the boys.'

'But we've only got a little time to get to the station,' Adele argued.

'We can still do it!' Lucy was clenching her fists.

'Well when is the next train? They could get that,' Melissa suggested.

'We're not leaving without them.' Lucy ended the conversation. Adele looked at Melissa but no one was going to say anything. We knew she couldn't be persuaded.

Then we heard a noise at the door. It was Mat, Felix and Brandon laughing. As they drew closer, we could see how happy they were.

Mat put his hands on his knees as he caught his breath. 'Guess what? We took the tube!'

'It was brilliant!' Brandon said huffing and puffing.

Felix was too out of breath to speak.

'Come on, let's get going.' Lucy was smiling again. 'We can still make our train. Daniel, you're back on lead, Sophie, you take up the rear.'

Our walk was more of a run. It was difficult to look like an organised school trip when Daniel had set such a fast pace. As we approached the pedestrian crossing, the lights changed to red and we were stationary. Lucy looked frantic.

'Nine minutes, guys!' Daniel called out.

When the lights changed, Lisa shouted, 'Forget the line everyone run for it!'

We ran for it, all right. At the next crossing, we ignored the lights and just held up the cars. We ran around people and got to the station in less than five minutes.

'Alright, everyone back in line,' Mat called out.

I think he called it too early as we still had to get to

the train and it's a big station.

As we neared the gate, I looked up and saw the clock we had three minutes. Mat held up our tickets to the guard, but he didn't really look and just waved us through.

We got on the train and then heard an announcement about having to be in the first four carriages. Everyone looked at Daniel. 'Yup, we've got time, follow me.'

We got off the train and ran up the platform. Near the end of the train, Daniel darted through the door and we all followed him. Within seconds, the door closed and we were off. We'd made it.

We sat down and tried to recover. No one spoke for a few minutes. We'd done it. Lucy was sitting next to me and I saw her close her eyes and breathe deeply, as if she were saying a little prayer.

I looked around and loads of people were eating McDonald's. Mat and Brandon looked at me looking at them eating. 'Is it me or is it hungry in here?' Mat said laughing.

'Yeah, I sure have worked up an appetite!' Brandon whined. And like magic, Lily pulled out a packet of chocolate digestives. They didn't last long, but Lily was the hero of the moment.

When we passed Battersea Power Station, we all looked on as it was lit up by the late sunshine. It seemed like such a short time since we had passed it, yet it was only a few hours before. It was such a welcome sight. We were going home.

It seemed like London had got a whole lot smaller,

as though we'd seen it all in just a couple of hours. I knew we hadn't, of course, but it felt as though we'd done something pretty amazing.

Lucy was quiet on the way back. I tried a few times to talk but she seemed to be thinking about something. The other children were really excited. We knew we couldn't speak about what we'd done – there could be lots of people on the train from Chichester. So we practised the art of talking in half sentences, not mentioning names and using facial expressions and gestures.

Mat asked Felix if he'd had a good run today. Brandon said he'd thought their school outing very educational. Adele said it was a shame, as their pyrotechnics would have been a lot better if it had been darker. But only a couple of us realised she meant fireworks.

Finally, I got to ask Lucy what was wrong. She went to the loo, and I followed her down the carriage and spoke to her by the doors.

'Are you all right?'

'We took quite a risk today, it got messy. We should never have split up, imagine how we'd feel now if one of us was missing.'

'But we are all here now.'

'Yeah I know… but it was more of a risk than I expected and…' She paused. 'Steve, I didn't expect to see him look so different. I think a lot of us just thought it was a bit of a laugh, a bit of excitement. But Steve looked lost, well a little bit crazy. He probably won't be going home tonight. He could end up in jail!'

Lucy was right, we all felt good, it was a day out, but for Steve it was the act of someone in a real mess. I thought of Dad saying 'poor mental health'. Steve was desperate. I remembered the message he gave me: 'Tell Oliver I love him'.

Perhaps Steve was turning into the man in *The Shining*, where he's lost touch with the people around him. Had he spent too much time on his own? Not necessarily from his own choosing. He'd lost something and he'd looked as though he'd given up hope of getting it back, of Oliver coming back home. I guess he had no one to talk about his fears, about what he'd lost, what he missed.

Lucy was deep in thought.

'There's something else isn't there? Something else you're worried about?' I said.

Lucy stared at me. 'Well... I need to tell you a secret.'

'Oh!'

'I was going to tell you on our walk but I couldn't... well, it's kind of awkward.'

'You can tell me, you know you can.'

'Yeah I know I can trust you, but it's just telling you.' Lucy looked up and to the right. 'I'm adopted.'

'What?'

'Yeah, I guess I should have told you ages ago.'

'No, I'm just surprised. But your parents are awesome.'

'Yeah, I got lucky.' She looked down.

'How does... what's the... how do you feel about being adopted?'

'Well, it's okay! And I guess it's weird that it *is* okay. I haven't known anything different. My parents told me when I was four or something. It wasn't even a big deal – I can only just remember being told.'

We sat there in silence for a while. It was such a big thing. Whatever Lucy said. 'So do you know anything about your…'

'Bio parents?' Lucy giggled. 'Yeah, it's a sad story. I guess it would be weird if it wasn't a sad story. My mother died giving birth to me and my father didn't feel he could cope. He didn't have what my mum calls a support network.'

'A whaty?'

'Yeah!' Lucy giggled again. 'You know the people around you that care.'

I watched her look out of the window and then back at me. 'I care.'

'Yeah, I know.' She squeezed my hand. 'That's why I told you.'

Curtains up

We all said our goodbyes at Chichester station. There was a great buzz of success, but we knew we shouldn't hang around. We had to get back to our normal lives before anyone noticed. One random thing happened: as we walked out of the station, Brandon assured me he'd seen a man who looked just like Mr Jeff, on the platform.

When I got home, it was a little weird. I half expected to have been found out. I thought Mum would be on the doorstep waiting to tell me off. But there was nothing. I opened the door and Dad was in front of the telly. He lifted his head but didn't turn to me.

'Alright, son?'

'Yeah, hi, Dad.'

I wanted to get to my room and fire up The Fountain of Knowledge and get an e-mail off to Lucy. I didn't know what I'd write but something to make her feel that everything was okay, that it had all been worth it.

Halfway through drafting my message, Dad called up. 'Sam, when are you getting changed? Are you getting changed there?'

'Changed for what?'

'For the Nativity!' I'd forgotten. The Nativity was

tonight. 'I'm doing a spaghetti bolognese early, so it gives you some time to digest before you're on.'

'Thanks, Dad.'

'Well?'

'Oh yeah! Yeah, I'll get changed here, Dad.'

'Don't forget I've got that purple shirt for you to wear.'

'Thanks, Dad.'

Kirsty came through the door. 'Where were you at lunchtime then?' I was trying to think of something but she carried on. 'It's weird about this bug, isn't it? Do you think they'll have recovered in time to do the Nativity? Miss Benny said that quite a few of the people in the show had it so it might be a bit of a flop.'

My head was spinning, what would we do about that? We'd all forgotten it was tonight. Could everyone have got well again, was that believable? I wanted to message Lucy to make a plan but Kirsty was still invading my room. In fact, it was Taylor, Felix and me? They wouldn't cancel the show just because we didn't turn up. But I felt bad for worrying Miss Benny.

Now Kirsty was picking up my gaming magazine, looking at the cover but not really reading it. 'I heard about your performance in the lunch hall. That sounded cool, to have everyone watching and cheering.'

This was weird. Kirsty was being nice but what a time to start! What was she after, had she guessed? What could I to say to make her go? 'What are you wearing tonight?'

272

'O.M.G, you're right, I don't want to go in uniform!' It was the perfect thing to say. Kirsty was out of my room in seconds.

*

I peeked out from behind the curtain. The hall was full. There were even some people standing up at the back. Mum, Dad and Kirsty had a seat right at the front. We'd got there earlier this year, what with Dad being at home and being able to start supper before Mum got home. As we arrived, Kirsty was telling everyone I was her brother and to wait for my 'wise men' routine. She even told me to 'break a leg'… in a nice way. Mum and Dad were chatting away nicely to each other in the car and it didn't seem to be an act. Dad had told Mum he'd found some jobs he could apply for and Mum said she really appreciated coming home and finding supper was ready.

From the side of the stage (they call them wings), I saw Mr Jeff walk on. He struggled to find the opening of the curtains to step through and we heard the audience giggle and then laugh. Mr Jeff finally found the split and walked out in front. I heard the audience magically sense his arrival and the chatter gradually stopped to listen.

'Ladies and gentlemen, boys and girls, thank you for joining us tonight to see our Nativity. We hope very much you enjoy our performance. Much work has gone into this year's production and Mrs Larkhill and Miss Benny have made us proud once more.

Before we begin, I would like to say a few words to set the scene of this story, which is part of our rich tradition and culture.

'Mary and Joseph, a man and a woman who have little: a donkey, some clothes, a little money. Seeking refuge in a place they did not know well, a safe place for the night in the coldest and darkest season. Away from family and friends they relied on the comfort and the kindness of the people around them, strangers. They had to rely on their own efforts, their own sensibilities. They took responsibility for themselves and each other. Looking back, maybe we can see the adventure and the excitement of making that challenge but on that day, with their child soon to be born, how worrying it must have been for them.

They had so little and their need for shelter was so great. In the end, the stable was all they needed: a lowly beginning for their child, who became a great champion for compassion, love, charity, hope, kindness and peace.'

Before the audience could applaud, the lights all went out and only the glow of the exit sign spoilt the perfect darkness.

It was a show that Mrs Larkhill could be proud of. Choosing the seventies theme proved popular with the parents, who loved the songs. The costumes had been easy to put together. It was dramatic and bright.

Lucy sat with her parents, right behind Mum and Dad. Every time I looked up from my performance to find her, she was staring and smiling at me. What a day we'd had. Taylor, Felix and I found the last bit of our energy and had a great night. It seemed even more fun for having spent the day together. When we were dancing in line, I'm sure we were all pretty much thinking of London.

I could see Mrs Larkhill and Miss Benny backstage enjoying the show and swaying from side to side with the music. Then at the end, the finale, they got on stage too and everyone stood up and clapped, which is called a standing ovation.

Then when we walked down into the audience, it was mad. Everyone was standing up and talking all the same time.

'Hey, Sam!' It was Daniel. 'Awesome show! Dad, this is Sam, we play football together.'

'Hi, Sam, I really enjoyed your performance, well done. It's great to see a modern interpretation, very fresh and creative. Did you know only thirty-two per cent of primary schools hold a traditional Nativity now? In fact, twelve per cent put on a play which dispenses with religious references altogether and at the other end of the scale, more than a hundred schools incorporate other religious festivals like Hanukkah and Diwali ...'

Daniel's mother coughed. 'I'm sure Sam doesn't need to know all that, dear.'

Daniel smiled. 'Sorry, it kind of runs in the family.'

'Sam!' It was Lucy behind me.

'Hi!' She was wearing her jeans and the white top she wore from the walk. She smiled and then grabbed my hand. 'That was so much fun, well done!'

And then a hand was on my shoulder. It was Lucy's

dad. 'Yeah well done Sam, great entertainment, I loved it when you were rocking the baby.'

Mum appeared. 'Yes it was brilliant, well done Sam,' and then to Tom she said, 'Well it was great catching up with you two, but I guess we'd better go!'

And then Lucy's dad did his thing: he gave Mum a little peck on the cheek. Lucy caught my eye, and we grinned at each other, and then Dad kissed Lucy's mum on the cheek and I thought I was going to burst out laughing.

'Come on, Lucy, Janice is right,' Tina said. 'This is a school night. We'll need you tucked up in bed soon.'

And then, casually, as though it wasn't out of the ordinary, Lucy took my hand and waited till I was looking at her and gave me a full smile. 'Well goodnight then, Sam.'

We both giggled, she was imitating our parents, but as I went to leave she pulled on my hand, pulled me closer and before I knew it, she kissed me on the cheek. I stood there and looked at her smiling and she smiled back. I realised that the parents were silent and looking.

Dad gave me a nudge on the back. 'Come on then, Sam, say goodnight.'

'Oh yeah, night Lucy.' And without thinking, I kind of just leant in and tickled her cheek with my lips. The parents all giggled and it was the most awesome moment. I thought about kissing her again, but decided that might be pushing my luck.

As we walked through the exit, Mr Jeff was shaking everyone's hand. When it got to Dad, Mr Jeff kept hold of Dad's hand and said that if he ever felt like it, they'd really appreciate his help to revamp the school website. I think Dad was pleased to be asked.

In the car going back, everyone seemed to be in a good mood.

'It was a great show, Sam,' Dad started. 'I didn't know you could be like that... quite a performance! I used to do that you know when I was in my twenties, a bit of am dram, amateur dramatics.'

'You sound like an old man,' Mum said. 'Come on, love, why don't you do it again then?'

'Oh no, it's all changed now hasn't it?'

There was a funny silence in the car as we considered what Dad meant. Mum broke it. 'You've been made redundant, Kevin. It doesn't mean *you* are redundant.' Mum waited for Dad to say something. Even Kirsty was silent.

'Yup, you're right! I have been thinking perhaps it is about time I turned the TV off.' Dad chuckled and looked behind to us in the seat. 'Okay, guys, I've been moping, haven't I? I'll call the school in the morning. Perhaps rebuilding their website will kick start my own business.'

And then, perhaps it's because we'd just finished a show and were in the habit of it, Kirsty and I clapped and Mum joined in too.

As we got back, Mum was quick with her command. 'Come on you two, it's really late, quickly to bed, please.' With that, Mum flicked on the TV. Dad and Mum always watch the *Ten O'Clock News*. I usually hear it while lying in bed.

It was late, and I did feel tired, but I was still in the buzz of the show and success of Operation Films and Fathers. To think that our plan had all come out as we'd hoped. What an achievement! To get to London and help Steve with something that was so important, and that might help Oliver get back with his dad. Or, at the very least, let Steve know that we were on his side, that he hadn't been forgotten. To get into London with hardly any experience, find Steve, deliver our message and then get back all without being noticed, that was pretty cool. But what had been the highlight of the day? Wasn't it spending the whole day with Lucy on an adventure?

I heard the music of the *Ten O'Clock News* coming on. I'd need to get upstairs before Mum had another go. As I wandered back from brushing my teeth, I stuck my head into the lounge to say goodnight and catch some of the news. I knew I could get away with seeing a bit if I was quiet.

'Night Mum, night Dad.' I'd stopped at the door. They hadn't said good night. I looked at the TV: it was London. It was Westminster Bridge. There was a man standing on a lamppost.

'Sam?' Mum said. There were a load of kids running around being chased by policemen. 'Sam?!' This time a lot louder.

And then I heard the commentary from the TV. 'Steve Bridle has been remanded in custody having caused damage and a public affray outside the Houses of Parliament. The widowed man explained that he was fighting for the rights of the stepfathers to have a right of access to their stepchildren. In a statement to the press, Mr Bridle explained that he had been a father to his stepson for the whole of his son's life, yet following the death of his wife, his son has been taken from him by the natural father.'

'Oh my God!' Dad stood up looking at the TV.

'In this one-off protest with no official organisation, Mr Bridle seemed to be supported by more than a dozen children who were drawing the attention of the crowd by laying out banners and letting off balloons and fireworks. The police captured none of the children and are appealing for eye witnesses to come forward and identify them.'

'Sam!' Dad watched as they replayed the clip on the bridge again and then showed the fireworks and the balloons going up. 'Sam, is that really you?'

Then Kirsty, at my side. 'Lordy lord.' She giggled. 'What have you been doing?'

'Kirsty, go to your room,' Mum said.

'What have I done?'

'Bedtime, Kirsty! Sam, come in here and sit down! Kevin, can you turn the TV off?'

So I sat down and explained. In a way, it felt better than having a secret. I didn't know how angry Mum and Dad would be. As I spoke, I tried to weigh it up. No one had got hurt or anything. There was the lying and not going to school. There was mucking about with the police and causing a disturbance. It was quite strange: Mum and Dad never interrupted and their faces didn't really give anything away about how angry they were.

279

I told them about writing the sick notes and asking for the bed sheet pretending it was a tent, and to get it all out I told them how we'd heard from Oliver's real dad – I didn't say Bio Dad – and how he'd told us to leave Oliver alone. I told them about Steve and what he'd said at the bridge, how he looked so thankful for our support. When I'd finished, there was silence. Mum and Dad looked at each other and then me.

Mum began, 'You do realise that you might be in a lot of trouble—'

'From the police!' Dad said.

'What kind of trouble?'

'I don't know,' Dad said almost to himself. 'I guess no one got hurt.'

'But... how did you organise it all?' Mum asked.

'How did you get there and back?' Dad asked.

'By train.'

'How did you know,' Dad continued, 'how to do the train, find the bridge, meet up with Steve and keep it from everyone? Mr Jeff didn't know you were doing this, did he?'

'No!' I thought for a moment. 'Well, it's from all the stuff you've taught me. Daniel is a walking encyclopaedia for travelling to London. Mat taught us about working as a team. When Sophie's got her make-up on, she looks about twenty. She pretended to be the teacher. Lucy is sensible, she kept us altogether.'

'Sensible!'

I stopped. Perhaps I was making it sound a little too ordinary.

'But,' Dad continued, 'you do know that it is very wrong what you—'

'It's our fault,' Mum said, looking at Dad.

'What?!'

'Yes, it's our fault.'

'Why, because we've been arguing, because I've been made redundant?'

'Err, no! Because Sam told us how important Oliver was to him and we didn't listen. We'd given up hope for Oliver and the kids hadn't.'

Wow, I didn't see that coming.

'Okay, Sam, you need to get to bed. We're all tired and this all seems crazy. I don't know what's going to happen... what we're supposed to do.'

I stood up and made to leave, but Mum grabbed my shoulder.

'Sam, promise me, promise me you won't do that again? We'll do what we can for Oliver and Steve, no demonstrations or anything, but maybe we could call Steve and find out where Oliver is. But promise me you won't do anything like that again?'

'Okay, Mum, I promise.' My head was spinning and Mum was right, I felt tired, exhausted!

There wasn't much time between laying my head on the pillow and dreamland, but enough time to think about Lucy and her secret.

Real Contact

In my dream, I was throwing flat pebbles across a pond where they skimmed across to the middle and hit a statue of Bio Dad. It's amazing that my mind remembered his picture from the file. Slowly, I drifted out of my sleep, but still heard the gentle tap tap of the pebbles hitting the statue. The sound was real! It was a gentle tapping on my window. Then I heard a faint 'Sam' in a whisper. I crept to the window and drew the curtains, but all I saw was the black of the night. I opened the window. It was cold.

'SamIam, it's Oliver.'

I looked down and there he was. I could hardly make him out.

'Come down!'

'Two ticks, Lolly Olly.' Carefully, I opened my bedroom door and tiptoed to the back door. Thankfully, I was used to creeping down so that Kirsty couldn't hear me. I knew which floorboards and steps creaked. I turned the key in the back door, which in the quiet of the night seemed to be far too musical, giving off a small symphony of noise as it reluctantly gave up its hold on the doorframe.

Before I could step out, Oliver was there with his arms around my neck. 'Sam!'

'Ha ha, how long has it been?'

'Seven weeks and two days. I saw you on the telly!'

'What?'

'I saw you running around the bridge when Dad was on the lamppost.'

'Not you as well! Half the world saw that clip!'

'I saw Dad too, he didn't look too good. Anyway, I left school.'

'What just left?'

'Yup, I had a load of cash from Piers.'

'Piers?'

'Yeah, Mr Chartwell, Piers Chartwell, my real dad. He was the weird one at Mum's funeral. You know, the one who kept on trying to talk to me.'

'Oh, you mean Bio Dad.'

'Bio Dad! Yeah, like it!' Oliver giggled. 'Yeah, he gives me loads of pocket money and I've been saving it up to run away. I ran away a month ago, but they found me at Dad's and that got me into loads of trouble. It means that Dad's not allowed to see me any more, otherwise he goes to jail. They call it an injunction.'

'That sounds pretty serious!'

'So, do your parents know what you did today?'

'Yup, it's pretty awkward. I don't know what's going to happen next. But it was worth it… to support your dad.'

'Yeah, thanks.' Oliver gave me another squeeze. 'I don't know when, but I'll get Steve back. I can wait, I guess. I hope Steve can too. Piers just wants a son. I know because he told me. He gives me loads of stuff, but he's not interested in me. He wants me to work in the city as a broker!' Oliver stared at me for my reaction. 'He doesn't know me and doesn't want to know me either, but he's decided who I'm going to be!'

'Whoa! That must be weird. What do you mean he doesn't want you?'

'I never see him, he's sent me to this boarding school.'

'What, after you got excluded?'

'No! I was never excluded!'

'Oh! That was what we all thought.'

'No!'

'I guess it's because you never came back. So what's this new school like?'

'It's all right… you've got to work hard, but there's loads of things to do, sport every day, four meals a day, skiing trips and stuff. You've got to pay to be there! The school fees would have taken Dad years to save up, you know, if he was working.' I looked at Oliver he had put weight on, he did look stronger too. 'But I could be going home to Dad every night, you know, in Portsmouth, and have a few laughs with. Even at the weekends Piers doesn't come. He says it's good for my independence.'

'Well, it sure made you independent, running away from school!' We both chuckled.

'You seem to have made some good friends.'

I looked at Oliver. 'How did you know?'

'On TV, you seemed to be having a great laugh.'

'Yeah, it was a good laugh, you'll never guess, we

284

all play football together! Hey and you know I turned up at your house and met up with your dad?'

'Yeah, he said you'd come around and that your parents weren't too pleased.'

'Oliver, I've got to tell you what your dad said. He made me promise to tell you. He said that he realises he wasn't a good father, but he couldn't cope with losing your mum. He said, forget biology, he's your real dad and he loves you.' I was glad to get that out.

Oliver sat there for a moment. 'He did tell me in Southsea. It's as though he thinks I'll forget. He's worried because he and Mum never got married.'

'What!'

'Yeah, they always planned to, they just never got round to it. And after a while people just thought they were married and so they went along with it.'

'Oh.'

'It doesn't change anything, he's still my dad.'

'So he's not really your stepfather?'

'I guess not.'

'So what do you call him?'

'Dad!'

'Yeah I know, but what would other people call him. Not Steve, what if they were saying something like, Oliver's dad? It can't be Oliver's stepdad.'

'Okay yeah, I see what you mean. Well, how about proper dad, you know like the one who's properly looking after me? Not just the guy who wants to call himself my dad.'

I didn't say anything, but we hadn't found the right word yet. 'He looked pretty bad, you know, on the bridge. Like when he has one of his off days.'

'Yeah, I know, it's not good. The truth is, we could do with being together. But if I go to him, it would put him in prison. Dad just needs some help. He's finding it hard without Mum. They said at school he's suffering from something called bereavement. He's trying to get me back, but the bridge thing doesn't look good on him.' Oliver sighed. 'Dad will wait for me. We'll find a way. This little act from Piers won't last long.'

'Sam?!' It was Mum's voice from the lounge and then the kitchen light went on. 'Sam? What are you doing? It's midnight!' And then she saw Oliver. 'Oh, Oliver!'

There was silence. I began calculating how much extra trouble I was in. What must Mum think!

'Anything else you're hiding from me, Sam?' Mum was wearing Dad's blue bathrobe.

'I'm sorry, Mrs Steepleton, I didn't mean to...' Oliver looked even more lost. 'I'm sorry! I'm so sorry, I didn't mean to get Sam into any of this.' And then Oliver began to cry.

'Oh, dear! Come here, love.' Mum went to Oliver and put her arms around him and then Mum sat down on the doorstep and just held him for what seemed ages.

'I'm sorry to cause so much trouble.' He sniffed. 'Life just isn't getting sorted out, Mum's gone and nothing's the same. It keeps on changing and then it changes some more.'

'Hello?' It was Dad at the door in Mum's pink

bathrobe and slippers.

Mum was abrupt. 'Put the kettle on, Kevin, we've got to get Oliver warmed up.'

'Oliver!' Dad's face was pretty neutral, I think he'd ran out of surprise. 'Well I guess that all adds up,' he said, as he turned around. 'Janice, come in, it's too cold to be out there. Oliver, when did you last eat?'

'I had a McDonald's, I'm all right thank you, Mr Steepleton.'

'Okay, well a hot drink then, you must be frozen.'

Friday 13th December

Oliver slept on my floor on the spare mattress. Mum told us not to talk for too long as it was already too late, but actually we were tired and pretty much went to sleep straight away. In the morning, it seemed weird as though Oliver had stayed for a sleepover. Oliver and I were chatting and having a laugh and Mum served up toast. But then Mum got serious and explained that she had no choice and that she'd call Oliver's school later on. She'd give Oliver a bit longer to recover and prepare himself.

'Mum, could Oliver stay here? I mean live with us.'

'It's a good idea, Sam, but I think you'll find Oliver's already in demand, by two dads!'

As I walked into school, Kirsty didn't ask about London. It was bizarre. Of all the people, I expected to get an interrogation from her. When we arrived at the school ground it seemed quieter, almost sullen. People were quietly chatting. Parents seemed to be staring. I finally found Lucy as we walked into assembly.

'You've seen it?' I asked.

'The news?'

'Yup.'

'Did your parents see it?'

'Oh yes!'

As we gathered for assembly, the atmosphere

seemed different – cold and silent. Like it goes before a storm. It was probably just the difference between last night's Nativity performance and another assembly, singing the same songs and saying the same prayers.

Mr Jeff stood up and looked very serious. 'Assembly is cancelled this morning, children.' There was a lot of muffled talking around the hall. 'I want the following people to stay behind.' And he began to read from a pile of papers. 'Sam Steepleton, Lucy Meddows…' Each time he read a name, he turned a page. The pile of papers were our sick notes.

I looked around and caught the eye of Melissa, Sophie, Tim and Taylor. We hadn't got away with it. Slowly, the room began to empty leaving us political campaigners behind. Lisa and Lily looked really worried and whispering to each other.

Mr Jeff stood there, patiently, waiting for us to be on our own. Usually he would talk to us, friendly chat. But he didn't look our way, and was keeping himself busy looking at his papers on the stand.

Mat caught my eye. 'Well it is Friday the thirteenth!' he whispered.

When the room was empty, Mr Jeff looked up. 'For the sake of clarity, you should know that where you were yesterday and what you did is known to the school. It is, in fact, public knowledge. The authorities are being called as we speak to let them know who the group of school children were on the Westminster Bridge yesterday… who set off fireworks and sent balloons into the air.'

As he said fireworks, he'd raised his eyebrows. 'This call is being made not through any lack of loyalty to you or the school, but because it is the right thing to do. It is what an organisation does when they have responsibility to those in its care and to the wider society. An organisation that recognises their place in that society and an organisation functioning within the rules that govern it and from the knowledge of the expected behaviour it should conduct itself within.' He paused looking at as all, catching all of our eyes.

'You've behaved like the kids in *ET* when they returned the creature to its kin and didn't turn it over to the American military for dissection. They defied the authorities with their own plan and commitment to a moral outcome.'

What was Mr Jeff's point, was he saying we'd done the right thing?

'Their actions were reckless, they could have been contaminated by alien disease. They could have attracted the wrath of an alien planet, and above all there was a government agenda of which they weren't party to, but which was designed to protect them. But we're not dealing with an alien matter here and we live in Chichester, not Hollywood.'

This was a funny kind of telling-off. This was more like Steve talk!

'I'd like to think yesterday you all forgot about our rules and what the expected behaviour was. But that would be wishful thinking. I believe you knew full well what you were doing. It was an act of defiance. And I have to ask myself: when making your decision to protest for Mr Bridle, had you considered the ramifications, the consequences of your actions? Did you consider that you would tarnish the reputation of the school? That you'd deeply upset the peace of mind of your parents and the other parents in the school? That you'd taken on the risk of your own physical injury?'

This was the telling-off I was expecting.

'Did the end justify the means? Was the cause just, was it great?'

In my head, I thought straight away that it was.

'Was there a wrong that needed to be rectified? These are questions you need to ask yourself when you make important decisions. Your actions may have consequences beyond that of which you anticipated, affecting the career path of the staff at this school and the inevitable effect on budgets to resource greater rigour in our security procedures.'

Suddenly, Mr Jeff's telling-off – if you could call it that – was interrupted by Mrs Ford bursting into the hall. 'I'm sorry Mr Jeff, but I couldn't stop them.' Behind Mrs Ford were at least forty parents storming into the room. 'One came in and held the door for all the others…'

Mrs Ford was drowned out by unhappy voices, all talking at once. 'Mr Jeff what's the meaning of this?' 'Have you seen the papers this morning?' People were pointing their fingers and some were shouting. 'Did you know what was going on?' 'When were you going to tell us about this?' 'Was this a school outing?' 'I knew this would happen with Mr Jeff in charge!' 'You have a duty of care'

'Please be calm. One at a time. Can you please—' Mr Jeff waved his arms like a bird.

'Oh no, you've had your chances!' someone shouted.

Mr Jeff put his hands on his hips. 'Actually, you're not allowed on these premises without permission!'

That made everyone shout louder. 'Are these the kids that were on the bridge? We want them excluded, and we'll have your resignation as well!'

Mr Jeff raised his hands. 'This is best dealt with when you've all settled down.' There was a sudden hush. But it wasn't Mr Jeff that silenced the crowd – it was three policemen in uniform racing into the room. Leading them was a tall man in a black suit, sharp nose and pale eyes.

Lucy nudged me. 'It's Bio Dad.'

And it was Bio Dad that came up to Mr Jeff first, not the policemen. 'Are you the headmaster?' He didn't look angry or upset, he looked serious. Mr Jeff was deciding who to talk to next, but Oliver's biological father continued, 'These kids know where Oliver is. They're in contact with him. One of them is Sam and my sources have informed me he was there on the bridge.'

The room was silent now as Mr Jeff turned to me. 'Is that right, Sam, do you know where Oliver is?'

I think my face gave it all away, I didn't say anything, but within a few seconds Bio Dad leapt forward and was inches from my face.

'Tell me where my son is now and I won't press

charges.'

Charges, what did that mean? Mr Jeff was at my side a second later.

'That's enough, I'll ask you to stand back, you've no right to be here. I don't know how you got in!'

But then the police constable stood between Mr Jeff and Bio Dad. 'Sam, you're Sam are you?'

I nodded.

'Do you know where Oliver is?'

I nodded.

'I knew it!' Bio Dad leered at me as though I smelt bad and then his face changed as though he'd scored a goal. 'Right! PC Woodward, can you please get this wrapped up? I want to get Oliver back to school.'

It was then that Mrs Blacknell marched in, her suit just like Bio Dad's. 'Mr Jeff, if I might have a moment?'

Mr Jeff looked up and didn't seem to recognise her.

'Mrs Blacknell, social services. Oliver is being dropped off here in a few minutes by Sam's mother, she called in this morning. It seems your children have been busy in London!'

Mr Jeff was still speechless.

'Do I understand that you hadn't worked out that a dozen of your children had disappeared for the day? This really isn't the kind of thing I expect from a school in Chichester!'

Bio Dad sneered. 'It doesn't surprise me, these state schools don't seem to have any control.'

I looked around at the guys and we all felt pretty miffed by that.

'Ah, Mr Chartwell,' Mrs Blacknell said. 'Can I have a word?'

'Not right now, Mrs Blacknell. I'll take Oliver back now and contact you later in the week. Where is he?'

Mrs Blacknell didn't look very happy. 'We can't release him yet, we will need to talk to Oliver and find out why he ran away.'

'I understand your concern Mrs Blacknell, you're being professional as usual, at least we can rely on you. But Oliver was a missing person and now he is found. Can we begin with the police questioning this school and find out what has being going on? Can you call that alcoholic in the spacesuit and remind him there is an injunction preventing him from talking or being anywhere near my son?'

'He's not your son!' I found myself shouting. 'You don't care about Oliver! You just want to win, and you treat him like property. Oliver wants to be with Steve, his proper father!'

Mr Chartwell sneered at me, I thought he was going to shout, but he smiled. 'I do understand, you must be very upset, especially after running from the police.' And then he bent over and whispered in my ear, 'Back off, you little twerp.' And then he stood back up again. 'I'm taking Oliver out of the path of destruction. I'm sure you wouldn't want him following that drunkard. Oliver will go far, he won't need to work until he's finished university.'

'That's no way to talk to a child!' It was Lucy's dad, and he placed himself between me and Mr

Chartwell.

Then Lucy walked up. 'Dad, this is the guy. The one that told all the lies!' Lucy had to shout over the angry parents.

Lucy's dad pointed his finger at Mr Chartwell. 'If you were any kind of a father you'd know that was inappropriate!'

'He may be a child, but he's also a trouble-maker, and he needs bringing into line.'

'And whose line would that be? Anyway this isn't about you, this is about Oliver.'

'Yes, Oliver, my son!'

'Your son? I've only seen Oliver with Steve, who are you?'

At that point, Mum walked in with Oliver. Mum was holding his hand. Oliver looked like he was being taken to the dentist, but as he approached, we all took over. It was Mat who started it, he shouted 'Oliver' as loud as he could and then Brandon, Melissa and Taylor were cheering 'Oliver! Yeah, Oliver! Yeah, Oliver!' Then we all scrambled. We pushed past Mr Chartwell, Mrs Blacknell and PC Woodward and ran for Oliver.

The cheers got louder, and we surrounded him. Adele and Lisa were hugging him and Mat clapped him on the back and Tim was shaking his hand. Oliver looked bewildered but happy, his smile spread wide and it looked like he was holding back some tears.

Lucy found her way to the front of our crowd. 'Oliver, we've missed you, we didn't know we would until you left. We didn't understand what you were going through.'

Mrs Blacknell was calling from the back. 'Okay, children, it's time for the police to take over now, you've said hello...'

Mr Jeff interrupted. 'Well there's no hurry, let them have a few moments they haven't seen each other in a while.'

Mr Chartwell was shouting now. 'They've spent long enough. I don't want Oliver spending any time with these children. Mrs Blacknell, please kindly use your authority.'

Lucy took hold of both of Oliver's hands. 'My e-mail is lucy2003@hotmail.com, e-mail me and I'll give you Sam's.'

'Mr Jeff will you take control of your children?' Mrs Blacknell called out.

Lucy continued, 'At the bridge yesterday your dad told me to tell you...'

'It's okay, Sam told me last night.'

'Well then don't forget it. You are loved.' And with that, she put her arms around him.

Then Lucy's dad appeared. 'Oliver, who do you want to be with, Steve or this guy?'

'Steve, Steve's my dad!'

'Then we'll try and make that happen. I'll do my best, Oliver.'

'Children,'—PC Woodward was clapping his hands now—'we need to bring this to a conclusion.'

With that, we unanimously and silently agreed Oliver needed another cheer.

'On the shoulders, lads,' Mat commanded. Oliver

was hoisted on to the shoulders of Mat and Brandon and they bounced him around, the rest of us raising his arms and holding up our own in triumph.

The crowd of parents just watched in silence.

'Oliver! Oliver, yeah, Oliver, yeah, Oliver, yeah, yeah, yeah.'

I spotted Mr Jeff, who was smiling, and then I saw Mum and she was too. I knew then we'd got it right. We were going to have to say goodbye to Oliver, but we'd given him something he wouldn't forget and it felt like someday soon we'd be together again. This wasn't an end, it was a beginning.

Dear Diary

~ Little acts together make big changes ~

I can't believe it's only a couple of months since Operation Films and Fathers, and it's all turned out right.

Lucy's dad went to London to bail Steve out of prison. Which means get him out while the police are deciding what to do with him. But when he got there, the police said they didn't want Steve and he could go. So then Lucy's Dad explained to Steve that he had lots of rights, as Oliver loved him more than Mr Chartwell and that was very important. He just had to tell the right people. Steve was still worried, or what Lucy called 'anxious'. So Lucy's dad, while Steve was there, contacted the social workers, the police, Mr Jeff and Mr Chartwell's solicitor.

Steve was over the moon. I got to see him the day after Oliver got back and he couldn't stop hugging him, and me too. He didn't have a beer that evening. He said 'whoever was in charge'– I think he meant God, but he might have meant the government – 'had given him a second chance and he wouldn't mess it up this time'.

Dad and Mum told me they hadn't understood about Steve and realised that they'd judged him unfairly. They said he didn't have the right support and that meant he was vulnerable.

The headmaster wrote to Steve and invited Oliver to return to school.

All the political activists, that's what Mr Jeff called us lot that went to London, were told to make a joint project that explained how we had upset our parents for lying and missing school. And how we realised now we'd put ourselves in danger.

The day before Oliver came back to school, Mr Jeff did a special assembly and explained how difficult it was for him without his mother.

When Oliver was at his school in Winchester, he saw a lady and spoke to her about losing his mum. About all his feelings that made him angry and frightened. They still see each other from time to time. Oliver and I are back LARPing and every so often we'll go to a cosplay event.

Mum and Dad told me they were completely shocked at what I did, and that they didn't realise how much I'd missed Oliver. But now they realised that they should have listened more. We all agreed that we would listen more to each other, so we would be stronger as a family; and when other families were in need we could help them too.

So it wasn't the adventure I'd planned, but it was amazing all the same. I didn't save the world or kill the aliens on another planet. But, like Steve would say, I'd found my tribe. Together we saw what was wrong and we fixed it. Lucy said she and I were special friends. So now, I have two good friends, and as Mum says, I only need one. So life's good and I'm looking for the next adventure.

About the Author

Luke McEwen was born in Chichester, West Sussex, UK in 1964, the second son of Andrew and Anitra McEwen. His father was a journalist for the Daily Mail for twenty six years, finally ending that career as chief diplomatic correspondent to the Financial Times. Luke spent four years of his childhood in Freeport, New York, and eighteen months in Brussels, where he attended the Common Market School. He finally returned to his home town nine years later in 1973. Luke went to the University of East Anglia and studied Politics and Sociology. Just to avoid any confusion, he sadly did not attend the UEA's famous writing course. But did attend Chichester College's creative writing course led by Julia Homan. Luke continues to work and live in Chichester with his son. He is a keen potter and painter, tennis and saxophone player.

Luke has also written an anthology of short stories called One Last Cruise.

He has a blog and writer's website at www.lukemcewen.co.uk

16808966R00180

Printed in Great Britain
by Amazon